DEATH ON THE D-LIST

DEATH ON THE D-LIST

NANCY GRACE

ToTo
press

TOTO PRESS / NEW YORK

TOTO
press

Reprint edition published in the United States by Toto Press.

Original edition published in the United States by Hyperion Books.

For information, address:
Toto Press
3384 Peachtree Road, Suite 575
Atlanta, GA 30326.
www.nancygrace.com

COVER DESIGN BY HSU + ASSOCIATES

ISBN   978-0-9906695-2-4
LCCN   2014913971

This is a work of fiction.
Names, characters, places and incidents either are the product of the author's imagination
or are used fictitiously, and any resemblance to actual persons, living or dead,
businesses, companies, events or locales is entirely coincidental.

TOTO PRESS HARDCOVER EDITION

10 9 8 7 6 5 4 3 2 1

To Bigness, Grr-Grr, and Man-Man.

Our love is forever.

IT WAS ALMOST COLD OUTSIDE. BETWEEN THE COOL AIR OFF THE OCEAN and the fact the sun set hours ago, you'd never guess it was nearly spring. The perfectly placed gravel covering the walkway around the side of the mansion crunched with each footstep. Anyone could hear it a mile away . . . if anyone had been home. But they weren't. That was step number one, to make sure the behemoth of a house was vacant while the owners were out in Park City making a spectacle of themselves at Sundance Film Festival.

It was.

They popped up on *Entertainment Tonight* last night, obviously stoned, at some red-carpet event. She had starved herself down to a bag of bones with a sprayed-on orange tan, and he was showing off new blond implants that had actually turned out pretty well, dipping his head toward the camera and brushing his hair back several times during the thirty-second clip. Everybody and their brother showed up at Sundance now. All the hot, sweaty wannabes cramming every sushi bar in town, hoping to connect with the stars.

Little did they know what was going on in their pool house at the very moment they were smiling for the cameras, sucking in every last drop of attention like two big, vapid sponges. They were completely full of themselves. Constantly throwing exclusive "private parties" only the celebrity elite were invited to.

Wonder what that was like.

The crunchy bleached gravel, which upon closer inspection turned out to be tiny shells of some sort, probably shipped in from the Coast and ridiculously expensive, gave way to damp, closely manicured grass with a stepping-stone walk. Walking around the pool, blue tinted water gurgled out of a fake grotto with a secluded hot tub in the corner. Why would they pay for running this get-up when nobody was here for weeks?

Whatever. It was their water bill.

It was so true . . . If you want anything done right you just have to do it yourself. Huffing up the steps and around the side of the house, the back sliding glass door facing the pool glided open without a sound.

There she was . . . thick, dull, silver duct tape securing her wrists and ankles tightly to a chair. Her trademark blue eyes edged in smoky gray liner widened when the door opened, even though she certainly couldn't see that far in the dim light. Nearly all the lights were out in both the guesthouse and the main estate. Thank God for Sundance.

At first she looked grateful . . . until she spotted the gun. When she saw the silencer being screwed on, she started struggling wildly against the duct tape binding her wrists.

Then, in just one flash, one sharp instant, it was all over. After all the hours, no, *days* of planning, calculating, scheming, and maneuvering, it was over. All that anticipation . . . Would there be pain? Sorrow? Regret? Elation? Or just simply revulsion when the trigger finally pulled and one, single bullet sliced through the gray matter of Leather Stockton's brain.

But now, in the dead silence immediately after the deed, standing there in the darkened pool house looking down at the macabre mask of human flesh and blood and gristle atop the actress's body . . . What a letdown.

It was nothing. Absolutely nothing.

Leather's left foot spasmed a few times, and then she was still. Okay. That was a lot quicker and easier than expected. Stockton's whole pampered life led up to this, the zenith of her career.

She'd end up more famous for being murdered in a celeb's pool house than she ever was for a string of mediocre TV series. It was always the same thing. Stockton lounging by a pool in a bikini.

Her in an over-the-top evening gown with a plunging neckline and a push-up bra. Her with tons of eyeliner and mascara to make her blue eyes pop on camera. "Saucy primetime soaps" had been her specialty, then there was a cop drama, and something after that—it all blended together.

Lately, Leather Stockton was only famous for her spread in *Playboy* and for crashing her car into the front window of a McDonald's while trying to order fries at the drive-thru. She was drunk out of her gourd of course and went straight to a $60,000-a-week "rehab" in Antigua.

Leather still looked pretty good, though. Not so much right now, of course, with her face blown open and the blood oozing down her neck and matting in her hair. But generally speaking, she was, and had always been, a looker.

This was not the time to dally. The sliding glass door clicked shut.

You could learn a lot on TV, such as how latex gloves were truly the best. Had it been touched with an ungloved hand, the thick glass on the sliding door would've definitely grabbed fingerprints.

Glancing at the wristwatch by the light of a glowing lawn lamp highlighting the fake grotto, it was clear there was plenty of time to make it across town to be spotted. Being seen around town as an alibi was really just the icing on the cake because by the time the morons got back from Sundance to find the decomposed mush, there would be no real way to establish a credible time line.

Fresh clothes and shoes were waiting in the car. Even the tiniest blood spatters could be picked up on a shooter's clothes, so they'd have to be burned, and thrown in the trash off the expressway. Dumpsters behind grocery stores or fast food joints wouldn't do. They had cameras. And nothing near those horrible freeway cameras that catch idiots cheating the tolls and so forth. That would be tough to explain.

All in all, the whole murder thing was really nothing at all.

A piece of cake.

THE FLIGHT UP FROM ATLANTA TO MANHATTAN HAD BEEN PRETTY painless. Of course, the security lines and hassle of traveling through the Atlanta airport were hell on earth, but that was a given.

Once Hailey Dean stepped off the Delta 757 and onto the jetport connecting the plane to the terminal, suddenly so much came rushing back. It had been a little over a year, but walking through LaGuardia past Nathan's Famous hot dogs, the magazine and newspaper stands, down the escalator and to the taxi stand outdoors, it felt like she'd never left. It felt the same as before.

Before two of her favorite clients were murdered at the hands of a man who was once her courtroom adversary, a man who not only passed as an upstanding and highly successful member of the Georgia State Bar, but before that, as an Atlanta beat cop. For just a moment, Hailey felt Matt Leonard's hands around her neck again.

Hailey shook the sensation off and moved forward a couple of steps in the taxi line. After a few minutes, the next cabbie approached and she hopped in the back seat. Although brusque as expected, he hoisted her only bag into the car trunk, slammed it shut and slid into the driver's seat in front of her.

"Where to?" The cabbie didn't turn around, just directed the question toward the rearview mirror.

She'd learned long ago not to speak too many words to New York cab drivers. With what was left of her Southern accent after living in Manhattan, they could hardly understand a word she said.

"Fifty-fourth Street. Manhattan." She clipped it out short and firm. Less words to misunderstand. It all came back to her without even thinking. The cabbie said nothing, just gunned the motor as dirty-gray snow churned up from the tires and out to the sides of the car.

Hailey buckled her seatbelt and leaned back against the seat of the cab, looking out as Queens raced by outside her window. The row houses jammed together along short streets visible from the Long Island Expressway, diners, apartment buildings, billboards . . . all blended together . . . not particularly beautiful but strangely familiar and somehow reassuring despite the fact it wasn't really her home. The Southland was home and always would be. But New York was part of her now, and she didn't realize she missed it until she saw it and smelled it and breathed it again. In that very moment there in the back of the cab, she was glad to be back.

They exited the FDR just before the UN rose into view, turned right, and careened around the corner and lurched to a stop. Hailey gave the driver cash, declined a receipt and pulled her own bag out of the taxi's deep trunk. Hailey always traveled light, so it wasn't tough to yank it out and let it drop to the curb. She turned and looked all the way up to the top of her apartment building to where its roof met the sky. Way up there, thirty-one flights above, was Hailey's cottage in the sky.

Taking the steps up as quickly as she could while pulling the bag behind her, she wondered briefly if the flowers would start up again now that she was back in Manhattan. Ever since two of her patients were brutally strangled, followed by her own false arrest for the murders, the arresting officer, Lieutenant Ethan Kolker, had tried to make amends. As best he could, anyway.

It started small with the old standby, a dozen roses. When she'd promptly had the florist pick them up as a "return," another dozen came, and then, another. When those too were returned, more thought was put into the order. Kolker tried it all, violets, calla lilies, somehow even finding her favorites, stargazers and Cherokee roses. They too had gone straight back from whence they came, to the florist . . . every last petal.

Although they were beautiful, flowers never impressed Hailey. In fact, flowers made her feel guilty, that such beautiful creations were cut and pulled from the fields (or hothouses) where they flourished, for the fleeting whims of a human. Hailey never responded verbally or in written form to the flowers from Kolker, nor did he ever include any written apology or explanation of his thoughts.

Then came the chocolates. A succession of treats, also including no communication of regret, sorrow or epiphany, arrived and were returned as well, this time directly to Kolker's precinct in downtown Manhattan . . . no note attached.

Kolker could always tell the boxes had been opened, then carefully repacked and returned with no comment whatsoever, always returned in the boxes in which they'd been sent, a new mailing address placed directly over Hailey's own home address.

Sure enough, when Hailey pushed through the heavy glass revolving door into her building's lobby, Ricky the doorman came from around the front desk to give her a big hug.

"Where you been? I missed you! Way to keep in touch . . . Not!" He ribbed her a tiny bit. Hailey had seen him graduate from college and doggedly follow his dream to become a sportscaster. She hugged him back tightly but before she could respond, he said, "And, hey! You've already got a package. Let me get it for you." He bounded back behind the front desk and into a storage area behind an open side door where the doormen stashed deliveries.

This time it was a box, wrapped, as usual, in plain brown paper. One look at the handwriting and Hailey knew it was from Kolker.

"How'd he know I was coming back?"

"Who's *he*? The dentist again? He didn't give up yet?"

Ricky had no problem getting up in her business. He was referring to Adam Springhurst, the dentist who practiced in the office beneath Hailey's down in the Village. They'd had a fleeting relationship around the time of the murders, but it left Hailey with the feeling she was cheating on Will by even considering dating again. Her heart wasn't in it, and she disengaged as best she could, sure she came off as cold and uncaring. It was actually just the opposite: She couldn't afford to care. It could hurt too much.

In any event, because Hailey ended up applying Adam's dentist drill, whirring at full force, into the temple of the defense lawyer who'd stalked her and murdered her two friends, things between them had been on hold, for lack of a better term.

"No, not the dentist . . . the cop."

"What cop? Not the one that arrested you? He's the only cop that's ever been here . . ."

"That's the one. How did he know I was coming back?" she repeated the question.

His eyes got wide to display innocence. "I don't know . . . It wasn't me! Ask the morning shift. You know how Julio is . . . He'll tell anything for a hundred bucks!"

"Don't you worry, I'll do just that."

"Don't tell him I told you! Hey, you need help with that box? It's kind of big. Want me to carry it up?"

"No. Thanks, though, I can manage." Hailey glanced at the clock sitting on the counter of the front desk. "Wait, on second thought, let me just dump my bag here. I've got to get across town. I'll pick them both up tonight. You hold it for me? The box and the bag?"

"You got it, sunshine."

Hailey turned and headed back out. She hurried down the steps and up the sidewalk to First Avenue. Looking into oncoming traffic and holding her right arm up high, Hailey quickly hailed a cab.

She slid into the back seat with nothing but her purse and her pad of handwritten notes.

"West Side, Sixth Avenue and 59th." Hailey rolled the window down to catch the breeze and the driver began inching through traffic across town to the West Side. All the television networks were there, HLN and CNN in the Time Warner Center looking down on Central Park and Columbus Circle. Fox there on the corner at Avenue of the Americas, with American flags flying out front, CBS, NBC, ABC . . . They all made their homes here.

Hailey was glad she stopped at her apartment, vacant nearly a year now. But after the murders of Hayden and Melissa, not to mention her own near-strangulation, she needed to leave the city. She wanted to go home and see the red dirt, smell the azaleas' perfume in the air, feel the hot afternoons heavy with humidity, see her mother and father.

The apartment sat there during it all, quietly waiting for her to come back. She paid Ricky to water her plants and crack the windows an inch or two every couple of weeks. Her mail had all been forwarded to a post office box in Atlanta. Not that she ever read it. It was all bills and catalogues and flyers. She paid nearly all her bills online, and as for shopping, she'd rather be beaten with a stick than set foot in a shopping mall, much less spend her free time thumbing through a catalogue.

When she left the courtroom years before, the need for new business clothes to wear in front of juries no longer existed. No more long-sleeved black and navy dresses, black pumps, hose. In fact, she hadn't forced herself into a pair of pantyhose in years and the clients she counseled in her psychologist's practice would suspect something very amiss, even downright wrong, if they saw her in anything but her favorite pair of worn jeans and scuffed brown cowboy boots. Living in Manhattan where everything was cement, she'd already had the boots resoled twice, but there was no way she'd break down and buy another pair. These fit just right.

Sights and sounds of the city glided past as she looked out the backseat window. Throngs of pedestrians at every corner waiting to flood into crosswalks, vendors cooking God knows what. Hailey called it "street meat"; she never really knew what it was, but it sure smelled good. Makeshift carts selling knock-off purses, watches, pashminas, scarves, and jewelry. The big avenues going north and south, up and down. The island floated by . . . First Avenue, Second and Third, Lexington, Park, Fifth, Sixth . . . before she knew it, the cabbie hit the brakes in front of GNE, Global News and Entertainment.

With her purse on her shoulder and her notepad clutched to her chest, Hailey wove through the people milling in front of the towering skyscraper that housed GNE. She'd never been in the building before, although she'd jogged by it many times in the past en route to Central Park. She rarely detoured off her regular jogging path up and down the East River. To get to the park from the East Side required ducking through hundreds of cars, thousands of pedestrians, and way too many exhaust fumes. Whenever she did do it, however, she was always struck by the park's beauty. The first time she ran through it forever stuck in her mind.

It was a brilliant Sunday morning and she'd been running over an hour when she unexpectedly came upon the park exit leading to the Plaza Hotel. At a distance, she saw a gold-plated statute, high up on a pedestal, shiny and glittering in the sun. It was one of the largest around. Wondering who deserved such glory, she stopped running and walked up to see it.

It turned out to be a shrine erected to William Tecumseh Sherman, the Union general responsible for literally burning a wide, sweeping swath of a path through the South, including the city of Atlanta, during the Civil War. The destruction of country so beautiful—carried out not to win the war, but out of pure joy at the South's devastation—remained a dagger in the hearts of many Southerners to the present day.

"Driver's license, ID" An old, gray GNE security guard repeated the phrase by rote without looking up from behind a long, glossy bleached wood counter.

Fishing through the deep leather purse hanging on her shoulder, Hailey pulled out her old District Attorney's badge, cased in a worn wallet holder. From behind the shiny gold badge, she pulled her Georgia driver's license and held it over the counter for the guard to inspect. He took it from her hand and began copying the information down on a sign-in sheet. Looking around, Hailey noticed several well-dressed security guards strategically placed throughout the lobby. They all wore blue sports coats with gray pants, with nearly invisible earpieces in their ears.

"Hailey Dean, Hailey Dean. That name rings a bell." He looked up at her and then lowered his glasses to peer at her over their upper rims. "Right. I remember you. I read all about you in the *Post*, saw you on the TV too. That nut-job lawyer almost did you in, but you got him good. Right in the head. Dentist drill, right? Man I'd like to do it to *my* lawyer. Made my divorce worse than the old lady did. Almost called the divorce off just to get rid of the lawyer!"

The last thing she wanted to talk about was the night she was nearly murdered. She remembered the feel of Leonard's hair, slicked back as always, when her hand, clutching the buzzing dentist drill, slammed into his temple. She never remembered actually turning the thing on.

Funny how little details like that can bug you for the longest time.

Hailey managed a smile, telling herself the security guard's heart was in the right place.

"Yep. Hailey Dean. Right in the head with a dentist drill. Wonder if the dentist used that drill again. He shoulda framed it. Right?"

Before Hailey had to come up with a response, she heard her name screeched out across the large expanse of the GNE lobby floor.

"Hailey! *Hailey Dee-e-an!* You made it! You're so much smaller than you look on TV! I thought you were at least five feet ten! *I just love it!*"

||||||||||||||||||||||||||||||||||||||||||||||||||||||| **2** |||||||||||||||||||||||||||

T HAD TO BE TONY RUSSO. SHE'D RECOGNIZE THAT VOICE ANYWHERE. It had been in her ear for hours on end for months. The Jersey accent had actually grown on her, but this was the first time she could attach a face to the voice on the phone.

She had imagined someone tall, dressed in a suit, businesslike, maybe like an on-air anchor. He couldn't be more different. Barely topping five-feet-six, he was dressed in a baggy pair of low-rider jeans working their way down. Fashion "trends" were not for everyone, and with that in mind, Hailey didn't want to see Tony's other side.

The show's host, Harry Todd, was Tony's polar opposite. Todd had to be in his late fifties despite insisting, even when confronted with evidence to the contrary, that he was only thirty. He'd undergone every plastic surgery procedure known to man and doggedly followed every trend to stay young. His current stab at youth was spiking his highlighted hair straight up in the middle, stiff with gel, like a mohawk. Ego aside, he was the undisputed star of daytime talk.

Somehow, Todd garnered a huge share of the daytime market and not only managed to hang on for nearly twenty years, but was still perceived as a ratings monster, and nobody dared suggest otherwise. GNE would go right down the crapper without Todd as the tent pole holding up the daytime numbers.

And Anthony Russo was Todd's chief booker.

Russo booked Martha Stewart on *Harry Todd* straight out of jail and even got her to wear the famous green poncho she knitted behind bars. He got Brad and Angelina, and every sitting president since Reagan.

The show was executive-produced by a female power broker by the name of Sookie Downs. Downs had come up through the network and landed at the helm of the biggest daytime talk show in the industry. She ran the show with an iron fist from her mansion somewhere in the Hamptons, literally smack in the middle of an apple orchard.

Rarely making the trek into the city, she relied on her henchman, Tony Russo, to hold the show together and do her bidding. He carried a private cell phone on his hip at all times so they could stay in constant contact. Right now, Russo looked Hailey straight in the eyes. "You're so beautiful. I had no idea! Do people just come up to you on the street and say 'You're beautiful'? *I love it!*"

Hailey gave him a hard look. Was he serious?

He looked so sincere . . . but glancing over at him as they walked side by side toward a huge, swanky bank of elevators, she noticed he had already looked away from her and was scanning the lobby of the building to see if there was anyone there he needed to gladhand before they got on. Meaningless compliments apparently just rolled off his tongue.

Okay. She sized him up pretty quickly. He was just one of those TV types she'd always heard about, shallow, frenetic, would say or do anything to get a story. Note to self . . . *Take Russo with a pinch, no . . . a box . . . of salt.*

The elevator was so spacious it felt like a room, oak paneled with high-def flat-screen color TVs installed flush on either side of the doors. Pretty luxe. Both screens were tuned to GNE and were flashing shots of dead civilians on a roadside in Afghanistan. The screen quickly dissolved into four old white men in suits, in boxes like *The Brady Bunch* intro, politicians arguing about White House strategy.

The elevator shot smoothly up to the thirtieth floor, where they stepped off and turned right. Russo swiped another security pad built into the wall next to huge swinging glass doors. Pleasant music piped into the area just outside the elevator banks ended abruptly and Hailey could hear raised voices in the distance. Even a long corridor away from the show's headquarters, tension was palpable. It hung in the air.

Walking along with Russo, she turned right into his office. The windows looked down onto a tiny park with cement instead of grass and some sort of statue in the center. It was surrounded by high-rises whose windows were grimy, many of them looking back vacantly, their blinds askew, suggesting they desperately needed tenants.

"Nice office, huh? *I love it!*"

He certainly *loved* a lot.

"Took me ten years, but I got the window!" *I guess beauty's in the eye of the beholder . . .* Hailey managed to keep that thought to herself. He seemed so proud of his window office, she felt guilty for noticing the bleak view.

"You'll just have to excuse me, Hailey. I don't feel so good today. I ate at the diner across the street, and I'm pretty sure there was a hair in my eggs. I've felt nauseous ever since. Has that ever happened to you? You know . . . a hair in your eggs?"

"No . . . I don't recall a hair in my eggs . . ." She could add nothing to Tony's personal horror story.

He went on. "Yep . . . I finally got the window office. Everybody wanted it, but they gave it to *me*." While Russo's face and body were angled toward her from behind a corporate-looking desk, the same as every other desk in the building, his eyes remained glued to his computer, its lighted screen glowing dimly back onto his face.

Something on his computer screen triggered Russo to leap straight up, rolling his chair back. "Hold on . . . I gotta get a printout right *now*! Don't move! I'll be right back!"

Racing from around his desk and out the office door, Russo left Hailey alone with the rows of TV monitors covering the walls. They were all tuned to daytime talk, and nearly every screen had a group of women sitting on a couch in front of a studio audience. Banners across the bottom screens screamed out shocking scenarios. One said *"Leaves Wife of 27 Years for Step-Daughter."* Sitting on the sofa were three women glaring across the set at a chubby, forlorn-looking man in a suit that was way too snug, seated beside a twenty-something girl in a low-cut top and tight jeans.

The second screen showed a group of women sitting around a table drinking out of large coffee mugs. The banner across the bottom read *"Wife Poisons Husband and Boyfriend With Antifreeze Hidden in Lime Jell-O."*

On the third, a former fashion model was seated on a sofa with a woman who was obviously a fitness trainer, dressed in scanty aerobic workout tights. They were cheering on obese women walking down a runway.

Before Hailey could focus on a fourth monitor, a door slammed, and she turned to look through Russo's glass office wall toward the noise. It was Tony, rushing down the carpeted corridor toward all the other cubies.

"I was right! I found it! A new story, people! A torso! A bloody torso stuffed in a suitcase washed up on the beach in Jersey City! Unidentified! White female! People! We've got a show! You're dead . . . We're *alive*!"

Hailey could only assume he meant the show was alive, not cancelled.

Tony waved a handful of AP wires over his head like a cannibal brandishing a bloody scalp still warm off a skull. A loud flurry ensued among the bookers, who pounced on their phones to start rounding up guests and booking satellites.

Hailey studied their reactions, hunching over their screens, some with a phone to each ear and, somehow, manipulating BlackBerrys at the same time. What about the torso? Wasn't anybody a tiny bit concerned that a once-living human being had been severed in half?

"What about the head?" somebody yelled out over the short walls of the cubicles to no one in particular.

"Shut up and book! If we're lucky, it'll wash up tomorrow and we can do that . . . or better yet . . . maybe they'll fish it up while we're live today!"

What was wrong with these people?

And how in the world did *I* get tangled up with *them*? Hailey stood up and stalked to the coffee machine. It was loaded with expensive Starbucks offerings. These people obviously had money to burn. She went for her usual, whenever she couldn't get Irish Breakfast, chamomile with skim. No sugar.

Stirring the tea in the Styrofoam cup with a red plastic stick, she thought back on just how she landed here, in the center of a towering high-rise in the heart of Manhattan, the vortex of the television news industry.

"It's a gift from God. A gift!" Tony popped his head around the corner.

"What gift?" Taking a first, hot gulp, she looked at him over the Styrofoam rim.

"The torso! We'll do it the first fifteen minutes . . . You don't mind being the second story off breaking news, do you? I mean, it's *a woman's nude torso! No head!* It's a gift from God!"

Tony took her by the elbow and began steering her down the corridor.

"So I'll have somebody walk you to hair and makeup, and then on to the studio. Harry can't wait to meet you! He's just thrilled! You're just what we need! You'll be an overnight star . . . The audience will *love* you! A lawyer-turned-shrink whose husband was a cop gunned down in the line of duty. And you're a fox! The camera's gonna love you!"

Hailey stiffened like she always did, even now, this many years later, when someone brought up Will out of the blue. It was like cold water thrown on her face.

"Mr. Russo, I've never been married. Will was not a police officer. He was in college studying to be a geologist when he was murdered."

"Who's Will?"

With that, Hailey turned on her heel. Walking as fast as she could without actually breaking into a trot, she made a beeline for a door that had a FIRE EXIT sign, along with the words ALARM WILL SOUND posted above it in red letters. Turning the knob, she threw the words back at him over her shoulder.

"I don't think I'll be able to do your show today . . . Thanks for the offer. I'll find my own way out."

Russo was stunned. A *Harry Todd* guest? Refuse to go on air? A no-name former prosecutor who didn't jump at the chance to guest on a nationally televised talk show? She was walking away from *the number one daytime talk show in the whole country*? He couldn't wrap his mind around it . . . *Someone who didn't want to be on TV?*

In all his years, Tony Russo had never encountered such a thing and took off, hot on her heels. She had the head start, but he was gaining on her, darting through the heavy metal stairwell door, which had coincidentally set off an alarm when she opened it.

The cement stair shaft reeked of smoke. The steps were littered with years and years of old cigarette butts from every employee who wanted to sneak a puff without having to go outside. Now she got the alarm. Sneaky smokers must have entered through another floor that didn't alarm. Hailey's abrupt exit was not so sneaky.

"Wait!" he called out after her, pumping his chubby legs furiously to catch up. Russo was going as fast as he could, but Hailey was an avid runner . . . only when Russo slipped on the third flight, skidding down eight or nine stairs on nothing but rump and elbows, did Hailey stop to look back up.

Everything went quiet. She no longer heard his footsteps. Hailey took a few tentative steps back up. Did he fall? Was he hurt?

After a half-flight up, from around the corner of the stairs, she spotted him. His khaki pants had slid down even farther than before, and his stack of papers had scattered the length of the stairwell. His glasses were missing, and to top it off, he looked like he was going to cry. Something that sounded like a muffled man-sob echoed against the walls.

Cry? He was a grown man, for Pete's sake. Hailey sprinted back up the steps.

"Are you okay?"

"Yeah . . . I just don't understand why you ran out like that. What happened? It took me so long to book you and fly you back to New York to be here on the set with Harry . . ."

"I'm leaving because you have no idea who Will is. Everybody, including me, we're just stories . . . stories to fill up your hour . . . nothing more. Will was murdered. *He's dead.* He was gunned down just before our wedding. And it means nothing to you. I won't let him be shilled out for ratings. The whole thing makes me sick, but now that I see you're all right, I'm leaving."

Hailey turned and started back down the stairs, but after only a few steps, she heard it again, louder. An outright sob, no longer muffled. Was he actually *crying*? *Shedding tears? Ridiculous.*

The sobs got a little louder. Tony Russo was outright crying. Hailey stopped, her hand on the railing. Was he that sensitive? Reaching into her bra, she pulled out one of her father's old white cotton handkerchiefs she always carried for good luck, turned, and headed back up.

When she reached him again, he was even more of a mess, now huddled against the painted cement-block wall, sitting on one of the steps with his head in his elbows resting on his knees. He didn't look up, although there seemed to be a brief pause between sobs.

"I'll lose my job over this. I know I will. I work like a dog, literally night and day. This job is all I have, Hailey. My parents live in another state, I never see them. I'm not married, I don't even have a girlfriend. Running *The Harry Todd Show* takes every spare minute I've got. It's all I have. And now, Sookie will fire me. I let the 'big get' get away. I don't know what I'll do. I don't have anywhere to go."

Standing at his feet, Hailey looked down at his head and for the first time noticed hair plugs and some sort of surgical scar that looked vaguely like the Atlanta Braves' Hatchet. After years of prosecuting and making her living as a professional "observer," she couldn't help but make a note of the plugs in three neat rows converging in a loose V shape, to resemble a widow's peak. As he was a few inches taller than she, she'd never had this particular bird's-eye view.

"You'll seriously lose your job if I cancel? I'm just one guest."

"But you're *the* guest for today. Harry was interviewing you alone, on the set. One-on-one. That's a big deal . . . and they've already promo'ed you '*Hailey Dean . . . for the hour.*' It's run for days on the network and the Web site. The whole world has seen it. I lose you . . . I'm screwed."

"You really think you'd lose your job? Over *one guest*?"

He did look pitiful sitting there on the cement step like a lump, a cigarette butt stuck to the side of his pants.

"Okay. I'll do it. But one condition. Not a word about Will. Don't have Todd bring him up, don't mention him, don't *anything.* Understood?"

"Yes! Yes! Anything! Oh, Hailey, thank you so much. I'm sorry I offended you, I'm so stupid. *Thank you, thank you, thank you!* And I promise, not a word about Will. It's totally on the up-and-up, nothing but integrity, all about justice, you'll see. I promise. I give you my word as a producer."

Hailey paused to take that one in.

"And by the way, I couldn't help but notice you don't wear jewelry . . . would you be opposed to slipping on a gold lamé blouse? I keep one in my office. You know . . . a little bling? It'll look great on camera . . . The viewers will love it!"

He didn't wait for a response. "And on second thought . . . I'd better *personally* escort you to hair and makeup . . . a little eye shadow wouldn't hurt a thing . . ."

Hailey shook her head, walking up the stairs ahead of him. She didn't bother shooting a withering glare at him. It would just roll down the side of his shiny little head, wasted.

But Hailey had her own plans. Ever since she left the courtroom, her life's mission, since Will's murder anyway, felt unfinished. Fighting back against what had happened to Will, *to her,* was all she really knew to do. Everything else was just filling time.

Now she had an opportunity to attack the violence, the hurt, and the anger in a new and unexpected way . . . on the airwaves. If someone had told her way back, say in law school, when Will's murder was still a raw, open wound, that she'd end up on television as an anti-crime crusader, she'd never have believed it.

Violent crime nearly destroyed her. Even now, not a day went by she didn't feel the acute pain of Will's murder. She'd already tried the courtroom route. It had worked, one case at a time. She even killed a killer with her own hands, something she tried very hard not to think about.

Could TV, specifically *The Harry Todd Show*, be any worse?

|||||||||||||||||||||||||||||||||||||||||||||||||||||||||| 3 ||||||||||||||||||||||||||

The Bayou, Louisiana

WHO IN THE *HELL* WAS AT THE FRONT DOOR? The doorbell hadn't worked in years, and he couldn't even remember the last time somebody actually knocked on his door. The rapping was firm and insistent. A-holes!

When he first papered the windows, he didn't realize how thin the *New York Times* really was. Poor quality paper. The *Post* was so much thicker. Bottom line, nobody could see in. He'd punched dozens of tiny holes in the paper with straight pins, then twisted the pin round and round to make perfectly rounded, miniscule peepholes, strategically placed so he could peer out when necessary, but so small they were useless to anyone who wanted to look in. Plus, he planted prickly holly in front of every window, which had grown tall and thick. Let the mothers wade through *that* if they wanted to find out if somebody was home.

He actually thought of taking out one of his guns and shooting straight through the front door. Just blow 'em to hell and back. He could always argue self-defense. He was in his own house, and an intruder was antagonizing him on his own front porch. If he hadn't duct-taped over the front door peephole, he could get a better look at whoever was standing there, but after reading about reverse peepholes used as spy techniques by the U.S. government, specifically the IRS and the CIA, he beat the Feds at their own game and duct-taped his peephole.

Tiptoeing across the den floor, he avoided every spot he knew made a creaking sound.

Ha! He made it to the front window without a noise. He picked his favorite pinhole, in an article about cancerous food additives in fast-food french fries. The *Times* was always exposing something. They should expose themselves. What a crock of simmering liberal holier-than-thou twits.

Staring hard, he spotted a goldish-brown sedan parked in his front drive.

Cocking his head and looking as far left as he could without shifting locations, he could make out the very bottom of a white short-sleeved shirt. Was it the Amway people?

He took another look, with only one eye at the pinhole, twisting his neck at such an angle it was unnatural. He didn't want to actually touch the newspaper, so as not to tear it. He could feel his breath hot against the yellowed article on french fries.

Holy crap. It was *them* again.

The Jehovah's Witnesses.

Either them or the fricking Amway people. He didn't want any of their stupid detergent. Plus, last time he'd waved his shotgun at the Amways, so he doubted they'd be back any time soon. More likely the Jehovahs. They didn't scare easy.

The Jehovah's Witnesses were a different animal altogether . . . God only knows what it would take to make them go away. He'd either have to sandblast them off the front porch or else answer the door and accept their pamphlets.

Several months ago, two of them caught him coming in with both arms full of groceries and trapped him on the front porch. They kept inching toward the front door, but he held his back to it. They actually made themselves at home on his porch furniture and started pushing their *Awake!* magazine on him.

The very first thing they told him was Michael Jackson had been a member of their congregation. Well, that didn't go far at all with Francis. True, Jackson was one of the greatest music icons that ever lived, but wasn't he a junkie? That's not a very good advertisement for the Jehovahs, but apparently they didn't agree.

Aside from their refusing to acknowledge birthdays, July Fourth, Christmas, Halloween and Thanksgiving, the only thing he knew about them was they were against blood transfusions, vaccinations, and all festivities in general.

And of course there was the mandatory door-to-door proselytizing. A mandate of which he was now a victim. How many others had suffered like himself?

Oh yeah, and they were run by an outfit in Brooklyn, New York. That didn't set well down here on the Bayou. Anything run out of Brooklyn, New York, could kiss his butt.

That very night he'd removed all the patio furniture off the front porch. It was 2 a.m. when he did it, pulling out the hardware where he'd bolted the wicker chairs to the porch's wooden floor. Without porch furniture to plop down on, the Jehovah's Witnesses would never get another piece of him.

He didn't want anybody to see his activities, especially his crab of a neighbor. Gladys Kravitz he called her. From *Bewitched.* Always looking through the fence at him and everything he did since his mother passed away and left him the house. He got sick of her watching him, too. He was convinced she was in league with the Feds, so he welded sheet metal over all the windows on the side of the house that bordered Gladys Kravitz's yard. Nosey crone.

He looked longingly back at the poster of Leather Stockton at the far end of the long hall running the length of the house. She was posted there at the end of the hall, at eye level so he could talk to her one-on-one whenever he felt like it. He'd just lit a vanilla-scented candle and placed it at her feet. She loved the vanilla-scented candles he bought at Yankee Candle Company. It made the others jealous, so sometimes he'd pick one up for a few of them, specifically his other girlfriend, the wholesome singing star Cassie Lake. Everybody knew Cassie had a jealous streak. He got lilac scent for her and lit it on Fridays. Like date night.

That was Friday. On Tuesdays, he communed with Prentiss Love. He had lots of posters of Love, but his favorite, and the one he had taped to the wall in his bedroom, was her as a Dallas Cowboys Cheerleader. So alluring, but at the same time so wholesome in that little navy blue and silver skirt. Yes, she shot to stardom, but she still looked best in the little cheerleading outfit. His all-American girl.

Wednesdays were reserved for Fallon Malone. Of course, just like everybody else in the country, he'd seen her in her famous screen role where she washed a red Corvette *sans* underwear. But there was so much more to Fallon . . . a heart and soul that only somebody like him could understand. She hurt a lot, he could tell. *Extremely sensitive,* that one. All of her sexual flamboyance was to cover up her pain and self-doubt. If only he had the chance, he could turn her life completely around.

Then there were all the others, but this was Monday and right now, the Jehovahs were keeping him from Leather. She was getting pissed, he could tell. He looked at the poster, glowing goldish in the candlelight. She had that look in her eyes. She was angry he was keeping her waiting.

He hated it when Leather got this way.

Beside the candle, he'd very soon lay the pair of Leather's underwear he swiped from the Shutters on the Beach Hotel out in Santa Monica. He read how she'd go there, and so he went there and hung out at the hotel pool for four weekends in a row, living out of his car the whole time. Well, technically, it was his mother's car, but she was dead, anyway.

Finally, on his last day there, Leather came walking out of a cabana and strolled beside the pool heading for the main lobby. He wound his way through all the lounge chairs and drinks sitting there chilling on classy little tables beside the chairs and chaise lounges. He wanted to talk to her, maybe just touch her arm to see what Leather Stockton's skin felt like.

Was that so wrong?

When he finally got close enough to talk to her, he called out her name.

"Leather . . . Hi! It's me!"

The guy with her, whose hair, by the way, was obviously styled with hairspray or some related hair product, pushed him back hard in his chest.

He didn't want to appear uncivilized to Leather, so he didn't kick the guy in the crotch like he wanted to.

"Hey! Leather! It's me! I sent you the roses for your birthday last month! The white roses . . . Your favorite! Right?"

She only slightly glanced backwards. The guy just grabbed her elbow from behind and pushed her forward a little forcefully, saying something into the back of her hair.

Francis tried to keep up, but in the process, knocked over one of the little white plastic poolside tables with four frosty little drinks sitting on it. The glasses slid to the cement, splintering into pieces as they made impact.

Idiots! You should never serve drinks in glass glasses poolside! *Plastic*, people! Plastic! Ever heard of *plastic?*

Now, two hotel staffers headed straight for him. One was short and chunky. The other one was tall and lean, his collar loose around his throat. Their black jackets matched each other.

He couldn't give up this easily . . . He was finally in her presence. Screw the black jackets.

He called after her. "Leather . . . *It's me!* You sent me the photo of you in the swimsuit . . . Remember? I love it! It's up on my wall right beside the greatest poster of you I got at Spencer's."

"Sir! *Sir!* Can we be of some assistance?"

Closing in on him from behind, the Shutters security guards stepped up, one on each side of him, firmly placing their hands around each of his biceps.

He'd better cool it. He couldn't afford another arrest. That last stunt back home with the makings for a pipe bomb in the garage nearly landed him in the Federal pen. It was all BS of course, he hadn't even assembled it. What happened to freedom of speech? That's what his public defender said.

But now, his mother wasn't around anymore to bail him out. *There could be no more arrests.* That was one of the last little nuggets of wisdom she shot at him from her deathbed in the hospital.

Old bag.

Assistance? He managed to keep it together and answer almost normally. "Oh no, assistance will absolutely not be necessary. I'm fine. Just thought I recognized her."

He saw them exchange glances. Two little snots. They apparently didn't seem to think he was "fine."

The short, stocky one piped up. "Sir, in which room are you registered?"

"Actually, I just got here, I hadn't even stopped in the lobby to register yet."

Who was he kidding? He'd been here poolside for days, trying to scope out Stockton.

"Sir, do you have any identification on you?"

"Well, not exactly on me, but I do have it in the car. I'll just go out to the parking lot and get it."

"Did you valet? We can get that for you . . ."

Hell no, he did not *valet*.

He wasn't about to part with $25 to have some moron dent his car. His mother kept it in pristine condition for ten full years and he meant to keep it that way, although it was currently covered with a thick coat of dust. That was only because of the long drive out here. He planned to take it to the Minute Car Wash way before Leather got into the front seat with him.

"We'll just escort you to your car, sir."

"No need! I can find it." They could drop the "sir" bull. He knew they were going to have his butt arrested.

"No problem at all."

S.O.B.s. They literally walked him off the property and then tagged along the full seven blocks to where he parked the Saturn on the side of a street with no parking meter to worry about.

The "guards" stood by the side of the car as he got in and pretended to shuffle through some papers. Within sixty seconds, he switched on the ignition, floored it and scratched off.

The two must have seen it coming, because they jumped back pretty fast when he gunned the gas. Good thing, or else he might have taken one of their feet with him. Too bad.

Fine. They wouldn't let him talk to Leather?

He got them good.

That night, after he'd sneaked back onto the property, he watched the cabana he'd seen her come out of earlier . . . It was damn miserable squatted down in a thatch of palmetto bushes. The plant was like a bushel of swords. And the automatic sprinklers had come on, too.

S.O.B.s.

Around 9:30 p.m., he heard the cabana door open and music come floating out from inside. She'd been all alone in there. If he had known for sure she was alone, he'd have gone right in. He saw her step out onto the lighted walkway and leave.

She was a vision, dressed in a beaded, white halter top that looked great against her tan skin and blonde hair, and tight, white pants. He didn't dare move an inch, crouched there on the wet dirt beneath him, watching her walk away from the cabana. The man from earlier at the pool appeared out of nowhere and walked along beside her. So he wasn't a boyfriend, he was a bodyguard or else he'd have been inside with her. She was single. In his heart, he'd already known it.

But what about security? They could kiss his ass. Even with the best hotel security, Francis found a way. He waited till the coast was clear and jimmied the lock on a secluded window behind a group of three thick palm trees.

Once inside, he looked around. Leather's clothes were tossed casually across the bed and one of the chairs, and a hair dryer was lying on a counter next to a tall, silver can of hairspray. A bottle of vodka was beside the bed, with a glass of melting rocks. So she *was* a drinker after all. Probably out of sheer loneliness.

There were the jeans she'd had on earlier at the pool. They were on the floor, as if she'd just stepped out of them. Shoes were everywhere. Who cared if she wasn't a neatnik? She could learn to be a good wife. He would be patient.

He couldn't help but stop to just breathe it in. Her perfume was delicious. He couldn't stop himself. He had to pick up the jeans and rub his face in them. The heady sensation sent tingles up and down his whole body. The touch of her jeans against his face . . . It was so much more than he could ever have imagined. He was overcome with love.

He stopped the sniffing and rubbing when, from beneath lowered lids, he spotted her bed pillow. This was the pillow where Leather Stockton had laid her beautiful face and luxurious hair.

There was no other word to describe Leather's hair than simply luxurious.

The sight of her pillow caused him to take several deep gulps of air. He stared down at it intently and walked toward it carefully, as if it might jump off the bed and run away frightened. Kneeling down on one knee at the top corner of the bed, he leaned in closer to the mattress, looking intently for a strand or two of Leather's silky hair, but didn't see any.

He scanned the bedside area. There was a stack of papers by the telephone; he'd love to look through them or better yet, take them in order to track her a little better, but he didn't have time and they were the kind of thing she'd likely miss.

Just like James Bond, with time running down to the last second, he scored. A red pair of silk thong underwear was lying on the bathroom floor beside the shower. The tiny shred of material was practically still warm.

That had been three years ago.

Ever since then, he'd kept them preserved in a plastic Zip Lock sandwich bag, only taking them out for their date every Friday night.

Standing there, trying to peer onto his front porch through the newspaper punch hole, the thought occurred to him . . . Could Leather have possibly *wanted* him to leave? She could have said something, *anything* to call her bodyguard off. Did she really have feelings for him, as she'd told him through the TV set?

Every time she was on, he set his TiVo to automatically record it just in case somehow he missed it live. She always sent him special, sexy little messages, all in code of course, like touching her necklace or earring or brushing her hair away for her face. It was so the Feds wouldn't pick up on it. But they were such dumbasses they never would.

Leather was very private that way.

But thinking back on it, he wondered: Had she purposefully allowed him to be brushed off? Humiliated there at the Shutters pool?

Was it part of some game she was playing with his head? He stared hard at the poster of her, smiling in a swimsuit.

Was Leather Stockton . . . . *a bitch*?

||||||||||||||||||||||||||||||||||||||||||||||||||||||||| **4** ||||||||||||||||||||||||||

WHEN QUINTON HOWARD ROUNDED THE CORNER OF THE POOL house, the stench hit him like a ton of bricks. He headed for the four giant plastic trash bins he'd emptied for the last eight months. Normally, the city provided curbside pick-up. All the rich people made their maids roll it down just before trash time, but the Saxtons paid a hundred bucks extra a week to the lucky sanitation worker assigned to their street so nobody would have to worry about wheeling it down the driveway.

Incredible.

The bins were just in sight. Quinton turned left, each step digging into crunchy gravel beneath his work boots. They were hidden from the casual eye by a decorative "modern-contemporary" façade to match the stark (bleak) lines of the mansion. They'd probably paid some uptight German architect God only knows what to design their huge monstrosity, all white and plain, with a cute little trash-bin hider to match.

Frank Lloyd Wright would vomit.

All the recycle bins were stacked neatly beside the garbage, something to make the rich people feel good about themselves. Quinton always got a laugh off the $15 bottles of sparkling water from Italy these idiots sprung for, tucked neatly into their recycle bins.

Oh, the dichotomy of the über-wealthy. Quinton graduated with a master's in philosophy from the University of Pennsylvania. He could tell you anything about the great philosophical thinkers, Thales, Aristotle, Plato, Socrates, Descartes, Hobbes, Rousseau, Marx, Nietzsche, Spinoza . . . he could go on.

His all-time favorite was Aquinas, of course, who shifted the focus from Plato to Aristotle in his attempt to fuse Christianity *with* Aristotelianism. Quinton's impressive, and unfinished, doctoral thesis had been on Aquinas's *Summa Theologica*. He was still deeply pissed he couldn't find a job expounding his deep thoughts on countless crops of philosophy majors at some, *any*, college or university. Hell, in the end he'd even have taken a *community* college offer . . .

But screw Plato, what the hell was that stench?

It seemed to emanate from the pool house. Quinton knew better than to look into rich people's windows, but it looked like they were either gone or sleeping off another late night of partying, although the hot tub wasn't still on and bubbling, surrounded by steam and booze bottles like it normally was every Tuesday and Thursday he was here.

Cocking his head to the left, he peered into the pool house with his right eye and there it was.

A woman. A dead woman. She was wearing a tight, pale pink miniskirt and heels, sitting in a straight-back chair that matched an uncomfortable-looking, modernistic table nearby.

In fact, she looked pretty hot with those legs, except for the fact half her head was blown off. Her hands seemed to be tied or taped to the chair, and her legs were sprawled at a weird angle out in front of her.

And she stunk. To high Heaven. No telling how long she'd been there.

Quinton pulled out his iPhone to call 911. But just before he hit "send," he had a thought. Instead of putting the call through to Emergency Dispatch, he scrolled down to "contacts."

Let's see, where was he, where was he? Frank LaGrange Hadden III. He met him at a bar a few weeks ago and kept his number. "Photographer to the World" he'd called himself. Translation: He was a photog for every sleazy tabloid in the country and then some. Hadden made it his business to know every waiter, waitress, maître d', beat cop, emergency dispatcher, and garbage man in town.

"Hadden." He answered the phone with two flat syllables, nothing more.

"Frank, it's me, Quinton. You met me at Muley's the other night."

There was a pause on the other end.

Quinton went on. "You know, the *trash man*."

"Oh, yeah! You work East Hampton, right? What's up, man?"

"I got something for you. I think it's big."

"Everybody thinks it's big. What is it?"

Not wanting to give away too much before getting a price quote, Quinton hedged. "It's big all right. If you think a dead body in a star's pool house tied to a chair is big."

"Holy shit. Where are you?"

"That's the million-dollar question. The owners aren't home. Don't know when they'll come back, but I know they weren't here Tuesday, either. That's when I was last here. No telling how long she's been here. May have been here then, I just didn't smell it until now and man, she *reeks*!"

"Million-dollar question's overdoing it a little, maybe a thousand's more like it." Hadden cut straight to the chase.

"Bullshit."

"Okay. If it's an A-lister, I can do five. Who is it?"

"I'm not telling till I get a number, dude."

"Have they ever won an award? You know . . . an Oscar, Emmy, Daytime soap? Porn awards don't count. But maybe they do since it's a dead body. You gotta give me more . . . or unless they're currently on TV, have a recurring role, have ever been in a movie, or if you've ever seen a story about them on *ET*, *Access*, or the *Insider*."

"Award, *Enquirer*, *ET*. Is that enough?"

"You got the five. I'm on my way. What's the address?"

"It ain't that easy, buddy. How do I know you won't get your shot and then leave me high and dry? I'll meet you a few blocks away and bring you here. Cash money up front. But, hurry, I gotta go or the others will get suspicious. I'll just tell them I gotta take a dump when you get close . . . But you gotta *hurry*, man."

"I'm an hour away. I'll do my best."

"Okay. Call me, and after you get here, I'll give you ten minutes before I call 911."

"Why do you have to call 911 at all?"

Quinton dug deep. What would Aquinas do? Or Spinoza?

Screw them. Seven years of devoting himself to them and he still had a roommate.

"Maybe I don't."

"On the other hand, if you do, then I could snap some long shots of cops arriving and bringing the body out. Coroner's office, the whole shebang. Hey, tell you what I'll do . . . You call 911 and I'll throw in an extra five hundred."

"A thousand."

"Seven-fifty."

"Done. See you in an hour." Quinton agreed to the price, having no idea a shot like this would be worth a lot more to one of the tabs. Seven hundred fifty dollars bonus money sounded great to him. All he wanted was a flat-screen.

"Forty-five minutes. I'm already in the car and on the highway. Traffic's light."

Quinton took one last peek at her. Poor broad. Nice legs, but, still, poor broad.

He crunched around the side of the mansion to the front drive and headed back to the truck.

"What the hell took so long?" They yelled it at him as they lounged against the back of the truck, waiting.

"Nothing, you lard-asses. Just checking the recycles. Empty again."

"Rat bastards don't give a crap about the environment." His trash partner muttered it under his breath, grinding a cigarette butt beneath his work boot there on the drive.

Quinton hopped on the back of the truck, held on, and off they went to the end of the cul-de-sac. The houses were few and far between. He eyed the digital watch on his wrist.

Forty minutes and counting.

T HIS HAD DAMN WELL BETTER BE GOOD. FRANK LAGRANGE HADDEN III didn't like getting out of bed before 10 a.m. He had been out developing "contacts" at a bar last night and didn't get home until after three in the morning. It was all a little bit of a blur.

Clutching a large, black coffee from a McDonald's drive-thru, he floored it, heading up the Long Island Expressway. He didn't really expect much, but a dead body in an out-of-town celeb's mansion couldn't be all bad . . . *Could it?*

Oh, hell. It was starting to rain. At least it wasn't a summer weekend or he'd be stuck in the thousands of city dwellers heading for the Hamptons for forty-eight hours, either to get a breath of sea air or make the scene. And man, what a scene. New Yorkers were convinced, if you didn't have a place in the Hamptons, you were nothing. They were willing to pay an arm and a leg for a hole in the wall just to say they had a place in the Hamptons. The ones that couldn't afford to buy or rent just went every weekend to free-load off the ones that sprang for a place.

Whatever. Pretentious boors.

He was just fine with his one-bedroom apartment walk-up two flights above China Fun on First Avenue. It was loud as hell so close to the street and it always smelled like duck, but it was fine. He missed his house back down south in the suburbs, but he lost it in the divorce. He got offered a free place to live with a friend here in the city for a few months, then he just stayed. It was easier.

This coffee was good. He didn't care what Dunkin' said. Mc-Donald's was the best. And the cheapest.

He'd been on the road for over an hour now and, without much traffic, was just about to pull into East Hampton. Feeling around in his pants pockets, he fished out his cell phone and hit "redial."

"Hello?" Quinton Howard asked it tentatively.

"It's me, Hadden. I think I'm just a few blocks from you. Wanna give me the location now?"

"Hey, man. You're late! Do you have the cash?"

"Of course I do. Do you have the dead body?"

"Shut up, man. It's not *my* dead body. I saw it. I wanna get this thing over with."

"All right, all right. Calm down. Where are you?"

"Hurry. I'll be at 43 East Shore Lane in five minutes. It's right on the water."

"Of course it is. You're a piece of crap if you're not on the water. Then they gotta have a pool."

"Yeah. Whatever, man. I'll be out back by the pool house."

"Whose place did you say it was?"

"I didn't. You'll see when you get here."

"Oh. Okay. Mr. Secret Agent Man. I'll find out when I get there. See you in five."

Hadden was pretty sure he knew how to find Shore Lane. The ritzy side was East Shore, which led down to the water. The "cheap" side was West Shore, which was not on the water but within walking distance. It was the supreme humiliation for the West Shore people to be caught walking through the crosswalk that divided the two, dressed in swimsuits and carrying beach gear. It identified them as the have-nots. Poor schmucks. They had to walk the quarter-mile to the dunes while the haves just looked right out the kitchen window and over their pools to the waves.

Winding through lane after lane of multimillion-dollar mansions, Hadden turned right onto East Shore. The tiny lane could barely handle two cars passing, but luckily, fewer people were around this time of year.

"Let's see, 37, 39 . . ." Hadden muttered to himself as he edged along, hunching forward over the steering wheel making out numbers on the mailboxes.

"41 . . . *Bingo!* 43."

He checked his rearview. Nobody there. Nobody ahead, either. Driving forward about eighty feet or so, he parked on the side of the street on grass that seemed unattached to any of the mansions.

Last thing he needed was to get towed out of somebody's driveway or reported by Neighborhood Watch. This bunch probably didn't have a Neighborhood Watch. Probably sprung for private security patrol. He better move it.

Walking casually, as if he belonged there, Hadden crossed the eighty feet and walked up the side of 43. Spotting a walkway on the side of the house, he slipped under an arched trellis and headed down the shelled walk out back. Walking the length of the house, front to back, he looked in several of the windows. It was empty, all right.

Wait a minute. He backed up and looked into a side window. They must have had their lights on timers. There, under a spotlight installed flush with the twenty-foot-high ceiling, carefully centered in the middle of a shelf with nothing else around it, sat an Oscar.

There was no mistaking it. The little statuette gleamed out at Hadden standing there on the sidewalk staring in.

Whose house was this anyway? He felt like he'd seen it before. He stepped forward a few steps and looked through another window. Gracefully arranged on the lid of a shiny black Steinway grand piano were a dozen or so family photos, all encased in similar sterling silver frames. There was the star, smiling out from inside a frame. It was Eric Saxton.

Holy shit. *Pay dirt!*

Eric Saxton! Yeah, way past his prime and all patched together with hair implants, lipo, and a full-on face-lift, but still a star. And so was the new Mrs. Saxton, Lisa. She was an actress and had to be twenty years younger than him even if she was lying about her age by, say, seven or eight years.

They'd met on a movie set. As soon as the affair took off, he dumped his wife, leaving her and his four kids, to move in with the actress.

He glanced at the photos again. Even though they were set up to look like candids, on vacations and such, they all looked like glamour shots from the mall. They had to be professionally touched up . . . or were people actually this beautiful?

He thought for a second about all the stars he'd caught without makeup and sold the shots to the tabs. The ones on the grand piano were touched up, no doubt about it.

Hadden felt a tingle in his gut. He was on the verge of a huge paycheck, but this was dangerous. Skulking around an old Hollywood star's place was a suicide mission.

And they were pretty freaky about that out here because of squatters, people from the city who came out here off-season and took up in empty mansions until they were busted. Sometimes they made it a whole season, living the high life, eating the food out of inlaid Sub-Zero fridges, watching TV in fancy home theaters, sleeping on the thousand-count Egyptian-cotton bedsheets, until somebody recognized they were out of place.

Usually they just ended up paying a fine. Owners didn't want to be bothered with prosecuting. Just wanted their maids to change the sheets.

Hadden better hurry. And Quinton better be out back and he damn well better have a dead body with him. Turning the corner, Hadden spotted him standing at the door of the pool house, guarding his find.

"Hey, man. Show me the cash."

"Not one for small talk, huh? Okay. Here, here's half. Show me the body and I'll give you the rest."

Hadden took a fat roll of cash out of his right pocket and peeled off three grand. With no fanfare, he thrust it into Quinton's right hand.

"Where's the other two?"

"Right here in my pocket and it'll be in yours the minute I see the body."

Quinton stalled for a moment, thinking over his options, but other than tackle Hadden right then and there, take the money and run, his only real choice was to hope Hadden would come through.

"Okay. Follow me."

He led Hadden through a set of carefully manicured wisteria bushes, trained to wrap themselves around a lattice arch.

And sure enough, there she was.

"What a set of legs. It's a shame." It was all Quinton could think to say as Hadden stared through the glass door to the pool house.

For a moment Hadden said nothing, and suddenly, Quinton was afraid he wouldn't get the remaining two grand. "Hey, man. You said five grand if it was in a celeb's house. And it is. You don't get a whole lot bigger than Eric Saxton. Plus, there's the wife. She's a star, too."

"Shut up, Quinton. You'll get the money. I'm just trying to place that tattoo she's got on her ankle. I know I've seen it somewhere before."

Quinton squinted again through the glass. He was right. Guess a photographer's eye caught it. There was a series of small, delicate, Chinese-looking characters down the inside of the girl's left ankle.

"What the hell? Who cares about a tattoo? She's got her head blown off in Eric Saxton's pool house!" Quinton didn't feel like getting philosophical about the woman's tattoo. He wanted to get his money, then get the hell out of here.

"Yeah. Here's the money." Hadden got out his money ball again and counted out two thousand.

Handing it to Quinton, he started to quickly assemble his Nikon, attaching a long lens to one end. "Now, it'll only take me a minute to get some up-close shots . . . Call 911. Pronto."

"What's my excuse for being back up here?"

"Tell 'em you're checking the recycle bins."

"But I already told the crew that!"

"Whatever! Tell 'em you missed one! Just call!"

Hadden didn't look over his shoulder as Quinton whipped open his cell and punched in the numbers.

"Wait a minute. Where's my seven-fifty if I call the police?"

"Right here, my man, right here." Hadden gave him the rest of the money and, without missing a beat, hopped up on a retainer wall beside the door and started getting shots through a window.

"Listen, Quinton, make the call. I gotta get these shots and get behind those bushes before the ambulance gets here."

Quinton chose the speaker-phone feature on his cell so Hadden could hear the whole thing, just to make sure he got the extra seven hundred fifty dollars. After punching 911, he pushed the "send" button.

The phone rang several times, followed by an automated message warning callers not to dial 911 if they didn't have a real emergency, and redirecting them. That way the cops could avoid, say, a mouse in the kitchen or a cat stuck up a tree.

"911 Emergency Dispatch. What's your emergency?" It was a female voice, crisp and cool.

Quinton Howard paused. Was it right to make money off a dead woman? Obviously murdered? Her face was nothing but a mushy pile of pulp on one side. From the glass door, he couldn't see the other side, but it probably didn't fare much better. It hit him, standing there: *What had he become? What had happened to his ethics, his values?*

He had a choice . . . he could hang up right now, give the money back, and walk away. Screw Frank LaGrange Hadden III and his filthy blood money. This wasn't right, morally, religiously, or philosophically.

Quinton pondered. It was the age-old problem first encountered in the Garden of Eden. Good vs. bad, right vs. wrong, evil vs. sublime. Eve was seduced by a talking snake, the magician Faust sold his soul for knowledge and power, and Tab Hunter, aka Joe Hardy, sold out in *Damn Yankees* to transform himself from a middle-aged baseball fan to a young long-ball hitter who could beat the Yankees in the World Series.

They were all a string of bad ideas. For once, Quinton Howard could learn from the mistakes of others.

But then . . . There *was* the flat-screen he wanted for his apartment.

"Repeat . . . 911 Emergency Dispatch. What's your emergency?"

Quinton dug down deep. For once in his life, he had to be strong.

"Hello? I need help. The cops need to come in a hurry. I think I see a dead girl. Her head's blown off."

W HERE THE HELL WERE THE COPS? EVEN AN AMBULANCE would do. It had been nearly thirty minutes and they were all no-shows. He himself had heard Quinton give the exact location, street address included. *Where was this bunch of hayseeds?*

Hadden had gone from crouching behind a hedge about fifty feet back from the pool house, poised to start snapping long shots with his Nikon, to sitting flat on his rear on a pile of pine straw, peering through some azalea bushes. He wasn't too worried about these nincompoops spotting him; they apparently couldn't even find Saxton's house.

Just as he whipped out his cell to check his messages, he heard voices. Hmm. So they hadn't used the sirens. Probably didn't want to cause a ruckus in a neighborhood like this one.

Hadden stuck his nose back in the azaleas. There they were. Two uniformed Hamptons cops, coming up the same walk he had. He could hear every word. Quinton was walking along with them and was explaining how he'd been picking up the trash, but was interrupted pretty quickly by the short cop. He had his back to Hadden, but Frank could still hear him clearly.

"But why were you back here? Don't you pick it up out front?"

"Oh, yeah. But I do this as a favor for the Saxtons when they're out of town, you know, so burglars won't see the trash cans on the road for days on end and come loot the place. You know, just to be safe . . . right?"

The cops just looked at him and started taking notes on little pads they both had. They walked up to the glass door and looked in. The tall one took one look and puked right onto a bush beside the walkway. It sounded like he was vomiting all the way up from the soles of his feet.

What an embarrassment. Hadden started laughing to himself, then it turned into a coughing fit. Damn cigarettes. He could hardly laugh without coughing like a wild dingo.

Hadden stifled it. Didn't want to explain to cops why he was sitting out back on a freaking pine cone.

After the tall, young one quit with the puking, the other cop just looked at him. The contempt for his weakness was barely concealed.

The short one held his hand to a shoulder police-band radio, barked a series of numbers into it, began asking the routine questions. What time did Quinton get there, was it his usual route, blah, blah *blah.*

Quinton was holding up pretty well. It was easy . . . So far he was just telling the truth. Not hard, or so you'd think.

Thank God. Here came the EMTs. The body would soon be out on a stretcher. The cops were already fiddling with the lock on the glass doors.

What was the hold-up? Even Hadden could jimmy a sliding glass door in no time. Then . . . They got it. The door slid open and they all walked in, including Quinton. Hey, maybe Hadden could actually enter the pool house after they all left and get inside shots.

Within forty-five seconds, the young one was back outside puking again, this time on a different bush. Who could eat that much this early in the morning?

Hadden couldn't hear what the other cop was asking or what the EMTs were saying over all the puking sounds. Plus, the puking cop was obscuring his view. He finally finished, wiped off his face, and went back in to the murder scene. A man in a blue sports coat—Hadden could tell it was polyester from fifty feet away by the way the material shined in the morning light—and gray slacks reappeared. He'd walked up along with the EMTs and started taking pictures with a black camera. Not a bad piece of equipment, either.

Hadden recognized it as similar to his own. Must be the detective for the Coroner's Office.

Hadden crouched into position, secured the long lens, and started snapping away. He was waiting on the body. They'd probably have a white sheet over the face but maybe he'd get lucky and they wouldn't. After he got shots of the dead body being rolled out, he'd take a few beauty shots from the front yard, a couple of side shots showing the walkway around back, and of course a few shots of the pool, complete with hidden grotto. He could only imagine what went on in the grotto.

Then, who would give him the best money? After all, it was Eric Saxton's house. Who knew who the broad was. Whoever she was, he had plenty of shots of those legs.

It came to him in a flash. Mike Walker with *Snoop*. That was the primo mag. Walker was no idiot. After a stint in the air force in Japan, he became the youngest-ever foreign correspondent for International News Service, which later became UP. He ended up as a foreign correspondent for NBC, then went for the big money with *Snoop*. They were the single largest-circulation mag in America. Over seventeen million readers weekly.

Hadden was nearly giddy at the thought of Walker and *Snoop*. He started snapping shots even faster.

Who knew what headline they'd attach to the story? One of Walker's fortes was headlines. Hell, Hadden didn't care what they printed, as long as they paid him. He could easily get fifty grand for this. He'd make sure to get a shot of the Oscar statuette, just yards away from a dead body!

Hadden had no idea how to reach Walker directly. He'd only spoken to underlings at *Snoop* in the past, and in all his years, had only gotten two shots published on *Snoop*'s pages.

He could hardly wait until they rolled the body out.

It had been over an hour now. Hadden could see the coroner's investigator down on his knees, measuring the length from the pool house door to the body, then from the window to the body. The others were also on their hands and knees, likely combing the carpet for a shell casing or maybe even a bullet. The head was so mangled, it would take an autopsy to determine if there was an exit wound. For all they knew, one or more bullets could either still be in her skull, or have shot out the back of her head onto the floor.

How long would they be in there? He had a cramp in his leg but didn't dare move a hair. Squatted there behind the bushes, Hadden was shifting positions when he spotted a dog. Oh, hell.

The damn thing came right over to him and started to bark. The cops turned around and looked. Hadden froze.

The dog nosed his way through the azaleas and actually started sniffing at Hadden.

What the hell? He must smell the McDonald's. Fast-food sausage biscuit smell could linger on clothes for hours. One of the cops stepped outside the pool house, looking back at the bushes.

Damn dog. Now he was sniffing Hadden's leg. What would be next?

The cop took a few steps toward the bushes where Hadden was trying his best to shoo the dog away before its sniffing got any more personal.

The dog looked him straight in the eye, raised its left hind leg, and seemed to enjoy taking a long, warm piss right on Hadden's shoe. There was not a damn thing Hadden could do about it. He could feel the urine soaking down through the ankle of his sock.

Static-laced squawks came out of the cop's shoulder radio. He stopped to talk back into his shoulder, turned on his heel, and walked back to the pool house.

Suddenly, it happened. They were bringing out the body on a gurney. Hadden could barely contain himself. He needed a cigarette badly.

The coroner's staff rolled her out, and sure enough, they had a white sheet over her body, including her face. Damn them to hell.

But then, in a moment of serendipity, her left wrist fell out.

The girl's dead, manicured, salon-tanned hand dangled there, as only a dead hand could. It was beautiful.

Hadden almost wet his pants.

"YOU KNOW WHAT A JPEG IS DON'T YOU? YOU'VE HEARD OF that, right?"

Walker was losing patience with the moron on the other end of the phone, but if he had a shot of what he claimed to have, this could be the winning lottery ticket for Walker. But you had to give the guy credit for persistence. Walker didn't know how Frank Hadden, whoever the hell that was, got his cell number, but he'd called it no less than fifteen times.

Walker noticed the cell lighting up on the bathroom counter when he got up to take a leak. Assuming it was an emergency that early in the morning, he picked it up even though he didn't recognize the caller's number. After a brief self-introduction, Walker could hardly make out, Hadden said one phrase loud and clear: *Dead girl, great legs, Eric Saxton, and pool house.*

Hearing those words together in the same sentence, alarms started going off in Walker's head. Now he was trying his best to walk Hadden through sending the photos to him via his iPhone. He'd been explaining for the last fifteen minutes.

It was way too early for this BS. Walker clicked the phone on speaker and turned to pour his coffee. Then, the magical "ping," the phone alerted him to a received message.

It was the first of Hadden's jPEGs.

"Hold on, Hadden, I think I got something."

Walker opened up the text. *Holy shit!*

He set down his mug and reaching into the pocket of his bathrobe, he pulled out his other cell phone, punched in a number off speed dial and put Hadden on mute with his other thumb.

"Jerry, get up. Hurry. Get out to the Hamptons right now. There's a dead girl in Eric Saxton's pool house. I've got photo confirmation. She's probably at the morgue by now. Don't stop for a shower. Get out there and try to get whatever you can. Take the coroner doughnuts, find the cop, do whatever you have to do, get something now. Find out who she is. I want it on the cover of *Snoop* but it's gotta be fast. We go to press in twelve hours."

Walker clicked off. Taking Hadden off mute, he broke into Hadden's monologue. "I'm sorry, I lost you for a moment. Look, let's cut the crap. How much do you want?"

The jPEGs kept coming. They were beyond fantastic.

"So how many do you have?"

"Over a hundred. I've got the mansion exteriors, shots of the family on the grand piano . . ."

"You didn't break in, did you? That'll screw the pooch . . ."

"No way! I'm not an idiot, Mr. Walker. I shot from outside, through the window! For all they know, I coulda been thirty feet away! No trespassing here!"

"Okay. What else do you have . . . exteriors, photos . . ."

"I got the backyard, the tranquility pool, pool house, about twenty-five or thirty shots of the girl, the cops arriving, and the jackpot . . . shots of the girl being wheeled out with a wrist dangling off the gurney!"

"Face covered?"

"Yeah. The S.O.B.s covered her up with a sheet."

"Damn. I hate when they do that. But you said a wrist was dangling out?"

"Yep."

"Okay. But we still have no idea who the girl is . . . She could be nobody . . ."

"*Who cares who she is?* It's Eric Saxton's house! This is at least worth fifty grand! Don't bullshit me. I'll go to another tab if you don't pay. I'll call right now you cheap son of a—"

Taking a closer look at one particular shot of the dead girl, the one where her leg was sprawled out from the chair, Walker abruptly stopped the bargaining, cutting Hadden off mid-sentence.

"No need for you to do that. No need to haggle about money. You're right. Your work is phenomenal. You have a real talent for, let me say, *capturing the moment* so well, so beautifully. Perfectly, actually, to be completely accurate. *Snoop* will absolutely pay you the fifty. I can wire it from my laptop in thirty minutes. Give me a number. Happy?"

Hadden was speechless. He knew *Snoop* was the best, but he'd expected a big argument, and in the end, he'd realistically hoped he could turn around fifteen large. This was over triple what he had hoped for.

"Just send the rest of what you've got. I'm firing up my laptop right now. E-mail the numbers so I don't wire to the wrong account. Okay, buddy?"

"I'm e-mailing now from my BlackBerry. Thanks . . ." Hadden didn't know quite how to end it, but he wanted to get off the phone before somehow, it all went wrong.

The phone clicked off. Man, what a morning!

Little did Hadden know that at that very same moment, Walker was yelling out to his wife, "Honey! Honey! Come here! Hurry! Look at this!"

When she arrived in the kitchen rubbing her eyes, Walker was standing by the kitchen window to get the morning light, squinting into his iPhone.

"Look at this dead girl . . ."

"Why do I want to look at a picture of a dead girl first thing in the morning? I haven't even had any coffee . . ."

"Okay. Don't look at the dead girl. Just look at her leg."

Marjorie Walker squinted in the light to get a look at a shapely leg attached to a dead woman's body, seated in a straight chair. The leg was sprawled at an unnatural angle.

"Okay. I see it. What about it?"

"The tattoo, Marjorie, the tattoo! Forget the head. *Look at the tattoo!*"

By now, Walker was on his laptop, to which he'd sent the photos. He punched a few keys and the photo was enlarged. He zeroed in on the ankle tattoo and blew it up. Along with some Chinese characters, the tattoo depicted two intertwined hearts. The hearts had initials in them. LS and KD.

Leather Stockton and her former husband, Kenny DePaul.

The dead girl was Leather Stockton.

"OMG! DID YOU SEE THE TWITTER? ABOUT LEATHER STOCKTON?" Sookie breathed it into her cell phone, barely able to contain the excitement.

"*Yee-es!* Of course I saw it! Twenty minutes ago!" He had to outdo her on the timing . . . Sookie had to think he saw it before she did.

He was a little stunned she knew about the murder. Sookie hadn't even known Reagan was dead for two days, while Russo booked like mad.

"Are you thinking what I'm thinking?" He breathed it right back into the receiver at her, his lips actually grazing the mouthpiece.

"Yes! Absolutely! Pull Harry's last interview with her . . . you know the one after her DUI? Or was it after her divorce from that Wall Streeter? Whatever . . . I think it was right after her DUI . . . Didn't you tell me she was drunk in the Green Room?"

"Yes, I definitely told you. You weren't here. You were in the Bahamas, I think, weren't you celebrating your fortieth? Weren't you on a yacht and you had that French Champagne you told me about? You know, a thousand dollars a bottle?"

"Tony . . . You're right! Again! I was in the Bahamas with Julian for my fortieth! The French Champagne! Your memory is *amazing*!" It hit neither that *all* Champagne came from France, or else it wasn't Champagne.

"I remember! I never forget a detail!" Tony desperately wanted praise. It didn't happen.

"But, please, Tony, don't get me started on Julian. He's dating a girl in college now. *College.* Some little tramp from Barbados. She's probably eighteen. That's sick. Please, I can't think about him anymore today."

Tony didn't bother to point out he wasn't the one who brought up Sookie's soon-to-be ex-husband, Julian. She did. As usual. No way did Tony want to launch another three-hour phone therapy session about Sookie's most recent marriage disaster.

"How do you know she's eighteen? Where did you see her?"

"Where? It doesn't matter . . . *Okay . . . from my car . . .* across a parking lot when they were going out to dinner. I happened to be there at the same time they were."

Oh, no, Sookie was stalking her ex again. Tony knew it.

"But Tony, let's focus on Leather."

"It's got to run today."

"No! Tonight! We'll stick with Hailey Dean and the torso for today daytime, then push the suits to preempt political coverage and go with Harry's last sit-down with Leather! That White House bunch, whine, whine, whine, it's always the same thing night after night. How do they *do* it?"

"Yes! Tonight!" Tony paused. "But wait . . ." *Stay calm . . . Stay calm.* Tony thought it through. "If we go prime time tonight, we won't get the credit for the big number . . . It won't be our time slot . . ."

"Doesn't matter . . . we don't have time to promo before air . . ." she reminded him.

"Okay. I'm on it. By the way . . . where are you?"

"At the salon . . . remember? The root emergency? I can't do everything . . . you'll have to handle it."

Sookie's attention was already drifting; she was looking in the mirror at her roots and, shockingly, observed they were more gray than dark brown. She assumed something was wrong with the lighting . . . probably the fluorescents beaming off the crown of her head.

"We have time! We can promo it as *Live interview with Leather Stockton.*"

"But it's *not* live, Tony. We can't."

"But Sookie, it *was* live when we shot it . . . remember? The viewers won't know . . . They'll think Leather Stockton *must not be dead* . . . and they'll have to watch because they'll have heard all day she *is* dead!"

"So when Standards and Ethics starts whining and complaining, that's our out. That it *was* live when we shot it?" Sookie feigned attention to the show's details, but couldn't peel her eyes away from several gray hairs along the part of her hair.

"Sure! Plus, better to ask forgiveness than permission . . . Right?! That's what you always say!" Tony had it all figured out.

"Okay. Handle it . . . I have to go . . . somebody's beeping in." She was gone.

Leather Stockton's last interview.

What would the lower font read? *Bullet to the Brain of TV Beauty?*

He had to get the dot-com people on the phone right now to start the promos. Picking up his cell and land line, he started punching digits simultaneously. Once one began to ring, he put it on speaker and started typing furiously onto his BlackBerry.

This would be tough. He'd need the whole staff on board. He'd order them pizza to make it okay.

Russo was in Heaven.

THE *HARRY TODD* SET WAS ICY COLD. GOOD THING SHE'D WORN A suit jacket and blouse to top her usual jeans and cowboy boots. Hailey noticed all the other women in the Green Room, totally decked out with intricate hairdos and over-the-top makeup and jewelry. Even though she knew she didn't fit in to the scene, no way would she have slipped on the hideous gold lamé blouse Tony Russo tried to force on her again. Ridiculous. Plus, it smelled slightly of sweat. He'd obviously used it on other guests that didn't meet his "eye" for TV ratings.

Whatever. She didn't want to fit in with this phony bunch, although she was looking forward to meeting Todd; she'd watched him for years.

After sitting there for about fifteen minutes on a sofa before a live TV audience who talked among themselves, occasionally stirred up by one of the producers on a megaphone who was trying desperately to get them riled up, Todd made his entrance.

He was flanked by three staffers who were prepping him even as he walked up on the set.

"Hello, Hailey."

Her first reaction was astonishment. His face seemed unreal and he was so tiny. His bleached-blond hair stood up in a stiff spike down the center of his head and the rest was combed thinly around it. A gold chain peeked from his open collar . . . He seemed so much more robust on camera. She'd heard rumors he stuck to some fad diet in the false belief that thinner was younger, but now she believed it.

Hailey stood and reached out to shake his hand. He conspicuously did not take her hand, so she casually let it drop by her side.

Hmm . . . Maybe he's a germaphobe. Poor thing. The staffers laid out several thick, yellow sheets of paper before him on his anchor table. Reading them upside down from across the table, Hailey realized they were the exact questions he was being spoon-fed to ask, word for word.

Within two minutes max, the intro music to the show started. The audience producer motioned everyone to start clapping.

Did that include her? She couldn't think of a reason to clap, so she sat completely still, trying to maintain a half-smile as the lights maxed on to bright, right into her eyes, to the point she could hardly look up.

A deep baritone voice came out of nowhere overhead, reporting the headlines of Stockton's murder and announcing the live show that night. The voice introduced Harry Todd first, then her.

Her chest tightened as she listened.

". . . and after being the target of a serial killer herself, she goes on the offense and *murders the murderer! In cold blood! Murder weapon? A dentist's drill!* Today, her secret past life *revealed . . .* Why she killed a killer! Because *she was a crime victim herself . . .* her fiancé gunned down! Now . . . she fights back against crime!"

Hailey was mortified. *She was no murderer . . .* She had defended herself, brought down a twisted killer, and nearly lost her life doing it. And why did they drag Will into it? Tony had promised this wouldn't happen. In the bright lights, she could barely see past the anchor desk. The studio audience, the aisles leading to the exit, everything was completely obscured by the harsh lights . . . She couldn't see her way out. After the quick intro, Harry Todd lobbed the first question.

"So, Hailey Dean, before you've been touted as a victims' rights champion, but you killed a man in cold blood . . . What's your response?"

Okay. That was it. Gloves off.

"Mr. Todd, I'm not sure where you're getting your facts, but you, sir, are woefully misinformed. I did not kill a man in cold blood . . ."

"That's what the reports say!" he broke in. Hailey ignored him and plowed ahead.

"I defended myself against a man twice my weight and a full foot taller than me, a man who murdered defenseless women in cold blood, strangling the life out of them, and ripping them open with a sharpened poultry lifter. Mr. Todd, maybe your producers should feed you the correct information, but that killer had his hands around my neck, and frankly, I'm glad he's dead."

Before she could go on, the studio audience burst into wild applause, *unprompted.*

She tried to look out past the blinding lights shining into her face and into the audience to signal a silent thank-you, but she couldn't see any of them. Instead, she made eye contact with Todd, who was obviously angry the audience was siding with *her* and not him.

What a pompous ass . . . Exercising immense self-control, Hailey did not give him a swift kick under the table . . . She could've always acted like it was an accident . . . These cowboy boots could really do some damage.

"So killing someone, stabbing them in the temple *with a drill* doesn't bother you . . . *You're happy about it?*"

"I'm happy to be alive, Mr. Todd, if that's what you're asking. And yes, while I never, ever condone violence, I am, let me say, relieved that a man who stalked, tortured, and murdered innocent women is now gone off the face of this earth and if by my own hand . . . Then so be it. I'll answer come Judgment Day, certainly not to you, Harry Todd."

His long, thin face was turning blotches of beet red, and Hailey spotted sweat trickling down the left side of his forehead, cutting through the thick, tan pancake makeup they slathered onto his face, neck, and hands to give him a more human skin tone.

Todd looked at the prompter blankly, the deer-in-the-headlights look, desperately listening for somebody, *anybody*, to give him a cue as to how to respond. He even held his right hand up to the nearly invisible plastic earpiece fitted in his right ear, in the hopes his line producer in the control room would give him a sharp comeback. Hearing nothing to bail him out, he looked down at the questions laid out plainly in front of him.

"So, Hailey, tell me about your childhood."

Hailey looked at him dumbfounded. Was he crazy? That question didn't follow . . . It didn't make any sense. *My childhood?*

At first she looked around for just a split second or two. Was this a joke?

Then, looking directly at Todd from across the three feet or so of table that separated them, she saw he was still looking down, red-faced, at the yellow cards lying in front of him. He hated her, she could tell, but *why?* Obviously, he was unprepared for the interview and was doing nothing more than reading canned questions some staffer had written for him, regardless of whether they were relevant to the conversation.

That was the first rule of questioning a witness on the stand, Hailey had learned in court. Be prepared with questions, but respond to the witness's answers, or any jury would have just as bad a reaction as she was having right now.

It was nearly laughable, how hard she had prepared for today, memorizing facts, figures, and statistics about violent crime across the country. She knew he was a virulent death penalty opponent, and having sent over a dozen or so killers to meet their Maker, she assumed that was the source of his animosity toward her.

Even though all these thoughts registered in just seconds, *enough daydreaming.* She shook it off . . . She was under attack.

"It was very happy, Harry," she replied sweetly. No need for vinegar when honey would do.

Todd obviously picked out another prepared question, re-shifting his weight in his chair. It was black leather and melted into the background of his set, making his appearance on camera even sharper under the bright lights and against the dark backdrop. Her own chair was beige. He leaned toward her to lob the next salvo.

Just as he inhaled for the question, music piped in through Todd's earpiece and also into the studio audience, signaling they were headed to break in one or two seconds.

He was thwarted. No time for an insightful comeback. In what had become a contest of sorts, she'd obviously won round one. Rather than chat during the break, Todd was listening to direction in his ear and pretending she wasn't there.

"No." He said it staring into the camera. "No. That won't work for me. What else do you have?" He paused. He still wouldn't make eye contact with her.

"No. Not that either. Send Rachel down."

Without looking at her, Todd got up unceremoniously and left the set.

Was this normal?

The audience was chatting among themselves. Even with the scorching lights bearing down on her, it was icy cold on the set. She felt a presence behind her, and turning, there was Tony, standing only inches from where she was seated, her back to him.

"Hi . . . How do you think it's going? When are we going to get to the fight against violent crime?" She looked up into his face and noticed stubble growing under his pale chin, where he had obviously missed a spot shaving.

"Cover your mike." He whispered it into her hair.

"What?" She whispered it back although she didn't know why they were whispering.

"Hailey, listen, *cover your lapel mike with your hand!*"

She did as she was told and looked back at him.

"I don't want the control room to hear me. As long as you're miked, they can hear you all over the building if they want to . . . on the in-house channel. Listen, Harry's got it out for you, I guess I should have told you before, but you know, he's got a record."

"What? A record?"

"Yeah. He's a klepto. He can't help himself. It doesn't matter what it is, shaving cream at Duane Reade, hair gel's his favorite steal, socks at Bloomingdale's, even a portable CD player he stuck down the front of his pants once at RadioShack."

"Down his *pants*?"

"Oh yeah, they have the whole thing on store surveillance video. All the security were watching him . . . I mean he *is* a celebrity . . . Then he stuffs the CD player down the front of his pants. I've seen the video. The whole staff watches it all the time. It's hilarious. He doesn't know we've got it."

Hailey tried to take it all in. That's one thing she hadn't thought to do before her appearance before millions of Americans: run the star's rap sheet.

"Then there was the iPhone he took right off a display at the Apple Store across from Central Park . . . Oh yeah, and some DVDs he put in his briefcase the other day at Barnes & Noble . . . in the music section. There's more . . . a lot more. It goes back for years . . . most of it gets swept under the rug, but he actually has a couple of convictions. He hates police and prosecutors . . . thinks they're all straight from hell. He never even wants them on panel legal discussions. I had to make him."

"Why doesn't the press make more of it?"

"The convictions are under his *real* name, Harold Isaac Finkler. He was booked under Isaac. Plus, they all plead down to citations or get handled behind closed doors. You'd really have to know where to look. Anyway, bottom line, he hates you."

"Then *why did you put me out here?*"

"Oh! Don't take it personally! *It'll be great TV!*"

If looks were daggers, Tony would be dead right now.

"Oh, and he's in the control room right now, up there." Tony gestured upward and ahead, into the darkness.

"*Don't look!* They'll know I'm warning you!"

She quickly looked down at the table and the handwritten notes she'd worked on for hours, then brought with her.

"Warn me about what? What could happen? More lame questions?"

"No. He's up there right now, and they're loading him up with some ammo to shoot you down. Be ready."

"Ammo? What ammo? For what? Shoot me down how?"

No answer. She turned to look at him, but he was gone, evaporating into the darkness behind her. She took her hand off her lapel mike and steeled herself. Literally within seconds, Todd came back and slipped into his chair, revealing nothing. She noticed his makeup was repaired, now thicker than ever. He looked like he'd just come off hours lying on the beach, his face an unnatural brown. His hands and neck were browner than before, too. She wondered if viewers would notice the difference.

The music started and the audience cheered when a pale guy in skinny black jeans, black tennis shoes, and a black T-shirt walked before them with an "Applause" sign. They clapped wildly, some wolf-whistling their enthusiasm for all things Todd.

When the music started to fade, Todd looked directly at the camera and read verbatim off the prompter as Hailey read along herself, silently of course.

"Welcome back. With us, special guest Hailey Dean. She went from small-town prosecutor to national headlines after the stabbing death of a well-known defense attorney . . . *stabbed dead at the hands of Hailey Dean*, who is giving us her first-ever national interview about the night *she committed murder.*"

Before he could finish the rest of the read, Hailey spoke up loudly.

"Mr. Todd, you continue to misinform the viewers and I absolutely will not stand by silently. That is absolutely not what happened. First, correction. Obviously you don't make it past the city limits of New York City or read the papers or you would know Atlanta is no small town. In fact, sir, nearly a million people live in Atlanta, not including the metro area. And, I did not commit murder. Whoever is feeding you questions in your ear needs to fact check. I was unarmed, and in self-defense stabbed a serial killer with a dentist drill, turned on, in the temple. It's as simple as that. Check the police report, if you know how."

Before he could interject, she went on.

"And, I was invited to be with you today to discuss the fight against violent crime in our country, crime that takes the lives of thousands of men, women, and especially, children. It can be stopped, I firmly believe. More people die of homicides in the U.S. each year than they do in our most current war."

As if he'd heard nothing she said, he blurted out the next question, trying to maintain his best newslike demeanor while trying to stop her from talking.

"Is it *because of Will?* Will, your fiancé who was *murdered just before your wedding?* The murder that *ruined your life, that changed you forever?* He was gunned down, right?"

He tossed the last question off casually, almost as an aside. The question clearly was not the point. The buildup was.

Even though she had been warned by Tony's whisperings in her ear, she didn't expect this. Hailey was speechless. She never allowed anyone to bring up Will's name. If she brought it up, which was never, she'd be mentally prepared. But to have it thrown at her like this was like having a bucket of icy water thrown in her face.

Mortified, she looked up on a screen directly to her right, behind Todd's head. Out of nowhere, just over Todd's slicked back hair appeared a huge head shot of Will.

He looked so young.

Will's eyes were brilliant blue against the light tan on his face and his teeth were pearly white, shining out from a big smile. The sky was a sapphire background behind him. It was a shot she herself had taken when they had gone to the beach, not long before he was murdered.

How had they gotten it?

Her chest tightened and a pain seemed to shoot out of her heart. This was not what she had signed up for. At first, tears sprang to her eyes and a huge lump seemed lodged in the front of her throat. But then, she pried her gaze down from the full screen of Will looming above them and looked Todd in the face.

There was no mistaking it. He was thrilled . . . a smug, self-satisfied grin played on his lips. She noticed for the first time he'd obviously had filler . . . probably Restylane . . . along what should have been laugh lines on either side of his nose downward toward the outer tips of his lips. Extremely unattractive in doses so great. And speaking of his lips . . . Weren't they a tiny bit . . . *too plump*?

It hit her there in her seat with an entire studio watching, and no telling how many viewers would likely see from their own homes, how little TV people actually cared about what they were reporting. Todd was actually smirking now, waiting for her to say something, to break down in tears, to blurt out her life story and the pain she suffered the day her world exploded and Will's world . . . ended.

So she did the opposite. Never taking her eyes away from Todd's, Hailey stood up, jarring the little table that sat between them. As she stood, she noticed Todd shrinking back in his chair, like *he* was afraid of *her*.

Hailey squeezed open the tiny microphone attached to her left lapel, let it fall gently down the inside of her blouse, and pulled it out at the waist. Setting it on the table, in one fluid motion, she picked up her purse sitting on the studio floor behind her chair and her notes off the table and turned to leave.

"Wait! You can't leave! Answer the question! You murdered a man because of all your pent-up rage! Isn't that right, Hailey Dean? It was all because of Will!" He barked it out, leaning forward in his chair, into the camera for emphasis.

Hailey froze.

Turning on her heel, she looked back at Todd, sitting there, so smug, so self-satisfied, so impressed with himself.

"You are not worthy to even say his name, you plastic freak. *Don't you even whisper his name to me again.*"

Todd opened his mouth for a comeback, but before he could say a word, Hailey picked up the huge glass pitcher of ice water sitting between them, along with two mugs emblazoned with Todd's name and logo. He recoiled.

He should have.

Aiming straight for the top row of fake white dental implants, she thrust out her right arm, drenching Todd's head with at least a gallon of clear, cold water mixed with slushy ice. He pushed back his chair; the matte-colored makeup, carefully patted onto his face and scalp so the bald spots wouldn't shine through, streamed down in rivulets.

"They're right . . . You *are* crazy . . . you're . . . you're . . . ," he had to stop and think since an appropriately outraged zinger wasn't provided on his cue cards, ". . . a *bitch!*"

Wow. That was original. If only Hailey had a dime for every time she'd been called a bitch in court, she'd be a millionaire.

She couldn't see exactly where she was going, but she didn't stop going. In the background, she could hear thunderous applause, wolf-calls and whistles from the audience.

They were a bloodthirsty bunch.

Hailey could make out the faint red glow of an illuminated exit sign over a door and headed toward it. Pushing it open, she could hear the applause still going in the background. She had walked into yet another stairwell, obviously the wrong one; she had no idea where it led. But before she had made it ten steps, she heard the door behind her open and there he was.

Tony Russo was lumbering after her as fast as his short little legs could take him. She braced for his anger at what she had done to his beloved Todd.

"You were *marvelous*! We *loved* it! The whole control room was cheering!"

There he was with the "*loving* it" thing again. But his words stopped her in her tracks and she turned around to look at him.

"*What?* I just threw a bucket of cold water on your boss. It made his hair and makeup run down the front of his face. You should be *furious*!"

"Furious? Are you kidding? You're a natural! *It'll make great TV!*" He was so excited, he was panting, gasping for breath. Or maybe it was the eight stairs he tackled.

"Great TV? So you don't care I just chewed out your boss on national TV? I don't get it."

"Number one, Harry Todd is not my boss. Sookie Downs is. All she cares about is ratings and *honey, this is ratings! I love it!*"

"Don't call me honey." She was trying to take in the depth of his disloyalty. Even from Russo, it was disturbing.

He went on as if he hadn't heard her. "Look, he's been in a ratings slump; no matter what we put up—politics, celebrities, angry housewives—it doesn't rate. This will rate! My gut says so and I have the best gut in daytime talk."

He brimmed with sheer excitement at the prospect of not only a ratings comeback for *The Harry Todd Show*, but more specifically, a guest and a story that *he alone had masterminded and booked.*

"I have to go." She simply could not think of anything else to say.

Once again, Russo chased after her as she exited the stairwell out into a common hallway lobby and a set of elevator banks. She recognized them from before and punched the "down" button.

She could find her own way out.

Stepping onto an elevator that opened right in front of her, she heard him as the doors were shutting.

"Wait! Hailey!! Wait! I want to talk to you . . ."

Suddenly everything was quiet. She was alone in the elevator. Alone with the thick carpet and the wood paneling, and on the two identical TV screens on either side of the door was a replay of her drenching Todd with the icy water going out onto the live airwaves. The banner across the bottom third of the screen screamed out *Violent Crime Vigilante Takes Aim At Harry Todd!*

As she looked at the screen, the banner changed. *Dean's Fiancé Murdered Just Before Wedding, Transforms Her Into Vigilante Crime Fighter.*

These people were shameless. The dousing kept being replayed over and over, including the brunette makeup running down Todd's forehead. They obviously would eat their own for a Nielsen number.

The elevator doors swished open and Hailey stepped out into the huge lobby. She kept walking straight ahead, clutching the notes she'd brought with her. She didn't stop to look either way, to the left or the right, her eyes locked on the huge plate-glass doors ahead of her and out onto the street.

Just before she pushed the doors open in front of her, she stopped. There was clapping. From a single pair of hands.

Hailey turned around toward the lobby. There, off to the side of the large, marble expanse, beside an indoor stand of perfectly manicured trees, was a cleaning lady. She was actually only a few feet away from Hailey. She was dressed in a light blue, short-sleeved dress with her name, Lorraina, embroidered across the left shoulder in deep navy blue thread. Under the dress, which came to a few inches below her knees, she wore a pair of black pants and tennis shoes. The woman, slightly built and barely topping five feet, rolled her plastic bucket and mop toward the front door where Hailey stood.

"They murdered my son. He was only seventeen. Nobody saw anything. Nothing ever happened. We've only been here in the U.S. a few years. I know who you are. I see you in the paper. I saw what you did to Mr. Todd. I'm glad."

Outside, the sun was shining and a huge fountain in front of GNE was shooting gusts of water up into the air. It caught the light as it hung there, just before it fell back into the fountain.

Sucking in a lungful of air, Hailey walked right past a long, black limo with her name written on a white placard in the window. She went to the corner, cars, trucks, buses, all whizzing by.

Holding her left hand high over her head, arm straight up in the air, she looked uptown. Within seconds, a cab swerved in dangerously close to her shins. Opening the door, she got in. Some type of canned music was blaring, repeating the same verse over and over and over, and the cab reeked of incense.

It was good to be back in New York.

"Fifty-fourth and York."

He didn't reply, just gunned the motor, and they were off.

THE CABBIE RACED ACROSS TOWN BACK TO THE EAST SIDE, weaving dangerously through parked and moving cars, catching lights just as they changed from yellow to red and growling out his open window at any pedestrian who dared to slow down in a crosswalk. Hailey paid cash through the plastic window partition between seats, opened the car door, and stepped up on the street's curb headed toward the front steps of her building.

Pushing through the heavy revolving door, she saw Ricky smiling at her behind the lobby desk, still here these hours later. It made her smile back. "How are you?" Hailey called out as she stepped in from the cold.

"Same as ever. Happy to be alive. How about you, Sunshine?"

"Good. Thanks, dear." She said it with warmth. It was nice to see a friendly face.

"Need help with the box and the bag?"

Hailey was suddenly reminded of the flight up from Atlanta, the luggage she'd dragged up the front steps, and the box wrapped in plain brown paper with Kolker's handwriting on the front.

"Nope, I'll manage. Thanks."

Heading toward the elevator, Hailey balanced the box on top of her rolling bag while keeping her purse on her shoulder and her notepad clasped in her left hand. Once off the elevator and standing at her own front door, she instinctively glanced over her shoulder before setting her purse and pad down on the carpeted floor beside her. She'd already pulled the apartment keys from her bag so she wouldn't have to fish. Sliding the key into the top deadbolt lock, she turned it to the right, and it slid to the side. She mechanically went through the same process with two lower locks and pushed the door gently open, scooping up the purse and pad, and rolling the bag over the threshold in one fluid movement.

The apartment was silent. Silent in an inviting, quiet way. The shades were up and from the entrance area, she could see the city lying beneath her. Hailey turned and locked all three locks and slid the door chain lock into place. Leaving the bag where it stood upright, she carried the box into her kitchen, glancing around her little apartment as she strode across the rosewood den floor and onto the smooth, green slate floor of the kitchen.

She automatically turned on her gas stove for tea, filled the copper kettle that was always there, and sat it on the stove's eye, now burning blue. Pulling a pair of scissors from the spoon and fork drawer, she slid them down the middle of the box, slicing it open neatly. Though she knew she'd return whatever he'd sent as an apology for her arrest the year before, she always looked to see if there was a note included. Something that would somehow explain what Kolker had done . . . something to make things right.

The flowers, the treats . . . It was almost as if he were courting a girlfriend. But what had passed between them, the murders of Hailey's two friends, the suspicion cast on her, her arrest, the night she'd almost lost her own life and ended up taking the life of her attacker . . . When she'd come to . . . his was one of the first faces she remembered seeing. She distinctly remembered the look on Kolker's face, the realization hitting him hard that Hailey was innocent and had nearly lost her own life while he pursued her instead of the real killer.

There was some sort of bond between Hailey and Kolker . . . something she couldn't quite identify, nothing as trite as a flirtation. Hailey remembered motioning Kolker down, to where she was lying alongside Matt Leonard's dead body. The others standing around had all parted, stepping aside for Kolker to kneel down beside her. Hailey remembered her throat ached so badly from

Leonard's attempted strangulation, she couldn't speak. But Kolker had . . . He'd said exactly three words as Hailey recalled, whispering the words against her hair, "Hailey . . . I'm sorry . . ."

The kettle whistled and Hailey moved it over to a cold burner. The box was full. She picked up each item . . . mostly CDs. The first was *The Otis Redding Anthology*, including "The Dock of the Bay." Redding was born in Georgia and grew up in Macon. Then there was *Forever Ray Charles*. Charles, also from Hailey's home state of Georgia, sang one of her favorites, "Georgia on My Mind."

The last CD in the cardboard box was by Johnny Mercer, the genius from Savannah who composed "Moon River." The lyrics and the haunting tune never failed to bring tears to her eyes . . . to make her heart ache for something she'd never had . . . a lifetime with her true love.

How did Kolker know such personal details? *They certainly didn't come up that night in the police interrogation room.* Hailey bristled at the vivid . . . and painful . . . memory.

At the very bottom of the cardboard box were two smaller boxes wrapped separately. Tearing at the same brown paper wrapping, she opened the larger one, obviously a book. She looked down at it in surprised silence. It was a hardback copy of Harper Lee's *To Kill a Mockingbird*. When she was just a little girl, Hailey checked the book out from the bookmobile, a library van that routinely traveled to visit poor and rural areas in the South. The librarian had warned her she was too young, that the book was for more advanced readers, but she let Hailey take it home anyway.

When Hailey turned to the first page, she couldn't believe her eyes. The book was signed by the great author and recluse, Harper Lee. A note fluttered down when Hailey opened the book. Leaning down toward the kitchen floor, Hailey unfolded the note and read it. It was Kolker's handwriting in blue ink and read simply

"I understand Atticus Finch was the first lawyer you ever met. That explains a lot. Kolker."

Then it dawned on her exactly how he knew so much about her. She'd agreed to a profile piece in the Atlanta paper several years ago when she won her hundredth jury trial. While the article focused mostly on her courtroom victories and various killers, dope dealers, and thugs she put behind bars, it also included a few personal details she allowed them to know. They were printed in a thin panel to the side of the article, including her favorite music and books.

Kolker had done his research.

The last item in the cardboard box was a longer, thin container. When she removed the brown paper, she immediately saw it was a trademark eggshell blue box from Tiffany's. Of course she wouldn't accept jewelry from Kolker. But true to her inquisitive nature, she at least wanted to look inside the box.

When Hailey gently lifted the lid, her lips involuntarily parted open in surprise. There, inside on its black silk cord, lay a small, silver necklace, a tiny Tiffany's ink pen. It wasn't new . . . It was hers . . . Hailey's . . . from long ago and another life she once had.

Hailey didn't have to look closer to know what was engraved on the pen . . . It had hung lightly from its silken cord around her neck for nearly ten years. It was a gift from Katrine Dumont, whose fiancé, Phil Eastwood, was murdered. It was one of Hailey's first murder cases as a young prosecutor.

A newly engaged young couple with their whole lives ahead of them had stepped out onto their patio to toast their new engagement. Two new parolees with long rap sheets ambushed them from behind a thick hedge surrounding the patio. Phil fought back and was immediately gunned down at point-blank range. His fiancée was dragged into the apartment and repeatedly assaulted.

Katrine was so traumatized, she was unable to testify at trial. In the end, Hailey found corroborating evidence, and even without an eyewitness, the jury convicted. After sentencing, Katrine came to see her and handed her a sky-blue velvet box. Inside was the pen, etched with the words, *For Hailey, Seeking Justice, Katrine Dumont-Eastwood.* For the next ten years, Hailey had worn the pen during every jury trial and often in between.

Then, as fate unfolded, Kolker discovered the silver pen years later . . . under the dead body of Hailey's own patient here in New York. It had been planted underneath the body to incriminate Hailey and was a big part of why Kolker arrested her to start with.

How did he ever get it out of police property this soon? Usually it took years to retrieve evidence in criminal cases, much less a serial murder case. Kolker had to have broken rules to get it out of the evidence room for her.

Hailey took the box to her favorite chair by a window overlooking the city. Studying the CDs, the book, and the pen on its silky cord, she slowly stood and walked to the apartment's front door, carrying the cardboard box they'd come in.

Padding down the carpeted hall in bare feet, she opened the door to the trash chute and threw the box to the foot of the tiny trash room. She wouldn't be needing it anymore. There would be no return.

*C*ABLE COVERAGE WAS AWFUL IN RURAL DAVIDSON COUNTY. Even though the county seat was Nashville, Tennessee, a major hub for the music industry, you'd never know it from the cable service. The motel room he rented by the week advertised it came with free cable. What a joke. Clint Burrell Cruise leaned forward and stared at the TV set he'd propped on a folding metal TV tray table.

But even through the bad reception, he recognized her. It was Hailey Dean. Her blonde hair was a little longer, now falling down around her shoulders. She was discussing what goes on inside the mind of a killer with the same intense demeanor she had in the courtroom. Her green eyes stared directly into the camera and she never looked away. Cruise shifted in his seat . . . it appeared she was looking at him straight in the eyes. The camera sat on the shot of Hailey, then music played and her face dissolved into a commercial break.

Suddenly coming face to face with Hailey Dean again, even if it was through a TV screen, was more than a small shock. Cruise had tried his best to stop thinking about Hailey Dean. It always got him nothing but trouble. Hailey Dean at the jail with a subpoena, standing there watching as his blood was drawn into tiny thin vials, blood yielding DNA to convict him for murder. Hailey in court, Hailey's shoulders and back as she argued to a jury, Hailey Dean reading his guilty verdict out loud in court, the moment he leaped across the defense counsel table and for an instant, just an instant, circled his hands around her neck until he was clubbed and dragged away by courtroom bailiffs.

He remembered the first time he ever laid eyes on her at the Fulton County Superior Courthouse. The courtroom was jammed that morning with attorneys, witnesses and inmates in prison garb, chained together by leg irons. Cruise was chained too, to a chair bolted onto the floor of the jury box.

When the clock hit nine o'clock exactly, double doors at the rear of the courtroom swung open, and Hailey Dean blew in. She wore a black dress just above the knees, her arms covered with long sleeves. He still remembered the blonde hair against the black of her dress. Nobody had to announce who she was, she strode straight to the State's table to remain standing. The judge entered, took the bench and the calendar clerk called Cruise's name and case number. Hailey Dean turned to look directly at him, shackled in his chair. Holding his gaze, Hailey announced in open court that the first arraignment of the morning was for him. He'd tried his best to stand, even chained. And then she said it . . . that she planned to try Cruise herself and that the State intended to seek the death penalty.

During months of court appearances, there were the constant TV shots of her, sound bites at local news pressers. He watched them all. She won the trial, of course. Then after the trial, she left him abruptly, dropping out of his life like he'd meant nothing.

Until he hopped a Greyhound bus straight out of Reidsville Penitentiary and headed to New York. When he'd landed that first blow to the side of her face it felt so good. Then at the end, he'd had to leave abruptly after his lawyer ended up going after Hailey himself. Cruise always hated Matt Leonard and oddly, hated him even more now. He was glad Leonard was dead. Good riddance.

The commercial ended and *The Harry Todd Show* resumed. An argument seemed to ensue between Hailey and Harry Todd. From what Cruise could make of what they were saying, Hailey nailed him.

Watching her in action again, his chest tightened. Being in court with her was one of his worst recurring nightmares. And now, here she was again, gorgeous, her blonde hair framing her face, her skin perfect and her teeth naturally white and barely showing between her lips when she spoke. Cruise noticed she never cracked a smile. Some things never changed. As much as he hated Hailey Dean, he stayed glued to his seat a few feet away from the TV, until the next commercial.

The chatter in the commercial break suddenly annoyed him and he wanted to kick the screen in. In fact, he wanted to tear the whole room up, kick in the walls, lift up the furniture and send it crashing to the middle of the floor, tear down the curtains, and put his fists through the windows.

Cruise clicked the remote and the screen went black. Who the hell did she think she was? He was living in a fleabag flophouse and she was on TV. He wondered if her hair still smelled the same as it did in court. He'd gotten close enough to smell her only once.

The thought of her made his whole body tense. For the first time in months, the old feeling was back . . . His hands were starting to tingle. He was superhuman . . . again. He had the power. Cruise forced his hands into balls and stuffed them down the sides of the chair's seat cushion. The electric sensation pulsed through his fingertips and into his palms . . . Even his wrists were on fire. In the dark of the penitentiary cell block, after lights out, he'd had plenty of time to think about Hailey Dean

Cruise walked to the front window of his room and looking out into the night, stood rooted at the curtain's edge, trying to shake off the electric sensation now tripping through his arms and chest. To hell with her. He was sick of Tennessee and sick of hiding out in the middle of nowhere. Seeing her again made him realize . . . He had unfinished business. In New York.

Two Weeks Later
Hell's Kitchen, Manhattan

I F IT WEREN'T AT THE EDGE OF HELL'S KITCHEN, SHE'D NEVER HAVE found a parking spot. Prentiss Love had just finished her "hot yoga" class and was headed for her shiny new, metallic sand-colored Mercedes SUV parked around back of the yoga studio. She needed to relax. The last season of her reality show *Celebrity Closets* had nearly killed her. The pressure, the fans, and of course the celebrities whose closets she was expected to magically organize and transform . . . It was all driving her crazy.

Couldn't they see she was an artist? She needed space . . . space to promote artistic thinking and creativity. She hadn't done anything really creative since she performed in a music video with an animated cartoon raccoon as a dance partner. Now that was something she was proud of.

She'd only recently discovered hot yoga, a series of intense yoga poses done in a room heated to temperatures of around 100 degrees. It was all about profuse sweating. It ridded the "bodily temple" of all the toxins introduced to it by consumption of toxic foods such as doughnuts, Twinkies, processed meats, and of course, Mexican food of any type.

Her instructor, Enrique, said the purpose was to make the body warm, and therefore more flexible. Prentiss was all about having a warmer, more flexible body.

This particular yoga studio was out of the way and word hadn't yet seeped out about it. It was only a matter of time before every woman in New York heard about Enrique, or "Rick-ay" to Prentiss, and flocked to him, completely ruining the ambience for Prentiss.

Rick-ay had promised Prentiss private hot yogas if necessary. She could hardly wait. He'd actually studied under the greatest living yoga master of all times, the genius Bikram Padhoury. Padhoury pioneered hot yoga, including *pranayama* exercises. Screw *pranayama*, whatever the hell that was, as far as Prentiss was concerned. She just wanted to somehow do the poses well enough not to topple over facedown into her yoga mat in front of Rick-ay.

Much less in front of the others, who seemed to Prentiss to be way too serious about the whole thing. She got the feeling they looked down their snouts at her.

She actually overheard one of them after class whispering about her at the water jug, a clear glass receptacle displaying filtered spring water with lemons floating in it. The tall one said to the short mousy one that she, Prentiss Love, smelled like red meat. How in the hell can somebody smell like red meat? What . . . The scent of lamb just oozes from your pores?

Prentiss knew for a fact she did *not* smell like red meat. She smelled like her favorite perfume, Sensuous Musk. She put it on before every class with Rick-ay.

Skinny bitches. They could take their mats and shove them for all she cared. But then, she got supreme satisfaction when she spotted them walking away from class. She took a little swerve at them in her SUV and they jumped away from the edge of the sidewalk. She just wanted to scare them a tiny bit.

But forget about them. As long as Rick-ay wanted her in class, there on the front row, Prentiss was happy. Rick-ay was totally committed and inspired. She loved that. Even though she knew he was from Milwaukee, sweet boy, he might as well have been from Calcutta. His heart and soul were definitely Bengalese.

Rick-ay was a devout follower who ascribed to Bikram Padhoury's teachings to the letter, including keeping his studio at exactly the precise temperature prescribed by Padhoury, 101 degrees, but insisted the same type mirrors, carpet, and exact text be used during each and every hot yoga session. His dream (that he had shared with Prentiss) was to bring his discipline to Park Avenue with his own Multi-Specialty Physiotherapy and Accupressure Padhoury Method Yoga Studio. It was all so exciting.

Plus, Rick-ay was ripped. She'd never seen a pair of glutes like what was on Rick-ay's caboose. She begged and begged for repeat instructions on the Virabhadrasana II, commonly known by the masses as the Warrior Two yoga pose. It specifically worked Rick-ay's glutes. Not that she'd ever do it on her own of course, but the view of Rick-ay in the Warrior Two pose was worth it.

But no matter how much she came on to him, he seemed oblivious. For her last effort, she'd worn the skimpiest outfit possible, claiming she had to wear practically nothing to class because of the extreme heat and clothes trapped toxins in her skin. They simply couldn't get out if she had on too many clothes. She approached him about her theories on yoga, then suggested they go to dinner.

He suggested she should focus on improving her downward-facing dog.

She hoped none of the paparazzi were straggling along, hiding in the bushes or between the other cars. They were relentless. And they'd do absolutely anything to catch her looking bad . . . or drunk. She parked out back and down an alley every single time she came, so as to hopefully avoid them and their long lenses.

Wearing dark glasses and a scarf over her hair à la Marilyn Monroe, she made her way alone down the alley to her SUV. No matter what she was doing or where she was going, the press followed her. But, so far, so good. Their favorite trick was to act friendly, take a series of shots one after the other, then pick the one where she was mid-sentence or in the middle of blinking her eyes, and print that particular one so as to make her look drunk or stoned, with her mouth open and her eyes half-closed.

The press was simply hateful. And when she *did* go to rehab, you'd have thought the world had come to an end. It was all "see, we told you so."

How she loathed them.

She took one quick peek over her shoulder . . . The coast was clear. She hopped up into the driver's seat of the SUV and glanced around for the gin and tonic she'd left in the glass holder between the seats. Ah, perfect, the ice was still floating around in the red plastic glass she'd pulled out of her kitchen cabinet that morning. She intentionally used the red plastic instead of clear so no one could see exactly what she was drinking.

Prentiss pushed in a New Age CD to bring it down a notch and turned on the AC. She was sweating like a pig.

Oh hell. Guess the sunglasses and scarf didn't work. Here came a fan, bundled up head to toe in coat and scarf, rushing up to the side of the SUV with something, a piece of paper for her to autograph.

Would it never end? Why did she have to be so famous? It was actually a curse to be a star.

Prentiss wearily put on a brave face and pushed the button to lower the electric window. She stretched her arm out for the fan's pen. She wished she had some lipstick. Maybe there was some in the glove compartment.

The gun came out of nowhere. In fact, she didn't even really hear the bullet being expelled from the chamber. The silencer on the weapon resulted in a noise just slightly louder than a trash can lid being dropped in the distance.

The bullet sliced through her head, left temple first, front to back, left to right. It exited Love's head just below and behind her right ear, lodging in the leather upholstered headrest cradling her skull. The coroner's office would have to dig that one out with a knife, if they even thought of it.

Behind her head, a dark, red stain was spreading down the car seat toward her shoulders and back, pooling at the seat. Thankfully, it was heading only down, not visibly out to the sides of her head. Blood came trickling down the left side of her temple. But delicately reaching inside toward Love's face, a quick, careful rearranging of her long dark hair covered the thin, red rivulet completely. The silk scarf helped a lot.

New Age music emanated out softly through the SUV's speakers and the sound of some sort of bell tinkled over hushed harp strings. Blood and blow-back had spattered the inside of the driver's side door, heading down to the carpet. Since the window was completely down at the time of the gunshot, none would appear on the glass to alert a casual passer-by.

Was that a tiny bit of grayish pink brain matter on her cheek?

The latex-gloved hand reached in once more, to wipe it away, opening the door just long enough to raise the window back all the way to the top, turn off the motor, and lock all four doors of the SUV with one punch to the automatic lock button located on the door's elbow rest. The driver-side door shut firmly, but quietly.

Walking briskly but casually down the alley to the intersecting street ahead, the urge to toss the latex gloves and gun into a big Dumpster just beyond Love's SUV had to be wrestled down. That was the first place police would search. A nonchalant glance over the shoulder and down the alley confirmed not a soul in sight.

Later on that morning and throughout the day, people passing by the SUV—the few New Yorkers who bothered to do a double-take—just thought it was Prentiss Love, poor thing, passed out drunk again.

"So, BOTTOM LINE, DO YOU THINK IT'S THE SAME SHOOTER?" O'Brien looked at Lieutenant Kolker over the width of the diner's table top, two cups of coffee steaming, black, between them. It had been a long night and this morning they saw the photos to prove it, in color, on the front of the *Post*. It was Prentiss Love, all right. Shot dead, and on his beat to top it all off. He worked the crime scene into the night.

Kolker's lack of response gave O'Brien the impression he was undecided, so he went on, more emphatically. "I mean, come on, first there's Leather Stockton, now there's Prentiss Love. Stockton's a star, kind of, a D-Lister, anyways. Love is sort of a star. Hey, they're both D-List celebrities! I hadn't thought of that one!"

O'Brien took a sip of the black brew, winced a little, and kept going. "I know we don't have all the evidence from the other jurisdiction, the Hamptons, but look. Stockton's a woman, Love's a woman. Both shot, one bullet to the head. Both with a handgun, don't know the caliber yet. Both within short range, well, fairly short range. Love was within twelve inches, based on the amount of gunshot residue, and a little stippling on the left cheek. Stockton within three feet. Not exactly the same, but still, Kolker, they're both close range. Both boozers, both just out of bad relationships. Too many similarities not to be the same killer. And both within a month. What, are you blind?"

"Sounds like you've been reading *Snoop*. Don't know how those S.O.B.s got the scoop. Suffolk County PD better be looking at the reporter and the photographer as material witnesses, if not suspects. How the hell did *Snoop* get to the scene before the cops?"

"Yeah. I was wondering that, too."

"But to answer your question, no, I'm not blind, O'Brien, I just want to be cautious and not stir anybody up into thinking we've got a serial killer stalking the city's celebs, even if they are D-List. We don't need that."

"Have you heard anything about forensics yet?"

"Too soon on the bullet."

"What about Stockton? There's been plenty of time on that one."

"It's Suffolk County. They gotta get their heads outta their butts first and figure out how to get the bullet to the crime lab without breaking the chain of evidence! Of course they haven't gotten the caliber yet. Or at least they haven't shared it with us! Last thing they want is NYPD trying to big-foot the only murder case they've had in five years."

"What about cell records and computer? Anything?"

"I told you, it's their baby. They're not sharing. But the only text Love got that we haven't been able to ID overnight is somebody named Jonathon. But from the body of the texts, it sounds like it's some kid she befriended, maybe in high school. He wants another signed photo, talks to her about *Celebrity Closets,* talks about his classes, you know, stuff like that. Harmless. So, long story short, nothing in the texts so far."

"Is he a stalker? High school kids are weird these days. Look at Columbine for Pete's sake."

"Nope. Nothing like that. They seem to have been texting for over a year. Must have given him her cell at one of those book signings or a red carpet or something."

"Yeah, that's weird a fan would have her private cell number."

"A computer geek could find it online."

"Yeah. I know. That makes him a stalker in my book. But bottom line, are they connected?"

"Nah. Doubt it. Just coincidence. Kid probably writes a lot of stars."

The waitress came by. "How much do I owe you, ma'am?"

"For you, Kolker, it's on the house. Come back when you can stay longer. We'll have your favorite lemon meringue pie this afternoon."

The notoriety he got from the Hailey Dean case had made him a little bit of a celebrity. Whenever she was asked about the cops arresting her for the murders of two of her patients, she never once blasted him. It had been his big case, and he'd been so damn pigheaded. He was convinced she'd gone over the edge and started rubbing out her clients . . . although even the police shrinks had a hard time giving him a motive. It had to have been her.

But it wasn't. That perv defense lawyer had been behind it all. To hear Hailey tell it, NYPD was just doing their job. She could have torpedoed him, ruined him . . . if she wanted to. But she didn't.

He'd never had the guts to go and formally apologize, just sent flowers and peace offerings. And she always sent those back, always in the same box he'd sent them in. He didn't really know what to say to her, alone, one-on-one.

"Thanks, Sheila. Save me a piece."

The two cops got up, grabbed their jackets from the coat tree in the corner by the door and headed out. In twelve hours, they'd be back on duty.

"**S**O WHAT DID YOU DO FOR THE HOLIDAYS?"

Fallon Malone's BlackBerry emitted a sound like a tiny tinkling bell being played in the distance. Another text message.

Malone looked down from one of the two TV screens directly in front of her elliptical machine. She was right in the middle of a Lifetime movie and didn't want to be bothered. But maybe it was her agent . . . finally.

It had been years since she got a script worth reading and now, due to her dwindling bank account and penchant for beautiful clothes, cars, and jewelry, she had to work.

She'd even consider TV. She'd be great on a prime-time soap. What did the *Desperate Housewives* have that she didn't? Ridiculous. They should be kissing her feet.

Even though she was in her mid-fifties, in her heart she knew she didn't look a day over forty-one. She'd managed to scam the tabs about her true date of birth with a fake birth certificate, and lived in mortal fear that somehow, they'd dig up the truth.

Maybe some sort of a reality series, focusing on her finding just the right Hollywood script, the right vehicle to showcase her talents.

Ever since the role where she soaped down a red Vette on camera without the benefit of underwear, most of Hollywood believed her "talents" lay beneath her belly button and above her knees.

The business was cruel. She had been stereotyped in the worst way. It was clearly a case of misogyny. They all hated her because she was beautiful. *A beautiful woman has a hard time making it in the business world,* Malone reminded herself as she reached for the BlackBerry.

Oh, hell. It was that kid again. Jonathon. How in the hell had he gotten her number to start with? It had all begun when he said he was collecting stars' autographs to fund some sort of Boy Scout charity. Or something like that. Maybe an illness was involved? Or a school project? Or the school band? He went on and on about the band.

Whatever. Now the kid texted her fifty times a day, it seemed. She usually didn't write back. And wouldn't you know that if she ever wrote him a nasty note cutting him off, it would end up in the tabs that she was an evil shrew. More of what she didn't need.

She wrote back brightly, *"Nothing much! Just enjoyed the holiday! Tried not to eat too much turkey!"* She'd long ago learned not to ask him any questions like, *"How's school?" "How's your family?"* Or even *"How are you today?"*

Even the most general and innocuous questions resulted in reams and reams of text messages back that totally clogged her BlackBerry. She dropped it into the elliptical's magazine holder and got back to her movie. It was all about a marriage that went bad and the husband turns out to be a stalker. Again.

She must have seen this one, or one just like it, before. But now she was invested in the characters and wanted to see the end. Damn Lifetime. That network sucked up every daylight hour.

Bling-ding-ding. The BlackBerry tinkled again.

"I thought you were a vegetarian!"

Damn! Busted by a fifteen-year-old boy sitting at home in his room. What? Had he read every single article ever in existence about her? You could dig up twenty-year-old articles on the Internet, and apparently this kid made her his own personal research project.

She'd told the press for years about all her healthy eating habits, how she did yoga for hours, went "clean" vegetarian, and only ate organic vegetables. No dairy, no gluten, no meat, no chicken, no fish . . . You had to live like a food monk to be "in" in this business. She had to hide if she even ate a French fry. If they ever got wind she ate cheeseburgers whenever she wanted, she'd be a laughingstock.

"Oh, just joking! Ha, ha! It was Tofurkey! A tofu substitute!"

Gritting her teeth, she punched in the letters and hit "send." This was ridiculous. Could she block his never-ending text messages? But if she didn't keep writing this kid back, the press could make hay over her breaking the heart of an Eagle Scout in Slidell, Louisiana, or wherever . . .

No sense risking that. Sweat was rolling down her back. Why did this actress get a lead role on a Lifetime movie? She was horrible.

She, Fallon Malone, would have been so much better. Were these people that blind? Couldn't they see what a box office draw she still was? She'd even be willing to wash another car without a stitch on underneath . . . or a van . . . even an eighteen-wheeler . . . anything . . .

Turning the volume up on Lifetime, she waited for the next BlackBerry jingle.

|||||||||||||||||||||||||||||||||||||||||||||||||||||| **15** ||||||||||||||||||||||||||

T HIS WOULD DRIVE HIS MOTHER CRAZY. THE FACT THAT HE, FRANCIS Merle McGinnis, was texting back and forth with Fallon Malone. And Malone wasn't the only one. He texted, e-mailed, handwrote letters to them all. And they wrote back. Why?

Because they were into him.

He made it a ritual to devote time to each one of the women every day; he recorded every TV appearance he could find, even going so far as having a satellite dish installed to get hundreds more channels than local cable offered. Now Francis had access to thousands of channels on which to find them. Even the repeats. Of course, live TV was the best because then he could get fresh signals, messages especially to him from the ladies via the airwaves.

It was their secret. The casual viewer would never catch on. A tilt of the head, a wink of the eye, pushing hair back from the face or behind the ear, touching a necklace or earring—each move had significance. He loved communicating with them like this, and told them so in all the letters he sent. It was in the letters that he pre-arranged what each signal would mean. There were different love signals from each lady.

They were into it.

He had loved watching *Celebrity Closets* over and over. Prentiss was always gorgeous, but over the last few months, he had gotten really concerned she was dressing a little slutty. She was totally coming across as a tramp. Not that he'd ever tell his mother he agreed with her even in the slightest.

He'd written to Prentiss several times about her image problem, nice, long letters. He had tried to stop her from looking so cheap, flaunting herself. She was ruining her image, plus other men could mistake the look for a come-on.

After all, Prentiss was already taken. They'd had an intimate relationship for years, since long before *Celebrity Closets* hit the airwaves. He stuck with her through thick and thin. And what did she do? Wear low-cut blouses, tube tops, mini-skirts, you name it. Plus, she flirted outrageously with the male celebrities and Francis was convinced she did a better job on their closets than she did for female celebrities. It was subtle, maybe the shelf liner was more upscale, more shoe space . . . Francis noticed details like these. Subtle . . . but important details.

She even flirted with some of the workmen on the show, construction guys responsible for tearing down walls and building shelves. But that was all for ratings, it didn't mean anything at all . . . and Francis had been very understanding and patient . . . up to a point. Then, he had to endure the trumped-up claim she'd had an affair with one of the young and talented celebrities whose closet she "designed," but Francis stayed strong and sure enough, it all blew over.

It obviously wasn't true. She'd never cheated, he was sure. At least, pretty sure.

But Prentiss wouldn't respond to his letters. She just wouldn't listen. She'd put her career before his wishes. She didn't understand his motivation. She refused to see it wasn't that he was *jealous*, he was trying to help her. But she kept right on with the slutty look no matter how much he warned her. She simply wasn't the woman he'd thought she was. She misrepresented. She basically lied to him throughout their whole relationship.

It finally got to be too much for him and he had to end it. He didn't want to, but he had to. There was just so much a man could take. He hated to agree with his mother, may she rot in hell. She'd never thought Prentiss would amount to much.

But his mother had hated them all and thought they were all sluts. She couldn't have been more wrong. Mother particularly hated Fallon Malone. She was absolutely livid over Fallon's part in her last big screen role, where she'd washed the Corvette. Of course he had disagreed with his mother vehemently, arguing that that bit of film was classic movie magic and would one day be considered an all-time great, like *Gone With the Wind* or *The Godfather.*

But since he'd had his mother buried far, far away on the other side of town next to the interstate, he'd taken the liberty of moving every single one of his girlfriend's posters from the confines of his bedroom, rearranging and distributing them throughout the entire house.

And why not? They were art. Tasteful, yet provocative.

After putting them all on prominent display, as they all well deserved to be, he methodically removed and destroyed all his mother's religious paraphernalia. The crucifixes, the saints, the ceramic figures of the Mother Mary, the giant oil painting of *The Last Supper* . . . It all went straight to the Dumpster.

Right along with his mother's collection of ceramic dogs, her vast collection of miniature spoons from all over the world, and dozens of cream-colored, crocheted doilies carefully arranged all over every stick of furniture in the home. Armrests, foot-rests, headrests, seat cushions . . . all draped with doilies.

Oh, how he hated the doilies.

Then there was the Elvis collection. It wasn't as irritating as the doilies, but there was so damn much of it. The pillows, the Elvis clock in the kitchen with the hips swinging back and forth on the second hand, the commemorative dishes on little stands covering every inch of the china cabinet. At least he could actually listen to some of the Elvis stuff. In fact, as he distinctly recalled, Prentiss Love was a big Elvis fan. Another thing they had in common.

Speaking of his mother's junk, he couldn't bear to think of all the cardboard boxes of Princess Diana stuff he'd lugged out to the corner of the street. He'd briefly considered a yard sale, but he couldn't stand the thought of strangers picking through all the dishes while standing around in the front yard. And they invariably wanted to come in for something, the phone, the bathroom, a glass of water . . . He couldn't stand the thought of those . . . *people.*

In less than forty-eight hours after his mother was safely six feet under, he had totally redecorated the home. Now he could finally breathe without having a mournful-looking Christ on the Crucifix staring down at him over the back of his head at the dinner table. On the other wall was *The Last Supper,* with Judas Iscariot obviously the bad guy.

His cell phone blasted out the theme to James Bond. He adored his cell phone, although with all the special bells and whistles it had on it, it cost him nearly his whole disability check each month. It was worth it.

And he loved the James Bond theme song. Bond always got the women.

Francis looked down at the cell phone's tiny screen. Fallon wrote back! He was getting closer and closer to her, and she didn't even know it! She'd be so surprised. Francis focused on the text. *She was a vegetarian after all!* She'd just been joking about the turkey! He knew it!

What about that, Mom?

IIIIIIIIIIIIIIIIIIIIIIIIIIIIIIIIIIIIIIIIIIIIIIIIIIIII **16** IIIIIIIIIIIIIIIIIIIIIIIIIII

H AILEY DEAN CROSSED THE FLOOR OF HER KITCHEN. TWENTY-plus stories aboveground, she looked out over the Manhattan skyline from her cottage in the sky, as she called it. It was beautiful from up here. She really missed New York during the months she was back home in Atlanta.

Of course, Atlanta was beautiful, too. Everything was in bloom, the cherry blossoms, the azalea bushes, the magnolias, the tea olive growing outside her childhood bedroom in her parents' home, the Confederate roses . . . The air was so sweet.

But there was nothing like New York. And she had to get back to her patients. Phone sessions and Skype would only go so far.

Hailey plopped down in front of the computer, booted up, and started reading the news. The national headlines were the usual,

Washington politics, troops overseas, and *Prentiss Love dead*? Single shot to the head, back alley from yoga studio, car locked from the inside, body cool to the touch, one degree below the ambient air in her SUV.

That meant her body had been there for some time. It took hours for the body temperature to drop, and then to dip below the ambient air in the body's environment . . . plus, she had apparently been working out at something called a "hot yoga" class.

Love's body had to be soaring hot when she came out of that. That is, if she went straight to her SUV. If she had shopped, strolled, stopped to talk to fans, especially outdoors, her temp may have already recalibrated.

The cops had their jobs cut out for them. Wonder who was on the case? Hailey preferred the hard copy of the *Post* to the online version, so she got up and walked back through the kitchen to her front door, turning on the stove as she passed by to brew a cup of tea.

Dropping a tea bag into her cup, she went on to the door. Glancing down the hall, she could see nobody else had made it out their door yet. All the papers—the *Times*, the *Post*, the *Daily News*, the *Journal*—lay neatly stacked in varied piles just at the carpeted foot of each of the eight doors surrounding her corner apartment.

Sitting on a kitchen barstool with the morning sun at her back, she unfolded the paper. On the front page was a shot of Prentiss Love, her head slumped forward in her car, cops surrounding it, wisely touching nothing, just looking at it first.

She recognized him immediately. It was Lieutenant Ethan Kolker. The lead cop on the murder cases of two of her patients. His back was to the camera, but he was the closest to Love's body, his face turned to his left as he addressed one of the crime scene techs. Hailey hadn't seen him since the morning she was found unconscious in the floor of a dentist's office, drill in one hand, covered in her own blood and that of former-cop-turned-lawyer Matt Leonard.

The moment came shooting back, so vivid it was if it were happening all over again. Next thing she knew, she was looking Kolker in the eyes. Blue eyes. It was all such a blur. But she knew that he apologized. Briefly. The look in his eyes had been so full of sorrow, regret . . . and it should have been.

Kolker had pursued her relentlessly as the killer of not one, but two of her own patients . . . patients turned friends. He wouldn't listen to a thing she said; nothing seemed to make a dent in his determination that she, Hailey Dean, had lost touch with reality and acted out a murderous fantasy on Melissa and Shannon.

Utterly ridiculous. Impossible. It was against everything she stood for . . . She'd dedicated her life to stopping violent crime after Will's murder. Hailey was incapable of violence.

Or was she?

Not only had she killed Leonard, albeit in self-defense, she also punched Kolker in the face when he'd arrested her. Then just the other day, she literally had to fight the urge to do the same to that idiot Harry Todd, settling instead for drenching him with a pitcher of cold water on national TV.

What had happened to her impulse control?

She could shrink herself later. Right now, she settled in with her tea and skim milk to read the local version of Love's death.

Hailey turned back to the front page. Kolker looked tired. Or was she just imagining that? It was only a profile shot. Maybe she was wrong.

Wow. Two celebs in one month. True, they were D-Listers, but still, they were stars. Both murdered with a single shot to the head, both women, both generally the same age, both murdered just about an hour's drive apart.

Now that was a coincidence. But one thing Hailey knew from her years in the courtroom, *there is no coincidence in criminal law.*

Picking up the remote control from where she left it the night before, she clicked onto GNE and immediately saw an ad for *The*

Harry Todd Show. The ad showed clips of Todd's last interview with Love. It was just after *Celebrity Closets* had shot through the roof, dragging Love out of obscurity and back into the limelight. Todd was capitalizing on Love's murder, of course. What did she expect?

Glancing at the digital clock on the side of the TV's control panel, Hailey realized with a start she was late leaving. Tony Russo had called sounding distraught and insisted he had to see her in person ASAP. Judging by the tone in his voice, she'd agreed to meet him in an hour at Century Plaza just a few blocks away. Sliding into her boots, out the door of her apartment, and walking briskly, Hailey pushed through the diner's tiny front door in less than twenty minutes.

From her seat at the front of the restaurant, Hailey looked out the window. Tony Russo was late. She picked up the diner's copy of the *Post*. It was only when she'd sat down to open it, expecting the Prentiss Love story, that she discovered it was one of last week's papers. The banner printed across the top of the *Post*'s cover page was in huge, bold, black letters.

"PLASTIC FREAK!" The headline quoted her from the set and the cover picture beneath the headline was a still-frame grab off *The Harry Todd Show* as she threw a gallon of icy slush onto Todd's head.

Hailey shook her head. She knew no good could possibly have come from appearing on TV. What a horrible idea.

But she still had a soft spot for Russo. He reminded her of every kid that got picked on, kicked in the lunch line, not invited to birthday parties, the odd one left standing alone when sides were choosing teams on the playground. She knew that he was the one that always got spiked first during schoolyard dodgeball.

Through the diner window, she spotted Tony get out of a cab at the corner, rush up the sidewalk, and hurry into the restaurant. His eyes scanned the room until he spotted her and came over.

"You look *amazing!*"

Didn't this guy have any other adjectives in his vocabulary?

"Thanks. How's Todd? Has he dried out? I guess he's still mad."

"Actually no, he's not mad at all. That's what I wanted to talk to you about. He wants to apologize for the way he treated you on the show. And it doesn't hurt that your episode turned out to be the second highest-rated show we've had in two years, and that's saying a lot!"

"Oh, really? What was the first?"

Russo glowed. "The Leather Stockton show! We had her last live, one-on-one interview, less than a year ago when she got drunk and ran her car into a storefront at a strip mall . . . Or maybe it was a McDonald's . . . or both. Anyway, it was right after her husband gambled away all the money, you know, that investment guru . . . What's his name?"

"I haven't kept up with Leather Stockton's marriage . . ." She said it with a hint of sarcasm, which was completely lost on Russo, especially when he was discussing ratings.

"Oh yeah, Kenny DePaul. Used to be a big deal on Wall Street, then turned into the financial planner to the stars. Tons of celebs lost money. Anyway, she got drunk after the husband lost all the money. Big mess. She came on to talk about booze and rehab, you know, image repair. We re-aired it the night she was murdered, patched in with the *Snoop* shots of her body being wheeled out to the ambulance on a gurney. Numbers through the roof . . . *amazing ratings!* I only wish she could die all over again! But now we've got Prentiss Love!"

"Congratulations, I guess . . ." Hailey didn't know exactly what to say about Prentiss Love's murder, on the heels of huge ratings over a dead body in a pool house. She'd read about Stockton's murder in the papers. "Back to Stockton. Wasn't her body found in Eric Saxton's house in the Hamptons? Has he been cleared? He was at Sundance, right? I think I read that . . ."

"Oh yeah. It was his house all right. He wasn't home. He had nothing to do with it, is what I hear. *Anyway,* what I wanted to talk to you about . . ."

"What can I get you two?" The waitress appeared at Hailey's elbow.

"I'll just have hot tea with skim and the chicken Caesar." Hailey had had plenty of time to look at the menu waiting for Russo to show up.

"I haven't looked at the menu, I'll just have the same but no tea. Diet Coke for me."

The waitress smiled at Hailey. "I read in the papers what you did to that slimy lawyer. I wish I could do the same to the one that closed on my apartment out in Queens. Right in the head, I'd give it to him. Right in the head."

She turned on her heel and still muttering to herself, pushed through the swinging doors leading into the kitchen before Hailey could begin explaining it was self-defense. Did it matter? People believed what they wanted and they seemed pleased at the thought Hailey murdered a lawyer with a dentist's drill. So be it.

Back to the business at hand. "So what's so urgent you had to meet and couldn't talk on the phone? I did what you wanted, I came on with Todd to talk about violent crime. It was awful. So what . . . He wants to sue me for throwing water on him? Bring it on. He'll be a complete laughingstock for a lawsuit over getting wet. Plus, I could always counter-sue. Don't start with me."

"No! No! That's not it at all!" Tony was alarmed at talk of a lawsuit with Hailey Dean. He knew she had a 100 percent win record as a felony prosecutor, she'd never lost a case. And that was on behalf of *other* people . . . much less if *she* were the target . . .

"No! Harry wants you back!"

Hailey couldn't believe her ears. "Wants me *back*? On the show? Why in the world would he want me back on? I don't believe that for one minute. What's going on? And don't try to lie about it. I'm beginning to know you."

"Okay. It's not Harry. It's Sookie. She wants you on. It's the ratings. They shot up when you were on. The phone lines lit up and the e-mails poured in. We've gotten *tons* of viewer response."

"But Todd hates me . . . hates everything I stand for. It was awful. Why would I do it again?"

The salads came. As the waitress turned to leave after setting the plates down between them, she said it again: "Right in the head. I'd do it if I could . . . right in the head . . ."

Hailey couldn't summon up another denial. People seemed to love that she killed a defense lawyer. The fact she stabbed him in the side of the head with a whirring dentist's drill only added to their joy.

"Did that waitress just spit in our food?"

"What?" Hailey had no idea what Tony was talking about.

"I think when she was talking to you, some saliva came out of her mouth. I think it landed in our food."

Hailey tried to take it in without laughing.

"Tony. She did not spit in our food. Plus, even if saliva did actually come out of her mouth when she spoke, which I did not see at all and I was looking directly at her, she was a good three feet away from our plates.

"Even gunshot residue only travels about three feet. So if I were you, I wouldn't worry about a little spit . . . or a sneeze coming from across a football field. And as to doing the show . . . no. Thanks, but no. I'd tell Sookie to her face, but I've never met her. Does she ever leave her mansion in the apple orchard and actually come into work?"

"No. She doesn't have to. She can think much better out there than in an office. Plus, she's got *me* to do everything for her. We talk *all day*." He was clearly thrilled he had the ear of the powers that be.

"Plus, she's busy. She's just found romance again after the husband ran off with a teenager. But I can't tell you who it is. He's a lawyer and he's married. You might know him."

"I have no interest in who may or may not be dating a married lawyer. And her job sounds pretty cushy to me. Sitting in a mansion looking out the window and *thinking* all day while servants wait on you . . . Whatever . . . I guess it works."

"How'd you know about the servants? You know she actually makes them wear uniforms."

"So happy to hear it. I was just guessing."

"She's going to be upset you won't come on." He sounded worried.

"Don't care. I was upset when Todd threw Will's murder in my face."

"Sookie sent you flowers! Didn't you get them?"

"BS, Tony. You did that and I know it!"

"Okay! I did send them! How did you know that? But it was *for her*; in her heart she *wanted* to!"

Hailey took a few bites of the salad, giving him a hard, long look while she chewed. Silence didn't bother her in the least, but Russo was the type who needed to fill the void with chatter. Hailey had learned a lot this way over the years. The less you talked, the more you learned.

"Come on, please. We can make Harry behave. You *will* get the chance to push anti-crime. Sookie wants you to be a regular, to come on at least once a week for whatever story we've got going on. Harry does what we tell him. He doesn't even know the topic till he gets to the studio each day. And that's just thirty minutes before air, just enough time for hair and makeup. He couldn't care less what we do. If he had his way, we'd do sports every night, seven days a week."

"I believe it. I saw you did another show on Liberace last week, How can he do the same thing over and over? I mean, *Liberace*? How long has he been dead?"

"The viewers love it! They absolutely *love* Liberace. They love the old clips of him, especially when we show him meeting Elvis; then there's Liberace in the white mink cape, and oh . . . the clips of Liberace and his mother . . . *They love it!*"

"So I'm just lumped in with Liberace, the next freak in Sookie's menagerie? Tell me something, Tony. Why do you do this? Why do you put up with being an errand boy for Sookie, taking her crap?"

He sat quietly for a moment before answering. "Hailey, when I was a kid, I had nobody. Both my parents worked all the time, I was alone so much . . . I guess I watched too much TV, and I fell in love with it. When I was lonely or afraid of being at the house by myself or of the bully at school, I escaped into the TV. It was like magic, I could be somewhere else . . . *be someone else.* My whole life, I wanted to make TV and now I am. I run one of the highest-rated shows on air, even though I don't get the credit. *It makes me somebody.*"

His answer struck Hailey as genuine, but sad in a way. She understood a lot more about Tony Russo now.

"And Sookie thinks you're authentic, that the viewers like you because you stand for something. I guess. What is it exactly that you stand for? You know, that'd be a great banner on the lower third of the screen when you're on . . . what it is you stand for . . ."

"Okay, I have to go." Hailey put down a twenty for her salad and tea.

Tony looked up. "I think I feel nauseous. That waitress definitely spit in my food. Oh, and I don't have any cash." Shaking her head, Hailey pulled out another twenty to cover Tony's lunch and lifted the sweater off the back of her chair. Russo somehow managed to get between her ribs and her elbow so as to intertwine his arm in hers.

"Just think about it, please? Look, I know you like me. This will do more to fight crime than anything else you could ever do. More than trying one thug after the next in some dingy little courthouse."

"The courthouse is not dingy." She snapped it back.

Actually, he was right. She just didn't want to admit it. The courthouse where she prosecuted was horribly dingy. The carpet was frayed in the halls, the marbled floors in the courtrooms themselves had long lost their luster, the wooden pew-style benches were worn and smooth. But, at that moment, she could feel it, smell it, breathe the courtroom again. Only there, striking a jury or cracking questions like a whip during a cross-exam of a defense witness, or whispering the final words to a closing argument, did she feel she fit in her own skin, like a bird out of a cage.

Tony went on. "Hailey, just hear me out. We have an emergency. We need you. Please, please come on today. We'll work around your schedule. The Love story . . . *It's incredible! She's dead!*"

"Yes. I know. You told me. Let me guess . . . You *love it!* Right?"

"What?" Russo didn't understand her gentle jab at him. He was oblivious, and Hailey didn't bother to explain.

"But what's the emergency?"

"Well, we're running the Love interview. It's gonna be fantastic. We'll work in video from the murder scene. We can't get any of the cops to talk . . . That's where you come in. We need the voice of Lady Justice. All we have right now is the lawyer who's representing Love's family. Leather Stockton's, too. Both of them. Sookie's so amazing! She personally booked their lawyer, Derek Jacobs."

Hailey recognized the name. Jacobs was a famous celebrity lawyer who managed to bungle every case he handled, but somehow maintained a high profile. Apparently, the stars just heard about the Who's Who list of his clients, never thinking deeply enough to notice he always lost the case.

"He's a sleaze bucket. Why do the families have a lawyer?"

"They're suing, of course!"

Hailey paused. "Suing who?

Tony nearly exploded at the suggestion there was no one to sue. "Are you kidding? They were murdered and cops don't have the killers yet! Can't the families sue the cops? Aren't they taking too long to solve the case? Or the yoga studio for poor lighting? I mean . . . There's gotta be *somebody* to sue . . . right?"

"No . . . there's not a lawsuit there against the cops and I don't know what lighting had to do with Prentiss Love's murder . . . probably nothing. Murder constitutes a criminal intervening act and a civil lawsuit probably won't hold up."

"See . . . I love it when you talk like a lawyer! We have to do the show in a hurry! Before they catch the killers!"

Or killer, Hailey thought.

"I'm not a civil lawyer; it's really not my expertise. I was a prosecutor." But that was another life . . . a life she left behind. All of it. The bloody crime scenes. The late night phone calls. The heavy case loads, the autopsies, those horrible stainless steel tables, covered with a sheet of white paper to catch the human decomp as it oozed from the bodies of dead victims . . . It was over.

They stepped out onto the sidewalk. Instinctively looking past Tony Russo for a cab as he continued talking, Hailey spotted two Park Avenue types, stick-thin skinny with hair perfectly coiffed to fall in shiny waves around their heads, skin-tight pants, and high heels. Both faces looked stretched unnaturally across the eyes, noses, and foreheads, their makeup was perfect . . . and their dogs were having a vicious fight on the sidewalk. A fight as vicious as two tiny Manhattan maltipoos could muster. The women were trying their best to pull the dogs apart by their leashes without chipping any nails.

Both the dogs were wearing miniature mink jackets that fitted over their torsos and came just short of their short little silky legs.

Mink jackets? For dogs?

This was horribly unnatural. She could only pray the two doggie jackets were faux. Maybe coming back to the city had been a mistake after all.

"Anyway, you don't want to do an hour show to fight for justice, but you have no idea what I've had to live through for the show. I just got back from a trip to DC. *Miserable!* Travel booked me in what I was told was a five-star hotel, The Pentagonian, and guess what happened?"

"What happened?" She dragged her eyes away from maltipoos in minks and looked back at Tony.

"Well, of course I was booked on the *Elite Club Level.*"

"What's the Club Level?"

He looked at her like she was an alien from another planet. "The Club Level is where the hotel has an open bar, food, TVs, magazines . . . a hospitality room for frequent guests, you know, or people that shell out premium rates for the rooms."

He looked put out having to explain what a Club Level was.

"Anyway," he continued on, "of course I had to be moved to a room at the very end of the hall because I just am not going to put up with the elevator opening and shutting at all hours of the day and night, people laughing and talking in the halls . . . Were they crazy?"

"They had to be crazy." Hailey egged him on.

"So then, when I get into my room, I just felt nauseous from all the travel and I went into my bathroom and there, hanging on the back of the bathroom door was this thick, white terrycloth robe with slippers attached . . ."

"Well, that was nice, wasn't it? I can just see you in a terrycloth robe and matching slippers . . ." Actually, she could see it.

"No! It wasn't nice! It was awful! Because then, I saw not only lipstick, but urine on the terrycloth robe, Hailey! Lipstick and urine! On the robe on the Elite Level of the Pentagonian!"

"Oh, no!" Hailey had to hold in the laughter. But it was hard.

He went on. "*Anyway* . . . about the show, this time will be different. We'll put you in a studio all by yourself. You won't even see Harry Todd. He'll be in a completely different part of the building. He wants to apologize. Even if you don't want to do it for me . . . don't you want justice . . . *You're* a crime victim. Don't you remember what *that* felt like? What happened to you speaking for victims and all that? What happened to that? I thought you were actually dedicated to something. *Do it for Will.* It's what he would want." Tony Russo blurted it out there on the sidewalk. It was his trump card, and he'd been waiting to play it.

Hailey stopped in her tracks and turned back to look at Russo. Normally, she would have been angry to be reminded of Will. But instead, it was like a dagger to her heart. Even now, she missed him so much it hurt.

By this time, she'd have been a mother, fixing dinner each night, helping with homework, reading stories before bed. Holding them, loving them, playing and laughing with her family that never was. No birthdays together, no pizza nights, no anniversaries with Will, shared with their children.

A gust of wind blew across the sidewalk.

"Okay. I will. I'll do it."

She turned and hailed a cab before anyone could see the tears spring to her eyes. She waved goodbye over her shoulder and stepped into the taxi.

THE PRENTISS LOVE SHOW HAD BEEN A HIT . . . A RATINGS monster. But that didn't stop Sookie Downs from staring miserably at the heap of clothes lying on the floor of her private dressing room at Bergdorf's. They were all awful. She had a meeting in less than two hours with the president of GNE and had hoped she could find just the right outfit to impress him.

Not that she needed a dress to impress Noel Fryer. She'd done that when they were "dating," to put it euphemistically. The affair ended badly, of course. Noel dumped her for one of the GNE receptionists, and Sookie had done her best to act nonchalant. It was years ago, but it still stung. He likely wouldn't even notice her ensemble. No matter what the size, shape, color, whether a duchess or a secretary, an on-air anchor or the cleaning lady, Fryer loved the ladies.

Whatever. Sookie always had good luck when she mixed Noel Fryer with a Chanel miniskirt. Worked like a charm. With a red suede mini, she got her show budget nearly doubled. With a blue velvet micro paired with a gold chain belt, she got a splashy, new studio built for Todd, plus new backdrops for satellite guests in every bureau, Washington, L.A., New York, and Seattle.

Real proof of the power of the mini occurred just a few months ago. Sookie had made the horrendous trek, starting in the heated garage of her home in the Hamptons. Her mansion and waitstaff were all bankrolled by her hubby before he discovered his new girlfriend. He still had to pay for it no matter whom he was shacked up with, her lawyers made sure of that.

The brown-bricked behemoth stood wedged in between the fabulous estates of the president of Universal Studios and a Wall Street whiz who reportedly had over a billion stashed in Turks and Caicos.

Sookie's journey from there to Manhattan ended at the huge, glass entrance of GNE.

The trip was worth it. For that particular meeting with Fryer, she carefully chose a black leather miniskirt paired with a sheer, low-cut, leopard print top. And they did just what they were supposed to. That get-up got Harry Todd one hundred hours use of the GNE corporate jet of his choosing, of which Sookie herself usually "borrowed" about sixty hours to jet back and forth to L.A., to shop Rodeo Drive or whatever suited her fancy.

Today was a disaster. Not a single outfit worked. She'd started at Chanel, had her driver then stop at Gucci, and ended here at Bergdorf's.

She was exhausted. If only the others knew what she went through to stay on top. She sat dejectedly in a soft, cushioned chair, staring at herself in the mirrors that surrounded her, rubbing her temples with her forefingers. At least her hair looked good. No dark brown roots tinged with gray peeking through the coppery red. She could have gone blonde all those years ago, but blonde was so . . . predictable. She'd have it blown out just before her meeting with Noel.

And from here, at least, she couldn't see a single wrinkle. She admired her long, pale legs, stretched out in front of her. Contemplating her thighs, she knew she absolutely had to find a mini. The show depended on it.

Sookie's cell rang. It was sitting there at her fingertips on a side table along with a clear glass of ice tea tinged with cinnamon that one of the salesgirls had brought her. Maybe it was Derek. He was always calling from unidentified numbers so his wife wouldn't know where he was.

"Hello?" She gave it a breathless, mysterious quality as best she could after all she'd been through that morning.

A salesgirl poked her head in between the two heavy damask curtains. Sookie shot her a look that would have killed had it been a bullet. The girl ducked and ran back to the showroom floor. It was too early in the morning to have a purse thrown at her head. Last time Sookie was frustrated over her choices of couture, she'd momentarily "lost it" and sailed a Chanel clutch aimed at the attendant's nose.

Luckily for both, she missed.

"Hello, Sookie?"

It wasn't Derek. Where the hell was he? She'd specifically told him she'd be alone, away from the rabbit ears of her children, her domestic staff, and her ever-present personal assistants. One of the few places in the world she could truly be alone was in a Bergdorf's changing room.

"Yes. What is it, Pressley?"

Pressley was her first and most intimate personal assistant. She served as an assistant, secretary, driver, girl Friday, and babysitter. Sookie managed to get her a supervising producer title and the fat salary that came with it, all courtesy of *The Harry Todd Show.*

The only thing Sookie hated about her was the fact she was stunningly beautiful. She was tall and slim, with dark hair so beautiful it didn't need to be bleached blonde. And she was only twenty-three.

Dreadful in every respect.

If she hadn't been so efficient and discreet, Sookie would have fired her long ago based on looks alone. Sookie knew Pressley desperately wanted to break into the TV business and would do whatever it took to please, all in the hopes that someday she really would be an actual producer.

"Noel's late. I just heard from his assistant. He's locked inside his condo again and he can't get out. They had to call the guy that designed the security system to help him get out of his bathroom. It'll probably be another two hours or so before he can get out thorough the powder room door and over to GNE."

Sookie let loose a string of expletives. Pressley knew it was coming and held the phone a few inches back off her ear. This, by far, was not the first time Noel had trapped himself in his own condo.

When Noel Fryer was named president of GNE, his already engorged ego puffed up to a much more dangerous level. He became convinced he needed über-security, and contacted one of the most elite security mavens in the world, Einst Schlager.

Schlager worked most of his career in intelligence with the Israeli Army. He had consulted U.S. Special Ops and ultimately, went into private security. His security designs were found in embassies around the world, homes of reigning kings, princes, and dictators, private yachts of the mega-wealthy, and homes of private individuals that could afford him.

Fryer's ascension to the role of GNE president, in his own mind, edged him into the ranking along with presidents, kings, and princes. His home-security design must be commensurate with his position. Fryer was sure there would be death threats of some sort. Or at least attempted bugs and wiretaps. So far, none of the three had happened.

Schlager's security design for Fryer's six-story condo in the heart of Manhattan's toney Upper West Side was a technical wonder, a fusion of art and science, complete with a steel-encased "safe-room," with metal window and door covers that shut automatically in the face of an attack. Similar metal casement closings protected the bedroom and bathroom doors, with sensors constantly measuring everything from movement to sound to temperature, from wine cellar to attic.

Video cameras out the yin-yang were a foregone conclusion.

But for some reason, the detectors were a little too sensitive, resulting in Fryer frequently tripping the silent alarm locking all the doors, inside and out, and causing the steel casings to close, making him a virtual prisoner in whatever room he happened to be in at the moment.

He usually tripped the sensors when in his own bathroom. The condo's electricity and phones were tied into the whole thing. Visitors to the home were given cell phones at the front door to dial for help, just in case they accidentally tripped the system and locked themselves in as they wandered from room to room.

A mere technician obviously couldn't handle the intricacies of Schlager's design. So at times like these, Einst had to be tracked down wherever he was around the globe. He then had to hook into the portable laptop he carried everywhere in an aluminum briefcase, and log into Fryer's security system to reverse the trip.

Fryer's insistence on a steel safe-room and automated steel casings straight out of *Star Wars* to cover various doors in his home made him quite the conversation topic among the other network bigs. His "eccentricities" were overlooked . . . as long as GNE stayed on top.

And it did stay on top.

"Have they found Schlager?" Sookie hissed it into the phone. "I busted my frame getting into the city this morning, much less what I've gone through trying to find the right outfit for the meeting. This is absolutely unacceptable."

"We think he's on a yacht outside Bahrain. Still trying."

"What the hell is he doing on a yacht outside Bahrain?"

"I don't know, Sookie." Pressley spoke calmly and soothingly to Sookie at times like these. She didn't want to agitate her boss any more than she already was. "Would you like me to find out the nature of his business in Bahrain?"

"No, you idiot, it was a manner of speaking. I don't *care* what Einst Schlager is doing in Bahrain. I just want Fryer to drag his tubby white ass into this meeting."

Sookie was now standing, spitting the last syllable into the cell phone, kicking at one of the designer minis lying in a pile on the floor.

"Okay. I'll keep trying. What about a phone conference instead of a face-to-face meeting with Fryer? I'm sure he could do a cell call from his bathroom."

"I didn't drive the whole way in from the Hamptons and spend three hours at Bergdorf's just to talk to Fryer trapped on the can. Call me when he gets out. Oh yeah, what floor's he on? Can he at least crawl out the window?" Sookie was screaming at this point, much to the delight of the two salesgirls listening outside the changing room door.

"Already checked. Sixth floor. Bathroom attached to the master bedroom. Can't crawl out. He had the fire escape stairs outside removed, remember? He was convinced the paparazzi would crawl up and get pictures."

"Yes, how could I forget that? As if the tabs want a shot of him lying on his sofa eating a bag of chips."

"Hold on, Sookie, Tony's dialing in."

"No! I can't take all his slathering this early in the day. Just tell me what he wants."

"Okay." Pressley momentarily put her boss on hold to find out what Tony wanted without increasing Sookie's frustration. "Hello? Tony?"

"Pressley, where's Sookie? I have to talk to her *right now*." As usual, Tony Russo was frantic.

"I have her on the phone right now, she knows it's you and wants to know what's up?"

"It's about today's show. Patch me through."

"Hold, please." Manipulating buttons on the phone, she put Russo on hold and went back to Sookie.

"He needs to talk to you right now about the show. It sounds urgent."

"Why can't he just leave a message?"

"I already asked."

"I'm going to shoot myself. I can't take it anymore. I'm getting a migraine. Patch him through." Sookie held the back of her left hand over her forehead and lay back on the pillows of a deep-cushioned sofa there in the changing room.

Maybe she would take a tiny sip of the tea, after all. Could she put some gin in it?

Tony's voice blasted into the cell. He'd never learned the concept of an "inside voice." Practically everything came out several decibels too loud. As a preemptive maneuver, Sookie had already dialed down the volume on her phone.

"You have to call Harry. I just booked Dean on the Prentiss Love show. But you know Harry'll threaten not to host if she's on."

"Can't you deal with him?"

"I tried already. Didn't work. He's threatening to do the World Series."

"Doesn't that happen, like, a year from now?"

"Doesn't matter. He wants to predict who he thinks will make it all the way. Besides the Yankees, of course."

"But that's a year away and there will only be one other team. What's there to say?"

"Then he can rail about the Yankee payroll."

"Why are we talking about this? Prentiss Love's body's still warm. *We are not doing a show about the World Series.*"

"I know that, you know that, but Harry doesn't know it. You have to call him. Tell him we need the numbers."

"Harry doesn't care about the numbers. He doesn't understand why we all get paid. He thinks viewers tune in for him. He doesn't get it's about the guests. And he hates Hailey Dean. She showed him up and made him look like an idiot. At least keep her away from him. Put her in a flash studio with the logo behind her."

"Done. I'll tell her it's to make her happy. Needless to say, the hatred is mutual."

"Okay." Sookie agreed. "I'll call him. We can't miss the Prentiss Love train. She's only gonna get murdered once. Same as Stockton."

"What time do you meet with Fryer? Want me to come?" Russo would give his eyeteeth to be in the same room as the GNE president.

"Not till he gets out of his bathroom."

"Locked in again?"

"Yes. It's totally ruined my schedule for today. By the way, where are you?"

"At the office, of course."

"Come meet me for coffee at Bergdorf's."

He knew what that meant. Sookie translation . . . *Come buy my lunch plus whatever I spot that I want, and don't you dare try to expense it.* He dreaded meeting her at any major department store, much less a little boutique. Sookie always spotted extremely expensive items and pressured Tony into buying them as gifts to her. He really couldn't afford it, but she *was* the boss, and she had the ears of not only Harry Todd, but all the network bigs.

"Now?" He could only croak out the one syllable. His budget really didn't include one of Sookie's "lunches," aka buying spree.

"No, idiot. Tomorrow."

Russo was already headed toward the elevator to go out and hail a cab. He had to. Sookie picked three of the minis off the floor, and sticking only part of her left hand out through the changing room door, she thrust the clothes into the arms of one of the sales girls.

"Ring it up." She said it through the door and the girl trotted off.

Sookie plopped back down into the soft, deep cushions of one of the massive but delicately flowered chairs. After a few moments of collecting herself, she gathered all her strength to lean forward and zip up her own pair of black, stiletto suede Dior boots. Pulling the zip smoothly up the inside calf, she once again admired her own legs. These Diors would look great with the new red mock-croc mini. It couldn't be longer than eight inches, top to bottom . . . perfect.

She exhaled loudly for emphasis, as if someone were listening. Sookie always imagined she had an audience.

What she did for The Harry Todd Show.

IIIIIIIIIIIIIIIIIIIIIIIIIIIIIIIIIIIIIIIIIIIIIIIIIIIIIII **18** IIIIIIIIIIIIIIIIIIIIIIIIII

IT WAS A BEAUTIFUL DAY ON THE LINKS. THE SUN WAS SHINING, THE breeze was cold but gentle, and the smell of the ocean carried from the shore all the way to the greens. Scott Anderson strode purposefully across some of the most beautiful grass the great state of New York had ever seen.

The greens and the "rough" as well were manicured to perfection by a fleet of horticulturists, landscape designers, and groundskeepers, and they all would have burst into tears to see Anderson digging his golf cleats into the tender shoots of grass as he headed uphill toward the driving range. Oblivious, Anderson continued off the hand-built path to his next lesson. He didn't want to be late.

Anderson was finally starting lessons with Fallon Malone. Her personal assistant had been trying for months to schedule times with him, and they had actually had a few lessons planned, written in stone, but for one reason or another, Fallon always canceled or no-showed.

Normally, Scott Anderson would have refused to reschedule a lesson after a no-show, but how often did a golf pro like himself get to teach the game to a movie icon like Fallon Malone? I mean, was there anybody left in America who hadn't seen her in the car wash scene?

She was a star. And he was going to be her golf guru. And hopefully, more than that. His good looks combined with the manners he'd picked up along the way had served him well. It was no secret Anderson loved the ladies.

It wasn't hard. The women who took lessons from Anderson wouldn't leave him alone. The way he saw it, he was doing them a favor.

At the top of the hill, Scott spotted a black limo outside the club house. It had to be Fallon. As soon as he got about thirty feet from the car, a burly, uniformed driver jumped out of the limo and briskly approached him.

"Can I help you, sir?" He stood, nonchalantly but menacingly between Scott and the limo.

"Hello." Scott beamed his best and friendliest smile, known to disarm cats, dogs, and women alike. It didn't seem to be working on the driver. He continued. "I'm the club's golf pro, Scott Anderson. You may have heard of me, twenty-fifth at Pebble Beach three years ago? You a golfer?"

"No, sir. I am not. But I am the driver for Ms. Malone. She's here for her lesson." Without another word, he turned on his heel and went back to the limo, opened the back passenger side door, and out she stepped.

Long legs, just like in the movies, swung out of the back seat. The rest of her followed. She took off dark sunglasses and held her left hand up to shade her eyes from the sun. Even without the stage makeup, she was a looker.

"Hello, Mr. Anderson. I hear you're quite the pro! I've simply got to learn to play some semblance of the game for a role I've got my eye on. But let me warn you, I've never swung anything but a water hose!"

"And I saw that! When you washed the Vette and you swung the hose around like a lasso at the end! You were tremendous! Obviously, I'm a big fan. I still say you were robbed at the Oscars!"

Did he say she was robbed at the Oscars? Those were the magic words to Fallon Malone's heart. *He loved her acting.* She beamed up at him and tossed her dark hair back behind her shoulders.

The limo driver rolled his eyes after he turned away from the two and headed back to the car. *Here she goes again.* He grimaced. He knew where this was headed. Another affair with practically a complete stranger . . . and in his limo. If he didn't get paid so much to cart Malone around, he'd demand she and Anderson go to a hotel.

And as it turned out, the driver was right. The mutual attraction was consummated immediately following Fallon's "coach-led analysis" to better understand her swing and reach her "full yardage potential." The two never made it to the personal club fitting so Anderson could precisely match Fallon's clubs to her swing. In fact, they never made it past the pro quarters adjacent to the men's locker room.

That afternoon led to rendezvous everywhere, from Fallon's apartment in Manhattan to Fallon's limo to the back of the local IHOP a few miles from the club. All the meetings were surreptitious, as Anderson was not allowed to "date" anyone he instructed at the club.

Fallon's driver predicted it. Same thing all over again . . . the gin bottles and the pantyhose in the back seat again. Gin bottles and pantyhose.

F RANCIS WAS REELING. HE PUSHED HIS DARK HAIR AWAY FROM his forehead with both hands, holding them tight against either side of his head. He couldn't take it in . . . Prentiss Love . . . *dead?*

His chest pounded and his mouth went dry. He didn't even try to fight back the tears.

The cable news networks were wall to wall with funeral plans. He couldn't tear his eyes away. He hated them. They were totally whoring out the memory of a beautiful, delicate woman that had been one of his great loves. They were dredging up everything, harping especially on her alleged problems with drugs and alcohol, which Francis was convinced were false. Old boyfriends were dragged on and off the screen like it was a parade. Harry Todd especially liked to delve into her romantic past.

But all Prentiss's so-called "boyfriends" turning up on TV were idiots. They didn't know her like Francis did. If Todd had a clue, he'd contact Francis. But Francis wouldn't talk. Not even to Harry Todd. Francis was a gentleman and always would be. He'd rather die than kiss and tell.

Sitting there in the early morning darkness of his mother's living room, he looked down at his own two hands, stretched out over the expanse of his two knees. They sat there, seemingly innocent. They were hands more befitting a surgeon or a poet . . . maybe a musician, possibly piano or strings.

These hands could never kill Prentiss Love . . . Could they?

True, the last week had been a big blur. He'd had "dates" with both Leather and Prentiss. The overpowering smell of the incense and candles he burned on those special nights still hung in the air. Then after that, he remembered the Jehovah's Witnesses skulking around on the front porch. He remembered being angry at Prentiss . . . But then it all seemed to fade away.

When he headed out to Dunkin' Donuts this morning, he found the gas tank of his mom's car completely empty, but he had absolutely no recollection of where he'd been. The *Post* had compared the two. Prentiss shot in Manhattan, Leather out in the Hamptons.

Could he? It was Tuesday morning. GNE said so and he had no reason to believe the network was part of the government's plan to eradicate him and others like him, those who believed in true and unfettered freedom.

If the cable network was to be believed, over two weeks had passed since his last clear recollection. Francis clicked the remote and changed channels to the *TV Guide* station.

He sat and thought, his head in his hands. *Yes,* he had to be honest, at least with himself . . . He'd had dreams of killing them . . . powerful dreams. When he'd thought Prentiss had had an affair with a guy on her show, he was devastated and yes, he'd thought of circling her beautiful neck with his hands and squeezing the life out of her. He'd had similar dreams about Leather as well . . . and other women, too. They'd often coincided with nights he'd argued with his mother. That she-devil from hell.

This was all her fault . . . if she hadn't harangued him over the years about everything from his meds to his haircut to getting a job, he wouldn't have had those murderous dreams or ever acted them out.

He still couldn't take it in. How could he go through with it? True, in the dreams he'd actually enjoyed strangling the women . . . but in real life? *No way.*

Francis had an idea. Rousing himself out of his chair, he checked the front porch to ensure neither the Jehovah's Witnesses nor the Amway reps were lurking, then went out to his mother's car. He always kept meticulous records of mileage, oil changes, you name it.

In fact, he'd kept every gas receipt along with every tune-up and oil change record for the last twelve years. Same for the tires.

He couldn't believe his eyes. Nearly two thousand additional miles were logged on the odometer. It could only mean one thing. Francis did it. He drove from here, Marksville, Louisiana, to New York and back. Obviously in a murderous haze.

Had he been drugged? He felt groggy. Maybe the government had drugged him up for some reason. S.O.B.'s. But no way he'd let the government get the best of him . . . They weren't going to drug him up, make him commit murders, and then frame him.

No way. Francis Merle McGinnis could certainly outthink the U.S. government. *He had to think,* and doing so, he became convinced his fingerprints would turn up on the crime scenes. The government probably knew he collected guns . . . and both Prentiss and Fallon were shot to death.

Should he hide all of them now? Was one of them the murder weapon? He could bury them in the backyard tonight. Wrap them in sheets and bury them. That's what he would do. Bury his guns.

Was this part of their plan to frame him?

Think . . . Think!!! He commanded his brain to work.

He was in agony. Had two of his beautiful ladies died at his own hands? The pain was almost too much for him to bear.

Tears rolled down his face. Did he himself do it? True, he'd had dreams of killing Stockton after being rebuffed, but those were just dreams, weren't they? Plus, in his dreams he never shot her; he'd dreamed he strangled her pretty white neck, not put a bullet through her brain.

He'd never disfigure a great beauty like that.

And then, there were the flowers he'd sent Prentiss. He'd gotten a form response. She didn't even bother to thank him herself. Was it too much effort for her to pick up a pen? And he'd paid plenty for those flowers, too.

But he didn't really expect Prentiss to blow their secret. Their love transcended the prying minds of her assistants, agents, and all the flunkies surrounding her, much less the general public itself.

He didn't need a handwritten thank-you. She spoke to him that night on the airwaves and thanked him from the heart. Her eyes, which appeared to be looking into the camera but were really looking at him, had melted his soul.

He would never hurt her. Not intentionally, anyway . . . the dreams were just that, dreams. No matter how vivid . . . how lifelike . . . right?

But just in case, Francis got up and headed to the kitchen. Leaning back against the kitchen sink, he studied the kitchen table. His worst fears were realized. The table was a few inches out of place, he could tell, because the table's legs were not sitting squarely inside the four indentations they made over time into the linoleum floor beneath it. Somebody had moved the table.

Dragging the kitchen dinette from the center of the floor, he turned back to where it had sat, knelt down on the floor, and placed his right hand between two of the linoleum squares. Lifting a four-by-five-foot block of linoleum upward revealed a crawlspace dug beneath the kitchen floor.

Francis crawled down into the space and pulled the dinette back over himself and the hole in the kitchen floor. He army-crawled the five feet or so to his cache of weapons and HCBs, to get rid of potential evidence.

There were over a hundred weapons down here and he'd lost count of the amount of ammunition he'd stockpiled over the years. Then of course, there were the Homemade Chemical Bombs.

Francis took great time and care creating them and when talking to friends online, he referred to them as his "babies." He loved them all equally, he swore when asked, but his personal favorites were the ones he'd made of toilet bowl cleaner mixed with Drano and tinfoil, poured into a screw-top Coke bottle for just the right amount of pressure. He had at least twenty-five of them already prepared, but he still wasn't sure he was sufficiently armed for the inevitable showdown to come.

After all, look at what had happened at Waco and David Koresh. Koresh thought he was ready too, until ATF blasted up in there.

Francis pulled the thin chain attached to a single lightbulb over his head. The bulb was wired into a series of two-by-fours running from underneath the kitchen stove above to the center of the dug-out room beneath the kitchen floor.

Although everything looked untouched, just as he'd left it the last time he was down here, looking around, Francis could sense a government intruder had been in his lair. Several of the long guns were laid out, just as he'd left them, on a wooden work table he'd brought down piece by piece and assembled by the light of the single bulb overhead. Before the murders, he'd always loved coming down here at all hours of the day and night, cleaning them, keeping them all on the ready.

Between his blackout the weeks of the murders, the vivid dreams about strangling his beloveds, the odometer reading, and the obvious tampering with his gun cache, Francis knew the truth. The papers were vague about the calibers. He hardly knew where to start. Could he leave all the guns here? Would it be safe? And more important . . . *Which one was the murder weapon?*

What he did for love.

E MORY DAVIS, MD, WAS ON DUTY THAT NIGHT WORKING THE graveyard shift. He was the newest medical examiner on the roster, and obsessed with dead bodies since childhood. It didn't win him many friends in school, but it did land him the chief intern spot, and then a full-time position at one of the busiest morgues in the country. At this hour of the night, all his youthful fantasies were fulfilled.

Over the years, Emory had graduated from dissecting flies at play school to frogs in high school biology to exploring the pulmonary and cardiovascular systems of his own, individual, aged monkey in pre-med. Then . . . the ultimate . . . he was assigned an eighty-year-old male cadaver in med school. But it all paid off for Emory. He finally made it, landing here at murder central . . . the New York County Medical Examiner's Office.

The diener, Jimmy the morgue assistant, hoisted the body onto the table, still shrouded in the white sheet, and unobtrusively left the autopsy room, waiting just outside the swinging doors until Emory called out for him. He was a tiny man who'd worked for New York County in the morgue for decades.

It always amazed Emory how Jimmy could single-handedly maneuver even the largest of the dead, some tipping the scales at nearly three hundred pounds, but he did it. It was all in the technique. Emory figured practice made perfect.

The sheet would have to be removed extremely carefully, just in case fibers or other evidence was still attached to the body. The majority of morgues, especially the older facilities, still sported the old porcelain or even marble tables. They were charming, true, in a nostalgic sort of way, but Emory much preferred working with the sleeker, modern versions.

And here in New York County, he had the top of the line. She was a beauty. The autopsy table itself was a waist-high, cold, spotless stainless steel fixture. Not a single scratch on her . . . yet.

She was also plumbed for running water, too. Nice.

Several faucets and spigots running along the width of the table facilitated rinsing away the copious amounts of blood released during the procedure. Blood flowed by the quart, depending on the mode of death, of course, down into long, slender receptacles unobtrusively located at the edges of the table.

This particular sweetie was basically a tray, slanted for drainage. And it had slightly raised edges, preventing blood and other bodily fluids from spilling onto the floor.

Without much preamble, Davis pulled his long, dark hair into a ponytail, secured a surgeon's cap over it, and flicked on one of the intense overhead lights above the autopsy slab. Taking a cursory look up and down the body, he inhaled deeply through his nose, breathing in the heavy smell of the woman's bloody leotard.

Emory Davis loved his job.

Cutting through the skimpy Danskin with a surgical knife, the autopsy began. He started speaking cordially but routinely into a handheld microphone, taping for the record the COD, formally pronouncing cause of death.

"Well-nourished Caucasian female, brunette, approximately thirty to thirty-five years of age, sixty-five inches in length."

Hmm. No personal effects like a purse with a wallet and driver's license inside to check the date of birth. He'd have to guesstimate the age. He was usually right-on with all of it at the first guess . . . age, weight, height.

He clicked off the recorder and pulled out his measuring tape. Just to double-check. He quickly extended the yellow ribbon from the top of her head, what was left of it, to the bottom of her heel.

His first guess was right. Five-five.

It was a little game he'd created all alone back in one of the morgues where he'd interned in med school. He guessed the exact length of corpses. It was amazing the acumen you could develop after years of dead bodies.

Well-nourished was a stretch. This girl needed to eat. "Well-nourished" was a term of art to indicate that starvation was not the cause of death and that the body was within the acceptable weight parameters for height. And those parameters were wide, indeed. Emory guessed this was just another anorexic New York woman who lived off drinking Perrier and picking at salads.

"Weight, one hundred pounds." Davis continued speaking into the handheld mike, detailing the autopsy as he went along. The overhead hot light bored into the brick-brown blood caked around the victim's neck.

He punched a button on the side of the autopsy table, rigged with automatic scales. The digital number shone dull red. Emory smiled. Dead on . . . again. A hundred pounds on the nose.

"Single shot to the head. Near-decapitation of victim suggests to this doctor subject is the victim of homicide."

Of course it was homicide. He'd spent nearly six months in med school in a class titled Methods and Assessment of Homicide and Suicide. Statistically speaking, no way would a white female of this age, and judging by the expensive jewelry, this income bracket, shoot herself in the face.

Maybe it was vanity or just pure instinct, but rarely did women shoot themselves, much less in the head, in order to off themselves. They usually went the pill-overdose-mixed-with-booze route, maybe gas from the car or oven; and sometimes he'd get a jumper; but shooting to the head?

Nope. It was homicide for sure.

Plus, there was the obvious trajectory, the path of the bullet or bullets.

That spoke volumes.

Emory paused to whip out the Polaroid camera from the lower shelf of the metal side table again, taking close-ups of the head wound. He had to take photos, even if a jury wouldn't be able to discern what they were seeing amid the bloody pink tissue in the Polaroid close-up.

Suddenly he stopped. There was something familiar about this autopsy. It was like déjà vu. He'd done it before.

Of course, he'd performed literally thousands of autopsies, but it wasn't that. It wasn't the repetitive nature of the autopsy. He suddenly had the intense sensation he'd done this exact autopsy of this exact woman before. Since Emory believed in nothing other than that proven by science, he shook it off and continued narrating.

Practically poking his nose into the woman's skull, he observed the gunshot wound had left her left temporal lobe totally exposed. Taking a close look, Emory continued narrating into the handheld.

"Bullet entry wound is through the deceased's cranium, left temple entry, angle front to back, direction is left to right, at a mildly lowered angle, from up to down. Bullet exiting victim's head just below and behind right ear."

He went back to document details of the entry wound. Carefully looking at the bullet's entry, Emory detected stippling, the gunshot residue, and markings on the skin. He spoke again into the handheld. "Stippling noted in and around the entry wound with maroon-tinted particles, likely part of the gunshot debris." He continued to make his way along the bullet's path.

Emory looked intensely, barely breathing. He delicately pulled away layers of brain matter as fine as tissue paper to precisely confirm the exact trajectory path, although a look at the outside of the head normally tells all. Based simply on bullet entry and exit wound locations, here, the entry wound was a huge, gaping hole, not a clean and tidy entry at all. Emory would have to burrow further into the head to get the exact angle. Details matter.

"Neither bullet nor bullet fragmentation is observed anywhere within the brain cavity or for that matter, within the entire cranium itself."

Wait. Without moving his head or averting his gaze to look up, Emory reached above himself and pulled down the bright retractable light hanging over the table. It was hot to the touch, and getting hotter by the moment.

There it was. Deeply embedded in brain tissue, he saw it.

A tiny, tiny metallic fragment. It had clearly splintered off upon impact with the skull. Disturbing the least amount of tissue possible, Emory reached over to the steel surgical tray he'd placed directly at his right elbow to grab a pair of tweezers.

Carefully, carefully, barely breathing, with the thin pair of tweezers, he plucked the speck of metal from her brain. Placing it in a tiny Zip Lock bag designed specifically for this purpose, Emory finally exhaled deeply, and then inhaled. The surgical smell of the room, combined with the tiniest whiff signaling the inception of human decomposition, didn't bother Emory in the least.

He did it. Many, if not most, doctors would have missed the fragment. It was extremely important, possibly crucial to the case.

If the fragment was not damaged beyond medical and forensic use, it could be analyzed at the crime lab. Actually, Emory could pretty much call the caliber of a sliver of fragment himself, but best to leave it to the experts in ballistics at the lab.

From the sliver, caliber could be determined and possibly traced to a specific handgun if that particular handgun's tool markings were registered in the national database.

The database, The Integrated Ballistics Identification System (IBIS), is a highly specialized computer program that compares markings on crime scene bullets to those in other cases. It accesses a database maintained by ATF, the Bureau of Alcohol, Tobacco, Firearms, and Explosives.

IBIS would scan the bullet for markings, then run those markings against a database of known weapons to identify matches that police and crime technicians might never have identified. Who knew if there was enough bullet to get a match, but at least Emory had done his part.

Good thing he taped his narration before dedicating it to writing for the formal autopsy report. He rewound and played it back, listening to his own words. "Neither bullet nor bullet fragmentation is observed anywhere within the brain cavity or for that matter, within the entire cranium itself."

Wrong! He re-narrated his discovery of the fragment sliver.

And to think, he actually got paid for this.

Incredible.

Just then, it hit him . . . the déjà vu . . . she was familiar all right. Emory looked at the toe tag. Holey moley.

This was Prentiss Love. He'd had a poster of her tacked up in his bedroom since he was twelve years old. Used to drive his mom crazy.

In retrospect, Emory realized it hadn't been the poster girl, but instead it was the tacks he'd pushed into the wallpaper to secure the poster to the wall that bugged her.

His mom, God love her, had gone to great lengths to personally spend an entire weekend cutting, pasting, and hanging sports-themed wallpaper up on his walls, covered in footballs, baseballs, and basketballs. His mom had tried anything, especially encouraging sports of all types, to get him to think of something other than dissecting bugs and animals.

So when she saw the Prentiss Love poster, she was probably thrilled he was dreaming about a girl . . . any girl . . . any *thing*, actually, other than dead creatures he could dissect.

But she was proud when he walked across the stage to get that med school diploma and a handshake from the president of the university. They talked on the phone nearly every Sunday. But this time he'd have something to talk about she'd be interested in . . . not just more dead bodies and where he'd gone to dinner to tell her about.

Wow. Prentiss Love. They'd never believe this back home. Emory took another Polaroid just for good measure.

|||||||||||||||||||||||||||||||||||||||||||||||||||||| **21** ||||||||||||||||||||||||

RACING UPTOWN ON MADISON AVENUE, SOOKIE DOWNS NEARLY vomited in the back of the cab. She wasn't used to this.

First of all, the cab stank. She couldn't distinguish the exact origin of the stink. Pursing her lips instinctively downward while wrinkling her nose at the smell, she had several candidates from which to choose. There was the white gooey pool of liquid on the backseat's floorboard beneath her feet. Sookie had no choice but to delicately levitate the black spiked heels of her Dior boots a few inches above the floor mat. She certainly did not want the smell to attach itself to her shoes.

Then there was the clear but extremely sticky substance on the seat on which she was sitting. Just because it was clear didn't mean it didn't smell. What was it? Some sort of soup? Chablis, perhaps? Spilled from a celebratory flute there in the back seat? Or was it just old urine? At least she hoped it was old. But did age matter? Was urine sticky? She paused to think. She'd never really changed her children's diapers herself, so she didn't know whether urine became gooey or sticky over time, left on a smooth plastic surface such as a dark blue car seat, unattended and unsanitized.

A strong possibility, obviously, was the previous passenger. He looked homeless, with a shock of dreads coming out from under a colorful Rasta hat. He very likely stank.

Sookie just couldn't be sure. Didn't Rastas refuse to bathe? Or was it washing their hair they hated? They certainly didn't take care of their nails, from what she observed in the fleeting moment when they had exchanged looks, each sizing the other up, each looking disdainfully at the other.

Why did *he* look at *her* that way? *He* was the one that stank.

Sookie smelled delicately of perfume that sold for $250 an ounce. She better smell good.

Then there was the cab driver himself. He also looked to Sookie as if he stank. His hair was greasy, from what she could tell in the backseat, separated from the driver by a dingy, scratched-up plastic partition covered almost completely with directions, warnings, fare notices, and a taxi driver identification card bearing the driver's name and photo.

He could be a terrorist. She couldn't even mentally pronounce his last name. It was nothing but consonants. And it was probably fake.

Maybe Harry should do a show on terrorists.

No, the viewers would hate hearing about *that* again.

But they'd love a show on body odor. Hmm. Who could they book, other than stinky people? Doctors, specialists, victims of physical eccentricities that caused horrible smells through no fault of their own?

Anyway, she hoped the smell in the cab did not attach itself to her. That's the last thing she needed. To absolutely reek in a meeting with Noel Fryer.

Noel was finally out of his bathroom and en route to his office. That's what his personal assistant had whispered into the phone less than five minutes ago.

Sookie wanted desperately to lower the window. She was so tempted to punch the electric window button there on the door beside her. But A, she'd have to touch the button, and she knew it was a virtual colony of germs more likely at home floating in a petri dish under a microscope. And B, the breeze could ruin her hair.

She'd come this far and she wasn't ruining her look now. Although vomit on the sides of her mouth would also destroy the look.

Sookie Downs lightly touched the window control, lowering the window only an inch or two so as not to get a direct breeze on her hair.

The cab suddenly took a violent left turn and there they were, in front of GNE.

Sookie handed the driver cash through a small, square slot in the cab's plastic partition. Not waiting for change, she grabbed the paper receipt he handed out the window to her, for expenses of course, balanced herself on the Dior spikes, straightened her spine, and walked coolly toward the network's giant, glass-front entrance.

A loud buzzing sound directly behind her made her turn back.

It was Fryer, for Pete's sake. So much for the casual but dramatic entrance into his all-windowed corner office up on the thirty-first floor. Here he was in the flesh.

She hoped her coppery hair was perfection.

The irritating buzzing sound was coming from Fryer's moped. Or whatever it was. A Vespa, he'd told her in the past. She'd acted like she knew what a Vespa was, exclaiming about his manly brilliance for purchasing it.

It sounded like "viper." So this was it? It had to be. No, Fryer's little motor scooter was in fact the Vespa he'd described. She would somehow work it into the conversation to look in the know.

Fryer dismounted the thing like it was a horse and he was in a Western. Sookie supposed that made him . . . who? John Wayne?

Or did it make him James Dean in motorcycle motif? Or Marlon Brando, who also looked great on-screen on a motorcycle.

But they were all dead. She'd look old and dated if she compared him to them. *Think! Damnit! Think of something brilliant to say! Brilliant . . . but light . . . . something witty . . .*

He left the Vespa parked horizontally in the space between two cars as if he owned the street. Noel Fryer took off his helmet, balancing it briefly on the seat of the Vespa, brushing his hair to the side, what there was of it, and unwrapping the scarf around his neck. Reaching into his front pocket, he pulled out a black cashmere beret. He had recently taken up wearing it around the office. While he unwrapped the scarf, he still left it hanging loose around his neck. He'd walk around the network like this all day, with the cashmere scarf hanging draped around his neck over his hand-tailored suit.

Who the hell did he think he was? Pavarotti?

Utterly ridiculous.

"Hello, you handsome man!"

Did she give it a *touch too much verve*?

"Hi, Sookie! I thought that was you when I pulled up. Glad you could make it into the city today."

"Well, Noel, I'm here every day. You know, for the show."

A chill went down her back. Did Noel know she actually never came in to the show? Why bother? She could think and direct just as well from her home out in the Hamptons. Her physicality had nothing to do with her talents. It was all in her head. Creative masterminds were all the same. They didn't fit into the confines of a nine-to-five workaday setting like all the others did.

They both walked through the glass doors and headed toward the wide expanse of the security desk.

"Good afternoon, Mr. Fryer." The security guard said it, barely looking up.

But, glancing over at Sookie, his face was blank. "Name and ID, please."

"Why, I'm Sookie Downs." How dare he ask for her ID. Didn't he know who she was?

"Beg pardon?"

"I'm Sookie Downs."

The guard registered not a hint of recognition.

"You know, *Sookie Downs*." She said her name slowly and with emphasis as if he were deaf. "I'm the executive producer of *The Harry Todd Show*? Certainly you've heard of Harry Todd. *The Harry Todd Show*?"

"Not ringing a bell. Name and ID, please."

This was not going as planned. Sookie fished around the bottom of her purse for her GNE ID pass. Certainly she'd brought it. Normally she was with Tony whenever she came in. He'd meet her at her limo and walk her in, already clearing her entrance with security.

She couldn't find the pass.

"I must have changed purses . . ."

"I vouch for her . . . You can let her up, Fred."

"Yes sir, Mr. Fryer."

Walking toward the elevator bank, Sookie breathed as evenly as possible.

"You know, I hate it when they put new guards at the front desk. *So irritating.*"

What else could she say? The elevator doors closed in front of their faces as they zoomed upward.

"I JUST WANT TO CONVEY HOW HAPPY WE ARE HERE AT GNE WITH THE *Todd Show*'s recent ratings." Noel Fryer sat back in his leather swivel chair, his feet up on his desk, the view of Manhattan thirty-one floors below him. He'd had the chair specially ergonomically designed several years before. He'd even had the leather seat and arms individually crafted in Italy, and told anybody that happened to come into his office. Today, reared back in his chair, he looked like king of the city and acted like it too, like it all belonged to him.

"I know some time back I had mentioned that, in light of Harry's, well, I hate to boil it down like this, in light of his ratings, maybe he should consider a graceful exit. You know, when that day does come, when your career is winding down . . . headed for a new phase . . . a new direction . . . and believe me, Sookie, it comes for everybody, even me, Noel Fryer, we would make it all look like Harry's decision."

"Noel, let me remind you that for years, Harry's by far been the highest rated thing you've got going and you'd be crazy to end his run now . . ."

"Correction, Sookie, he *was* the highest-rated thing we *had* going." Noel Fryer came down off his perch and put his feet on the carpet in front of him for emphasis. Sookie winced.

He went on. "There was the little slump . . . not so little actually, sixteen months of Todd's ratings in the crapper. And we stood by him."

Hardly. The moment Harry's ratings dipped, they started circling like wolves and Sookie knew it. If Harry hadn't had an iron-clad contract locking them in for another eighteen months, he'd have been on the streets, and Sookie with him. What about *her*? *What would become of her?*

"But that's all behind us, Sookie. That's why I called you in. Todd's ratings are up. He's leading the network again. It's fantastic . . . we're . . . ," Fryer searched for just the right word, " . . . *thrilled!*"

Sookie was still defensive, but kept it together and smiled brightly, pointing every single one of her veneers across the huge expanse of desktop separating her from Fryer. He was now kicked back in his chair again, the soles of his feet balanced on the desktop, directly impeding Sookie's view of his face. She kept peeking around his left foot to get a look at him.

Was he doing it on purpose? Was this some sort of mind game? Fryer was famous for messing with your head . . . and with Sookie, it didn't take much.

She smoothed down the edges of her mini, not that she wanted to show less leg, she just didn't have anything else to do with her hands. From this vantage, Noel couldn't even *see* her legs. To remedy that, she got up and casually walked toward the window running the length of the office. She leaned against it, keeping a serious look on her face as if she were pondering his every word.

"In fact, research sent me an analysis of Todd's numbers and, frankly, they look great." Fryer reached down into the lower drawer to his left and, opening it, pulled out a stack of computer printouts labeled with yellow stickers. As he flipped through, Sookie could see some of the numbers highlighted in pink.

"And based on what we're seeing"—"we" meaning only Fryer himself . . . he always talked as if he were a group—"you spike on the nights you feature Hailey Dean."

Hailey Dean? He had brought her up here to talk about Hailey Dean? Todd hated her . . . wouldn't even have her on the same set with him. And Tony said the feeling was mutual. For her own part, Sookie didn't think Hailey Dean was *all that.*

But she knew how to play the game.

"Oh, yes. She's fantastic." Always better to play along with the suits, tell them what they wanted to hear, and then go do whatever you wanted. "I'll definitely have her back on the show. She's great as a legal panelist." Sookie consciously smoothed back her red hair, glittery with product in the sunlight.

"It's more than that. I've watched when she was on. It was the Prentiss Love show. Hailey Dean practically jumped off the screen. She's got it! She's electric. Then there was the ah . . . what was it . . . the ah . . . the first one, the ice water. And she's been on a few of the days you did follow-up shows. Police aren't saying much, but you've done pretty well with the old boyfriends, neighbors, you know, the usual suspects. But that Dean, she's got *something* . . ."

"Oh, Noel, you're absolutely right. She's lightning in a bottle. You're so right, Noel . . . she's . . . positively electric."

It pained her to agree about Hailey. But the Prentiss Love show was huge. And Hailey did light up the screen. Sookie managed to shift her legs while leaning back against the window, crossing one over the other, trying to re-direct his attention back to her own calves and thighs and off Hailey Dean's *"something."* It didn't seem to be working.

"So, I want you to make her a regular and pay her out of the *Todd Show* budget."

"What?" Sookie was appalled. "We can't afford to take money out of our budget for *Hailey Dean!*"

"You can and you will. You've already got the fattest budget at the network, and up until Dean came along, your numbers simply didn't justify it."

"Well you know, Noel, we did have the very last interview ever done with Leather Stockton, right after that DUI. And Prentiss Love had just been on with Harry about *Celebrity Closets*, and he got in a lot of questions about her personal life. You know, no steady boyfriend, no husband, doesn't cook, lives with her four cockapoos type interview. It was great. We sliced and diced them and turned them to make fantastic shows. I think the numbers had *nothing* to do with Hailey Dean. They had *everything* to do with my producing," she said icily.

She remained perfectly silent, motionless in fact, waiting for Noel to acknowledge her talent. That was what it was all about. No one in their right mind would imagine the success of *The Harry Todd Show* had anything to do with the host.

"Enjoying the GNE jet? It's nice, isn't it?"

She was thrown off. Noel had completely failed to take the cue. He didn't even bother to agree with her.

How rude.

"I wouldn't know . . . You know Todd uses it. He *loves* it!" She strutted back across the carpeted room toward his desk and re-settled herself into her original perch.

"When I was on my way to Arizona for the sales meeting last week, the pilot happened to mention you used it to hop down to St. Martin."

"Oh yes . . . that's right . . . thank you for reminding me, Noel . . . I *did* take a little jaunt." It had actually been a five-hour flight each way. "Harry is just so generous, as are you, Noel." Damn the pilot to hell and back. Big mouth. Wasn't there some sort of pilot-passenger confidentiality? Whatever happened to discretion?

The rest hit Sookie like a ton of bricks. Had the idiot pilot mentioned she'd taken a man along with her to St. Martin? Sookie made absolutely sure his name was never mentioned, not once on the flight, so certainly *that* didn't leak. And she never had to show ID to take a private flight, just get on and take off. So . . . no written record. But there was also the corporate jet log . . . and Noel Fryer kept it. He could easily see how often she mooched the jet.

This was just what she didn't need right now . . . a scandal with a married man at the very minute her divorce settlement was being hammered out.

She was taking Julian to the cleaners, come hell or high water!

And she wouldn't let one long weekend with a married boyfriend ruin it all. Julian would reopen all the depositions and suggest she was having an affair during their marriage. She absolutely did not have an affair, but her behavior wasn't the point. The point was that Julian had flaunted his girlfriends all over town, and that *did* matter very much.

How dare he make her look bad, after all she'd done for him? He had money all right, he was "in yachts" as a business, but she gave him credibility, standing. He didn't know a salad fork from an olive tray before Sookie Downs got ahold of him. She got him into circles he'd never dreamed of before, largely due to her position on *The Harry Todd Show*.

She created Julian. And they were *a couple.* They'd been featured in dozens of magazines and interviews together . . . you know . . . the "*it*" power couple. No way was a single weekend romp going to foul up this divorce settlement.

"Yeah, that plane is fantastic. It's my own personal favorite. Its like you're in your own private den, but you're twenty thousand feet up in the sky."

Noel Fryer's voice jolted her back to the here and now. Sookie stood up and walked alone to the window again, slightly sitting on the sill, her legs angled toward Fryer.

Did he notice the red mock-croc mini? Did he think it clashed with her hair? She thought she caught him looking at her shins, but wasn't sure.

"So, long story short . . . we want to renew both you and Harry. We're so knocked out by the numbers, we want to re-up. What do you think about that, Sookie?"

She was thrilled. Beyond thrilled as a matter of fact. The ratings were published every day. Anybody could look them up, and Harry Todd was barely holding on by the skin of his teeth, resting on his laurels. But the recent numbers changed all that.

"I'll relay the message to Harry. I'm sure he'll be just as excited as I am." She said it with a smile. Still working the mini, Sookie walked to the door.

"Oh . . . and one more thing," Noel said.

"What?"

"Get Dean."

Sookie nodded and closed the door gently as she backed out of the office. She managed to keep the same smile glued to her lips, and it would take a lot more than Hailey Dean or Noel Fryer to knock it off.

In her own mind, the mini had worked. Just an hour before, when Sookie was coming up the elevator, she'd actually been afraid Noel might initiate a conversation about ending Harry's run at GNE, and symbiotically, her own.

She made it down the elevator and walked through the thick glass doors onto the sidewalk, passing Noel Fryer's Vespa. If she hadn't known for a fact that security cameras were trained on every square inch of cement surrounding GNE Headquarters, she would have kicked the damn thing over.

He looked like a damn fool on the little bike, with his butt hanging over either side of the seat cushion when he rode it . . . that damn scarf around his neck, the hand-stitched Italian leather riding gloves . . . *moron.*

"**H**AILEY, I KNOW YOU'RE FIGHTING VIOLENT CRIME. I UNDER-stand, I really do. But the way Harry Todd spoke to you, well it was just rude . . . *rude.*" Her mother was referring to Hailey's appearance a few days before on *The Harry Todd Show* about the murder of Prentiss Love.

"I know, Mother, but I feel it's what I have to do. I've been given this opportunity. You know I've had a lot of angst about leaving the courtroom . . . no longer fighting violent crime. That door was shut, but maybe God opened a window for me through this plat-form. I just couldn't say no. Does that make any sense?"

"I do see it, I do. But it seemed to me that Todd gangs up with that . . . what's his name? That . . . *ambulance chaser?*"

"Derek Jacobs." Hailey answered without much emotion. Derek Jacobs had been arrogant, rude, combative, and, frankly, wrong about the law on several points during the show. She'd taken great delight in correcting him on every turn.

"Yes. That's it. Derek Jacobs. He's awful. Everybody at church just thought he was horrible, and that Harry Todd seemed to *agree* with everything he said. I even caught them shaking hands at the end of the show."

"Yeah . . . I saw that, too, even though I was several floors above them in some little studio. It was really like a dark little closet with a camera in it. But it was better than being on the set with Todd. And that idiot Jacobs."

"Well, if it makes you feel any better, they both looked like jack-asses. And you looked completely prepared and completely poised. I was proud of you. But I just don't see why you would torture yourself and do that show ever again."

"I don't know that they'll invite me back. But if they do, and it's a chance to expose violent crime defendants and their sleazy lawyers, lawyers like Jacobs, for what they are, I don't see how I can say no."

"But *why*? *Why* for Pete's sake? Why does it have to be *you* on the firing line? I had hoped and prayed that when you left the courtroom, your troubles would be over . . . You'd be out of danger . . . but now . . ."

"Because of Will, Mother."

Hailey's mom went silent. After all these years, she knew it was best not to argue about anything even remotely connected to Hailey's fiancé.

"I understand, sweetheart. I just love you so much, I want you to be safe and happy."

"I know. It's just what I have to do."

"Well, it seemed to me that Todd just sat back and let Derek Jacobs grandstand, but every time they came to you, you shot them down."

"It was like shooting two fish in a barrel."

"It showed."

"Mother, I think you're biased!" Hailey started laughing out loud.

At that point, her father picked up the receiver somewhere in the back of their home in Georgia. "I just wanted to punch that Harry Todd in the face! The way he talked to you! And that lawyer . . . What's his name, Hailey?"

"Derek Jacobs," Hailey answered.

"Where did they dig him up? Is he some famous defense attorney? I've never heard of him."

"Well, he represented Hit Man Number One—you know, the rap star that shot his business partner . . ."

"What happened to him?"

"Hit Man got life in prison. Let's see . . . Then he represented that actress, you know the one charged with DUI."

"Oh, *that* was famous . . . I remember that," her mother chimed in from the kitchen phone.

"Well, that was what it was all about, really. I think Jacobs just wanted to get famous and have his face plastered all over TV walking her in and out of the courthouse. I've never seen a lawyer so disappointed as when the trial judge refused to let Court TV cover the trial live."

"Oh yeah, I'm starting to remember him now. Always out in front of courthouses giving press conferences. Right?"

"Right."

"But why'd they put him on? Seems like he loses all his cases." Her dad was pretty observant.

"I know, Daddy. He's some close friend of the executive producer, Sookie Downs, I think. I really don't know why they'd use him. I guess he got famous and the show wanted a celebrity lawyer for the ratings. Makes me wonder why they picked me. I guess either because of Will's murder or because of the press after I killed Leonard."

"No! No, baby! It's because of your perfect record in court!"

"Mother, I wish that were so, but TV's not like that. Anyway, somebody's beeping in and I have a patient in a few minutes."

"Did you put that extra bolt on your office door?"

"I sure did. And I got those thick drapes for the windows like you wanted for when I'm working here alone, Mother."

"I know I don't need to remind you, Clint Burrell Cruise is still out there." Cruise was the serial killer Hailey had prosecuted in her last jury trial. He'd gotten a conviction at trial, but the Georgia Supreme Court had engineered a reversal. Cruise jumped parole and hadn't been seen since Hailey stabbed his lawyer.

"I know, believe me, I want him found and monitored, too. But I can't hide in my apartment under my bed just because Pardons and Paroles can't find Cruise. If he wants to stay out of trouble, he's probably gotten as far away from me as he can!"

Hailey laughed into the receiver, acting for all she was worth as if she wasn't worried at all about the released killer who'd come looking for her.

"Let me see who this call is. I love you!"

"Bye, honey."

"Bye, Mother. Bye-Bye, Daddy. Talk to you later."

"Promise?" her mom asked as if she really wanted an answer.

"Promise."

Hailey clicked off and considered Cruise . . . still on the run.

||||||||||||||||||||||||||||||||||||||||||||||||||||||| **24** |||||||||||||||||||||||||||||

F ALLON MALONE DIDN'T THINK SHE COULD LIFT HER LEG ONE more time. This damn elliptical. She hated it. But what else could she do? She had to feel the burn. Or else.

Or else go down the path of all the other aging stars. Flabby, jowly, and unemployed. They either became bag ladies, accepted scraps in movies for parts as grandmothers, witches, or otherwise . . . crones . . . or they got elected to some position at the Screen Actors Guild.

Not for Fallon Malone. She loved the attention her body got her. She only felt alive when she was admired, loved, desired. Which is exactly why she'd already scheduled her third lesson with the golf pro . . . What was his name?

His name didn't matter. Nor did golf. She just needed a few lessons to convince some eccentric producer she was good for a part in yet another big-screen production centering around the game. The adoration of the golf pro just made it all that much easier.

Fallon understood her assets and what they could do for her. She'd have never gotten her breakthrough role if it weren't for her body. Those who mocked her for it were simply jealous.

But there was so much more to Fallon Malone than her physique. She needed the idiots in Hollywood and the tight little clique that ran Broadway, so damn pleased with themselves and looking down their noses at her, to see that.

But in addition to the compliments and the adoration, Fallon loved the high life. Without a rich husband anymore, she actually had to pay for it herself. She'd downsized as much as was presentable. She got rid of two of her cars and moved from a five- to a three-bedroom apartment here in Manhattan, and to top it all off, leased her penthouse in Beverly Hills.

She even did a commercial. A TV commercial, at that. In Japan. She prayed like hell nobody in the States saw the thing. It would ruin her reputation as a serious screen actress.

What more could she do?

Obviously, her agent wasn't doing her justice. Stu had so many clients in his stable, she should really think of dumping him, but every time she called him, he acted like he was on the verge of securing a part for her.

They just had a way of falling through.

Her legs were feeling the burn, all right. At least having the elliptical here in her apartment, she didn't have to go to some horrible gym where she'd definitely be spotted. And photographed.

Fallon switched channels to QVC. She adored the shopping network and had memorized her American Express card number by heart, expiration date and secret code number included. That way she could order straight from the elliptical, speaking into her Black-Berry, which she of course had on speaker phone setting so as to have her hands free. Her arms must also be in continuous pumping motion along with her legs. It wasn't just butt and legs and boobs anymore.

Triceps mattered. No one wanted to look at flabby arms. And she certainly didn't want to end up in one of those horrible *Snoop* exposés with a shot of her coming out of a plastic surgeon's office following a brachioplasty. She'd never heard that word . . . *brachioplasty* . . . until her plastic surgeon put it in her head. Translation . . . an arm lift.

It was the industry's dirty little secret. Face-lifts, nose-jobs, and of course, boob-jobs, were all givens. But arm lifts were still considered a little taboo.

As if Fallon cared.

If she'd just go ahead, bite the bullet, and get the arm lift, she could drag this damn elliptical onto the elevator and dump it out on the street. In New York City, it would be gone in three minutes. Some Dumpster-diver would take it away and put in his own cramped little apartment. Speaking of New York, Fallon couldn't wait to get back to Beverly Hills, it was so dark and cold here. If it weren't for work, she wouldn't even visit, much less keep this dreary little *downsized* apartment.

But back to the elliptical: If she got the arm lift, the torture of two-hour workouts every other day would be over. But there was always her butt. What about *it*? Wait . . . maybe she could get those butt-enhancement things, like the silicone balloons they insert in your rear end . . .

Fallon heard the maid coming in the side door to the apartment, through the kitchen. She turned her head and yelled out, "Don't forget to clean *between* the tiles in the sauna this time! Use some-thing . . . a toothbrush . . . I don't care what! That's not my job! But

I do not want to sit my bare butt down on mold! That's why I pay *you . . . So I don't have to sit on mold!"*

These people. They come to America. Then they don't clean your sauna. Ridiculous.

Her BlackBerry tinkled. One glance and she exhaled, even more irritated. It was that horrible, horrible high school boy again. Jonathon. Why wouldn't he leave her alone? He'd mentioned he wrote for his school paper and wanted more facts about her for a profile on her he was doing. When would he finish? He'd been writing about her for six months, it seemed. *Ugh!*

The questions never ended with this kid. It wasn't a newspaper profile . . . It was a *book.* What's your favorite color? Do you like animals? What does your bedroom look like? And why did some kid want to know what her bedroom looked like, anyway? Little perv.

Fallon pointed the remote toward one of the two flat-screen TVs positioned on the wall at angles so she could watch both at the same time without turning her head. She hated it though, because by flicking one remote, more often than not she'd change channels on both screens.

So irritating.

Juggling one remote in the left hand, another in the right, and both feet pumping up and down on the machine, she was trying to get Lifetime on one screen and QVC on the other. If she was correct, it was Beauty and Age Prevention hour. Not that she needed any more such lotions and potions; her bathroom shelves, counters, and drawers were packed full of them, as were her bedside tables, but you never knew what you might need until you saw it on QVC or the Home Shopping Network.

Ah, she finally got both screens to her two choice channels. First, she focused on QVC. She'd been right. It *was* beauty treatment hour. She'd apparently just missed two hours of linens. The screen flashed up a grouping of facial creams, all different sizes and shapes, but all the slender bottles and tiny round pots were in the same pastel pink. A gorgeous set of hands, beautifully manicured with mother-of-pearl-tinted fake nails.

Hmm. Age-defying lotions. She already had plenty of those. Wonder if there was anything to that pure oxygen treatment to the face? Fallon had heard about it recently; it was the next, new thing.

Of course she'd done time in one of those hyperbaric oxygen chambers, just like everybody else. Hers was at a spa in Arizona. It worked wonders. She woke up feeling years younger.

It was a simple concept, really. A Hyperbaric Oxygen Therapy Chamber, a cylindrical tube in which the patient sleeps, delivers 100 percent oxygen at a pressure greater than that at sea-level atmospheric pressure. In essence, the patient breathes 100 percent oxygen while covered under a hood, or wearing a mask. Athletes used them all the time; then the skin industry got wind of them and now they were the rage.

But other than going to a spa and being caught on camera doing it, her only other choice was to buy one of the huge, coffinlike things to sleep in at night. Now if that didn't hit the gossip pages, nothing would.

She could see the headline now . . . Fallon Malone's Desperate Bid to Stay Young. Or worse yet, she could be associated with some type of illness, which was generally the kiss of death in the business.

There were now allegedly oxygen treatments applied directly to the skin at a doctor's office. And she certainly wouldn't be driving to the doctor's office and traipsing through a parking lot. He'd come to her.

With both hands free again, Fallon scrolled to the voice note recorder feature on her BlackBerry and spoke into it. "Note to self. Home oxygenation treatments. What are they? Do they work? Where can I get them? And how much do they cost?"

The bullet tore from its chamber a few feet behind Fallon just as she was about to lower the BlackBerry from grazing her lips.

The device ricocheted out of her right hand upon bullet impact, and the bullet, taking two of her long, fake nails with it, burst the PDA into a hundred shards of black plastic and bits of metal, some slicing the delicate skin of her face, tiny bits of it lodging around her mouth and nose.

The bullet tore through the skull, upward through the mouth cavity and out the front of her face, just below the bridge of her nose, glancing off the BlackBerry, and finally slamming into the wall a few feet in front of the elliptical.

The bullet took several of her teeth with it, three of them hurtling out of her mouth to the floor, landing underneath the TV screen. The hostess on the screen smiled lovingly out at all the millions of purchasers of age-defying moisturizers at that precise moment, and then moved on to exfoliators.

|||||||||||||||||||||||||||||||||||||||||||||||||||||||| **25** ||||||||||||||||||||||||

"THERE'S A MATCH? OH, MAN . . . *ARE YOU SURE?*" BEFORE Kolker could answer, his partner, O'Brien, went on . . . "Does the press know? Now what do we do?"

"I know one thing: Before this gets out, I want to nail down every single detail, you know, dot the i's and cross the t's. I need to get it all figured out before we take it to the District Attorney's Office. They leak like a sieve. It'll go straight to the *Post*. Just like the Prentiss Love crime scene photos. Just like *Snoop* got the Leather Stockton shots of the body being wheeled out of the pool house. Somebody's tipping them off."

They didn't want to talk about it at the office and had ended up back at the diner in their usual booth.

"Coffee, black?" Behind the counter and looking over a display of pies on a three-tiered plate underneath a glass cake cover, Shirley aimed the question in the general direction of Kolker's booth.

"Make it two. Thanks." Turning away from Shirley, he looked back at O'Brien.

"There's no doubt about it. The medical examiner managed to fish one sliver of fragment out of Prentiss Love's head, and bingo . . . it's a match. He did a consult on Stockton. I've never seen anybody so fascinated with dead celebrities as that ME."

"Same shooter?"

"Same shooter. No doubt about it. Kelley Trent over at Ballistics had it under the microscope for hours. He's the best. I went over and watched him do it. Saw the markings myself. They definitely came from the same weapon. And whoever it is, he's a decent shot. You know, even at close range, amateurs screw up." Kolker kept his voice low even though no one was in the booth behind them.

"You know Trent's thorough. Even tried to get prints off the one bullet from out in the Hamptons. No good. It was a long shot, but Trent tried. And the sliver from Love's skull was barely big enough to analyze, much less get a print."

"IBIS match?"

"Nope. Already sent it. Trent knows somebody. Got a rush. No match."

"Well, did Trent keep it quiet?"

"Did he keep what quiet? We don't have the murder weapon, so we didn't have to do any shooting. Just looking under the microscope."

To make a positive ballistics match to a specific gun, the tester takes the weapon in question, uses the same caliber as that in the murder, and fires the gun, usually into a tub of water with padding at the bottom. The high velocity of the bullet, hurtling down the gun chamber, causes distinct, identifiable tool markings on the bullet itself. Like a fingerprint, each gun leaves its own unique markings on the bullet. The inside of the barrel is made of metal, metal that cools after being heated in a molten state. Each gun has one-of-a-kind markings on the inner barrel left during the cooling process; hence, those unique markings appear on the bullet.

"I don't mean the testing, and I know we don't have the murder weapon . . . yet, that is. I mean, did Trent keep it on the QT that we think there's one shooter? And who'd want to shoot these two, anyway? I mean, they're D-Listers at best . . . What's the draw?"

"Don't know. I need to run it by some sort of strategist, maybe one of the profilers, somebody that knows what they're doing. Somebody that can keep their mouth shut and has nothing to do with NYPD." Instinctively, Kolker looked around to confirm no eavesdroppers.

"Good luck with that one." The coffee came. "Motive?"

"I'm not even close. I haven't even started with that one. I just found out it was from the same gun a little under an hour ago." Kolker stared down into his coffee, at the little tendrils of steam floating up.

He'd turned into somewhat of an overnight local hero after the Hailey Dean case, despite the fact he arrested the wrong person for double murder. Hailey had always been tight-lipped about what happened and actually praised him and the Force in the press. So, while the public at large liked him, he couldn't afford another screw-up. Kolker had to nail this one or he'd be looking at a desk job till he left the NYPD, which would probably be forced on him earlier rather than later.

They weren't subtle about these things at the NYPD. He'd be directing traffic in the middle of First Avenue and Fifty-ninth, if he didn't solve the case *before* he handed it over to the DA.

Kolker had a fleeting, horrible vision of the traffic piled up, snarled bumper to bumper, horns honking, exhaust spewing, radios blaring . . . Everybody trying to get on or off the Fifty-ninth Street Bridge. His insides turned hot and it wasn't the coffee.

Then, it came in a flash. *Hailey Dean . . . Would she help him?*

Was there any way? Probably not . . . but he could try. He could at least try.

She could have blasted him to hell and back over what happened . . . the way he'd treated her. She was in the hospital the first time he questioned her. He'd been so sure she was the killer. And he needed the collar so badly.

But what was he thinking? Knowing Dean, she'd probably punch him right there at the front door of her apartment when, and if, she opened the door. Or worse. He'd heard she was a pretty good shot. She could take aim at him and claim she thought he was an intruder . . .

He tried to make reparations. Bombarding her with flowers. That was pretty good for a cop, wasn't it? But never any response. Now that she was back in the city, he'd tried again. But, after seeing her drench Todd, he definitely remembered her temper.

Kolker rubbed the side of his face, reliving the moment Hailey Dean had punched him right in the nose. It wasn't the first time he'd gotten a snoot full of knuckle, but it had been, by far, the most memorable. And the only time a woman had ever decked him. Dean packed a pretty good punch.

And it had to hurt her hand, but he never even saw her rub her knuckles. Later, when he was questioning her at the station, he saw they had bled.

And you know what? He deserved the punch.

Maybe that's the first thing he'd say, if he actually went to see her in person.

"Hey! Kolker! Where you going?" Kolker had gotten up from the booth, taken his jacket off the coat stand, and was heading toward the diner door.

"Is it something I said?" O'Brien was smiling, but he was confused. They had just been brainstorming . . .

"Hey, pay for the coffee this time. We'll start getting a bad reputation as freeloaders! Tell Shirley I'll see her tomorrow."

"But what about breakfast? Aren't you going to wait?"

"You can have mine. You always try to get it anyway."

"You can't wait five minutes?"

"Nah . . . I think I'm on to something."

Let's see . . . It was only 8 a.m. Bet she'd still be home. Kolker walked across the sidewalk dodging the New Yorkers who *never* look up when they walk along with the tourists who are *always* looking up.

He unlocked his unmarked squad car and got in. No reason to radio back to headquarters where he was headed. They didn't need to know.

The less said . . . the better.

D AMN THE GROUNDSKEEPER TO HELL AND BACK. WHY WOULDN'T he go away? Why wouldn't he *leave*?

How long had he been here, anyway? Sitting crouched down in a cold, moldy-smelling mausoleum, Francis had a bird's-eye view of the Crestlawn Sacred Grounds groundskeeper. He'd had the guy in his crosshairs for nearly an hour now, and Francis's knees were all the worse for it. He was squatted down behind one of the crypt's ornamental windows, windows which were really nothing more than tiny slivers cut in the mausoleum's marble walls.

Why have windows at all? Like the dead want to enjoy the view? Absolutely no need for the dead to see out. Hunkered down on the cold stone floor, keeping his eye trained on the grounds-keeper, Francis contemplated the need for windows in a crypt.

Was that a big, fat doobie the guy was smoking? Oh, hell! If it was, Francis might as well dig in for the duration.

Francis had tried his best to get rid of the arsenal he'd been amassing under his mother's kitchen floor. He really had. But he couldn't. The guns were his friends. They were even indexed in long, elaborate journal entries.

And his collection of HCBs, Homemade Chemical Bombs as the Feds insisted on calling them, were almost like his children. He'd spent hours upon hours researching them on the Internet, watching online videos about how to create them, days collecting just the right ingredients, and weeks finally putting them together. They were dangerous and beautiful. He adored them.

But now, knowing the Feds were coming down on him at any moment for what had happened to Leather Stockton and Prentiss Love, he had to do *something*. But what?

He wasn't about to destroy them. A storage facility was out . . . that's the first place the Feds would look. Attic? No. Basement? No. Hole in the backyard? No. Friend's place? No. Other than his girlfriends, he didn't have any friends anyway. And he didn't want to jeopardize them. He *loved* them.

Crestlawn Sacred Grounds was his only alternative.

The few times he'd been here, mostly to visit his mother's headstone and rub it in to her how great he was doing without her, he noticed the door hanging wide open at one of the mausoleums down the row. He'd never seen a single soul visit whoever was interred there, so the intermittently open door creeped him out all the more.

Was the dead person opening and shutting the door to his own mausoleum? It could happen. Francis believed firmly in the spirit world. So finally, he mentioned it to Danny, the groundskeeper.

He and Danny were somewhat kindred spirits, although Francis knew immediately that Danny was by no means his intellectual equal. They first met when Francis's mother was buried. Danny caught him spitting a big glob down on the fresh dirt just raked over his mother's casket. Instead of judging him as so many others would have, Danny started laughing.

They bonded instantly.

For one thing, they both hated the government. They both hated their mothers and they both had a thing for Prentiss Love. But Francis wasn't jealous of Danny; he obviously didn't have a relationship with Prentiss like Francis did.

Francis wasn't one to kiss and tell, so he didn't brag about himself and Prentiss.

During their long discussions about their mothers, Francis learned from Danny that the particularly creepy mausoleum was not only empty, but also a point of legal contention within the deceased's family. Hours of conversation over the pint of gin Danny snuck into work every day yielded a lot of information about burials, cremations, grave diggers, dead bodies, and the like. Swapping off the bottle swig for swig, Francis learned all about the intended resident of the ornate crypt.

Specifically, she was ninety-six years old, Aunt Matilde Coco from Bayou Blanche, Louisiana. Aunt Matilde had a knack for plucking up the wealthiest men around and had been through quite a few husbands, each one richer than the last. Neighbors swore she put a love hank on them to make her irresistible in their eyes, because by all accounts, Aunt Matilde was not much too look at.

Maybe it was true. Plain and simple, Matilde, as Danny told it, practiced the ancient art of Santeria, or voodoo for short. Even though traditional Catholics frowned on sorcery, and the Vatican was firmly against it, Aunt Matilde was forever cooking up some foul stench on the stove in order to heal the sick, bring home a loved one, or seek Christian vengeance on an enemy. "Enemies" were normally gossips, cheats, liars, ne'er-do-wells, other members at St. Joseph's Catholic Church, evil neighbors, or anyone and everyone she believed had mistreated her beloved nieces and nephews.

On good days, her huge home smelled heavily of flower-scented potpourri, Glade PlugIns, and Creole cooking. On others, it reeked of boiling chicken entrails stirred up with God knows what. Aunt Matilde was notorious for smearing the gooey stuff near the target's front door at an opportune moment, or in special cases, actually feeding a tiny voodoo replica of the enemy to the stank as it boiled on the kitchen stove in the apartment. They all knew better than to ask Aunt Matilde what exactly stank, but for safety's sake, never, ever, casually grabbed a bite from the fridge.

Matilde never bore her own children, although she wanted them desperately. Outliving all five of her wealthy husbands, Aunt Matilde ended up with a fortune, which she left to her nieces and nephews and the rest to St. Joseph's Catholic Church, Bayou Blanche Parish.

Half the family swore the old lady wanted to be buried aboveground in case of flooding. They were all from Cajun country down in New Orleans, where apparently, the dead face a distinct possibility of their own human remains floating away if buried six feet under.

The other half of the family insisted departure by water was not a possibility for Auntie in the casket. They insisted she keep pushing up the daisies. They were all a little afraid Aunt Matilde might have the power to visit them from the Great Beyond, and nobody wanted that.

With all of them steeped in Cajun tradition and brainwashed in voodoo superstitions, they'd nearly come to blows at Auntie's funeral over the whole thing. The family finally had some money thanks to Aunt Matilde, so of course, a lawsuit ensued. With a pack of lawyers involved, it'd be years before Auntie was dug up and hence, the mausoleum inhabited, if ever.

Just think of all those billable hours.

Another thing for Francis to contemplate here on the floor of an empty crypt. Lawyers. Oh, how he hated them.

The court-appointed one he'd had for his last court case made him sick. He wanted to punch her out the moment she started talking to him. She looked at him as if he were crazy. She was the crazy one, not him.

The crypt was the perfect place to stash his guns and HCBs. Temporarily of course. He'd bring them home and stow them back under the kitchen table as soon as things cooled off. Plus, he had no idea which one was the murder weapon. It had all happened during one of his "episodes," as his mother used to call them.

But it was true, he'd had plenty of blackouts. Hours, sometimes days where he couldn't remember exactly where he'd been or what he'd done. He was known to drive around, sometimes great distances, make purchases, hold long conversations, and even check in and out of motel rooms during these periods. He'd checked the odometer on the car afterwards, when he'd come out of it, and sometimes there would be over a thousand miles registered.

Francis naturally kept a log of daily mileage on the old sedan, as well as every time he got gas, tune-ups, oil changes, even car washes.

You could never really be too careful.

All the shrinks called his episodes "psychotic breaks," but they were all asses anyway. They just made their two hundred bucks an hour when they saw him, paid for by the government of course, after his court-ordered mental treatment. The judge was also an ass. A woman judge of course. That explained a lot.

Francis knew he didn't have any such thing as psychotic breaks. He himself blamed it on the lithium. He'd taken it for years before he realized he could refuse to swallow the stuff. It was only after the old bag (his mother) died that he'd learned how she'd sneak it into his food when he chose to go off his meds.

But now, she was gone and he was off it for good. Things were so much clearer now.

Auntie Matilde's vault was perfect. The Feds would never think to look here. Now, if he could only get out of here without Danny seeing him and becoming suspicious. He liked Danny well enough, that was true. But if it got out he'd hidden the murder weapon, if Danny found out somehow and got a subpoena to testify in court, their friendship would likely go straight down the crapper. Danny would sing like a bird if he had to.

Francis's neck was cramping, and so was his left leg. He finally unfolded himself from his squatting position there at the slit of a window and sat down, stretching his legs out on the cold stone floor of the crypt. Leaning back against the wall, he forced himself to relax. No need to be anxious. He just had to wait.

Sitting there, he finally had a chance to admire his handiwork. It had taken days (and nights) to hollow out enough storage space to stash all the guns. But he did it, all right. After being kicked out of regular classes in high school, he'd been forced to go to shop classes to learn a trade. Well, guess what, Mother? They paid off. No one would notice the drill marks in Aunt Matilde's vault.

To start with, the mausoleum was large and, of course, way over the top in predictable Cajun Catholic style. The Holy Mother Mary took center stage in the crypt; a large ivory-colored statue of her stood in the middle of the room, hoisted up on top of a large, square base. Around it were three separate benches, solid, oblong, rectangular seats. The benches, the statue's base, even part of Mother Mary herself were now hollowed out and chock-full of guns wrapped in thick burlap sacks.

Perfect.

True, it had been hell lugging all these guns into the mausoleum. And especially his little babies, the liquid bombs in plastic Coke bottles. They had to be carried in just two at a time, each wrapped in layers of towels and stuffed down the front of his jacket.

They could all rest easy here, because with lawyers involved, it'd be years before they got the family lawsuit settled. Anyway, Francis had no reason to doubt Danny, and even though he'd witnessed the door left open on several occasions, he'd never actually seen anyone visiting. Plus, as far as he could tell, he was all alone in the crypt . . . No indication it was inhabited by a dead body. Just Francis and 253 guns, to be exact.

He had to be more careful. Just last week, with one of his last loads of guns stashed in his mother's car trunk, Danny had noticed Francis lingering there. Danny had actually made a crack about how Francis was spending a lot more time lately at his mother's grave.

It was totally out of character, since Francis, on many occasions, complained bitterly to Danny about how his mother had ruined his life. He better come up with a damn good explanation as to why he had a change of heart and was suddenly visiting now.

Details, details, details. The devil truly was in the details.

Francis peeked through the slot just in time to see Danny's back disappear around a corner of tall hedges. He knew for a fact it was the spot where Danny hid when he wanted to take a nap.

Must have been a doobie he was smoking after all. Francis waited and watched for just a few more moments to make sure the coast was clear. With one last, quick glance around the vault, he headed for the door.

Just as he was stepping out, Francis stopped. Turning, he quickly stepped back into the vault just a few steps . . . just far enough to kneel down on his knees in front of the Mother Mary. She looked down at him mournfully. She looked sad, disappointed, as if she knew exactly what Francis had been up to. She looked like she knew about the red panties he'd stolen out of Leather Stockton's bungalow at Shutters *and* what Francis did with them on a weekly basis.

He crossed himself three times because, you know, you just can never be *too* safe.

K OLKER PAUSED, THEN GRITTED HIS TEETH AND BUZZED THE doorbell.

Standing at the threshold of Hailey's apartment was like déjà vu. Kolker had come here immediately after following her ambulance to the hospital that horrible morning. He'd found her lying on a dentist's floor unconscious, the dead body of defense attorney Matt Leonard sprawled beside her.

As soon as he'd learned she was safe, he'd come straight to her apartment, used the spare key from the lobby after badgering Ricky, the doorman. Ricky had taken quite a bit of persuading in order to get him to give up the key without Haliey's permission. But after Kolker told him what had happened and how he feared Clint Burrell Cruise could still be lingering around, Ricky relented.

The truth was, Kolker still felt the whole thing was his fault. If Kolker hadn't fallen for the obvious clues Leonard planted for him to find, and had listened to Hailey, none of it would have happened. Maybe, just maybe, one of Hailey's patients would have been saved.

He heard a chain being slid across its lock and two separate deadbolts clicking open. The door opened and there she was.

Hailey Dean.

Half of her anyway; her right arm, shoulder, and leg were still behind the heavy door. She said nothing, but didn't look the least surprised that he was there.

Neither spoke, but neither averted their gaze from the other. After a few moments of silence, Kolker reached into his coat pocket. He took out his wallet. Unfolding it, he pulled a newspaper clipping from behind a layer of cash. Still gazing directly into her eyes, he handed her the yellowed slip of paper.

The article was about the kidnapping of a young girl, twelve at the time. In what appeared to be a school photo, her delicate face shined out, smiling. Hailey looked at the date of the article . . . it was over twenty years old. The girl's skeletonized remains had been found that summer so many years ago. The little girl would be middle-aged by now.

The article went on to say the girl had three survivors—parents and one sibling, a younger brother who went unnamed. Hailey assumed the parents hadn't wanted the boy's name out there for safety reasons, but the girl . . . the girl's name was Susannah Kolker. Kolker's sister was kidnapped and murdered.

Kolker was looking down at the floor. He couldn't seen to meet Hailey's gaze. "I loved her so much. I guess I never got past losing her. That's why I became a cop. My family hated it, they didn't want to lose the only child they had left . . . but I had to. When I arrested you . . . I thought I was doing the right thing. I was trying so hard . . . I was blinded by what happened to Susannah. I just didn't . . ."

He didn't seem to know how to finish the sentence.

Hailey still said nothing and now that he'd looked up, she looked him straight in the eyes. How the hell could she look at someone for so long without blinking? It was just plain weird. He'd forgotten that little detail about Hailey Dean, but now that, and so much more, came rushing back.

He knew what he had to do to get in the apartment.

"Hailey. I don't know what to say . . ."

She wouldn't help him at all. He knew she wouldn't, though. There was no other way. He just had to say it.

"I'm sorry."

Much to his humiliation, Kolker's voice cracked when he said it. Damn. He had to say it again.

"Hailey, I'm so sorry."

He thought it would taste like a dirt sandwich, but when he finally did it, it felt right.

"Come in." Hailey didn't need him to say anything more. The article about Susannah Kolker said it all.

She turned her back to him and started walking across the slate-floored entrance hall. Now he knew why she hung back at the door. In her right hand, pointed casually down as she walked, was a shiny, black, snub-nosed .38. She had a black Velcro shoulder holster on her right shoulder. He'd never seen one exactly like it. She must have had it specially made.

She sat down in a big, caramel leather chair slanted to face both the door and one of the windows looking down over Manhattan. She put her bare feet up on a matching ottoman. Setting the gun beside her on a side table to her right, its barrel facing away from them both and back behind her toward an old, upright piano, she looked at him calmly. Now she understood the connection between them, the bond that for so long she couldn't identify. They had both loved and lost. They were both survivors of brutal crimes and living with the pain, the memories, and, sometimes, the survivor's guilt at simply being alive. Neither verbalized what they were both thinking; a re-hash would be too painful.

"Please. Sit down. I've got some tea brewing. What would you like?"

He still stood.

"Why the gun? Leonard's dead."

"Clint Burrell Cruise. He's still on the run. Parole can't find him, neither can the best bounty hunters I could dig up. Nobody buzzed you up and I wasn't expecting anybody this early . . . I didn't know it was you."

"I understand." Kolker came around the corner of a love seat and sat down in front of her.

"I wanted to come before, but I really didn't know what to say. But there is nothing else to say other than that. I'm sorry. I was so wrong. I put you through hell. You tried to reason with me, but I was so bull-headed."

"You were actually worse than bull-headed, but since you *did* apologize, I won't bother to go into all the details about what *exactly* you did wrong."

"And, you covered for me in the press. They wanted me crucified, strung up in Times Square for what I did . . . but you never took the bait. You stuck by me and didn't feed me to the sharks. Why?"

"I'll keep that to myself for now. But you can also thank me for not filing a wrongful arrest suit. That may have won me a little money and I wouldn't have to work anymore."

"I know . . . I know."

Kolker was looking down at the hardwood floor of Hailey's apartment. The anger had melted away. Now she saw things differently.

"And Kolker, I appreciate the flowers and the music. But most of all, thanks for getting my pen back. I know you broke the rules to get it for me. And oh yeah . . . How's your nose?"

Kolker let out a short laugh. "It's fine. That was a pretty good clip. I'm glad you kept the CDs. I got all the other gifts back in the mail. I wondered why, but I think I know."

Hailey didn't want to delve into it all. It was just too much for this morning. She shifted gears. "I saw you in the *Post* a while back. Still on the Prentiss Love case? Any leads?"

"Well, actually, I'm now on Prentiss Love *and* Leather Stockton."

"But I thought Stockton was murdered in some mansion out in the Hamptons . . . Oh, no . . . you're on both. That means it's the same killer?"

Man, she was sharp.

"Let me guess . . . ballistics match?"

He didn't have to tell *her* anything. "Yep. Same killer."

Hailey stood up, leaving the .38 where it was beside the chair, and heading over to a kitchen island. Her den sort of melted into the kitchen, like one big room, kind of like an artist's loft, no walls between rooms. She leaned upward into a cabinet to pull out coffee cups.

"So, what do you think about the cases, Hailey?"

"You mean Love and Stockton?"

"Yes, the two dead D-Listers."

"Hey, they were stars in my book. Wait a minute . . . Is that why you came here? To get a download on how to proceed on the two murders?"

"No. It's not. I've wanted to come to your doorstep for a long time to apologize, but you stayed in Georgia for so long . . . Then when I heard you were back . . . I lost my nerve."

Hailey smiled and poured the hot water.

He went on. "But the truth is . . . you're right. I'm not really sure how to proceed. I haven't even told headquarters about the ballistics match. I just found out. I don't want it to leak, and once the press gets ahold of it . . . God help me."

"So you want help? Is that it?"

"Hailey . . . I do. I need help. I can't afford to bungle this one. Of all people, I can't believe I'm asking you." There was a long, quiet pause.

Sensing her silence as a "no," he stood up, literally holding his hat in his hand. "Hailey, I'm afraid this was too much of an imposition. I realize that now. I'm sorry again. Just accept my apology and I'll be on my way." Kolker started edging toward the door.

Hailey didn't stop him.

Turning the doorknob, he headed out toward the elevator halfway down the hallway. He didn't hear her behind him, but a firm hand grabbed his shoulder and turned him back.

He looked down. Her eyes were so green.

"I accept the apology. And, Kolker, of course I'll help you. Come on back in. Okay?"

They stood there for a moment, silent. So much had passed between them. The murders, Hailey's arrest, him finding her there on the floor, bloody, beside Matt Leonard's body. He had thought for a moment she was dead and he'd never forgotten the sick feeling he'd had in his chest . . . until she'd opened her eyes.

"Thanks, Hailey."

She turned toward her front door and tossed back over her shoulder, "Plus, I hate to waste a tea bag . . ."

Unlike before, when he refused to hear Hailey out, this time Kolker had a new strategy. He was actually going to listen.

They sat down and Kolker began outlining what he knew so far. He had his investigative file with him, the only copy. In just a few moments, the two moved to Hailey's dining room table in order to spread out crime scene photos, charts, measurements, ballistics reports, and autopsy data.

Two hours and two cups of tea later, after going through everything he had, Hailey started rattling a "To Do" list off the top of her head for Kolker.

"Look, I know you've probably thought of all this before . . . but have you pulled all the recent video, appearances, cell phone records, home phone records, credit card receipts, and checks for the past twelve months; travel information; where they've been lately, what they have been doing? You know . . . their full itineraries for the past six, seven months. Have they been to memorabilia signings? Celebrity autograph events? You know a lot of spooks hang out at those things . . ."

Hailey was talking so fast, in a kind of stream-of-consciousness train of thought, that Kolker didn't dare interrupt. He was writing down what she said as fast as he could. A lot of it he'd already thought of . . . but not all of it.

"Any similarities at all about the crime scenes themselves?"

"Well, Stockton was killed in the pool house of an out-of-town movie star and Love was shot in her SUV behind a yoga studio down in Hell's Kitchen."

"I mean the forensic findings."

"Other than the caliber, single shot to the head, close range. Both are contact wounds; we found some tiny particles, maroon tinted, apparently part of the gunshot residue, in both of them."

"Hmm. Wonder what that is. And of course, there's the obvious question . . . other than both being on TV, what do they have in common? Same grocery store? Same gym? Same doctor? Same plastic surgeon? Boyfriends, exes, grocery store delivery boys, florist deliveries, mailmen, carpet cleaners, maintenance, air and heating workers . . . You know . . . anybody and everybody that may have been in and out of their apartments."

Hailey was looking out the window, thinking as she spun it all off. "Also . . . any wacky New Age religion or meetings the two had been to? It's probably going to be more basic than that, but you never know." Turning her head back, she watched Kolker scribbling into his notebook.

Just as she was about to broach the likely murder weapon, Kolker's police band radio interrupted the two of them with static.

"Kolker, Kolker, please respond. What's your 54?" The question was followed by another blast of static.

Instinctively, Kolker stood up to speak into the handheld police radio.

"Kolker here. Location, Midtown Manhattan. Repeat, Midtown."

"Lieutenant Kolker, proceed to West Side. Proceed to West Side. Columbus and Sixty-seventh Street. Repeat, Columbus Avenue and Sixty-seventh Street."

"Copy that. What's up, Dispatch?"

"You got another one, Kolker, pretty sure. Fallon Malone. Shot dead, single bullet to the head, in her apartment. Crime Scene Investigators there already. Won't touch a thing, waiting on you to get there."

"En route."

Kolker looked down at Hailey. "Want to do a ride-along?"

"Sure. I haven't been in a cop car since you arrested me."

He knew she said it jokingly, but he couldn't muster a comeback. The guilt over Hailey's arrest was still raw.

Hailey picked up her jacket and hat, both hanging just inside the entrance hall closet. Walking out the door, Kolker said, "I know that name . . . Fallon Malone . . . Fallon Malone . . ."

"Kolker . . . are you kidding me? From the Vette scene?" She spoke over her shoulder toward his general vicinity as she turned toward the door to lock the two deadbolts with keys.

They stepped onto the elevator and headed down, and the name Susannah Kolker was not mentioned again . . . nor was Hailey's arrest. Both would hurt too much.

||||||||||||||||||||||||||||||||||||||||||||||||||||||||| 28 |||||||||||||||||||||||||||

AFTER BADGING THEIR WAY THROUGH A FLEET OF DOORMEN AND walking through a rarified lobby complete with colossal floral arrangements on inlaid wood tables and huge black-and-white marble-squared floors, Hailey and Kolker made their way up the elevators to the penthouse where Fallon Malone kept her New York apartment.

Winding through the maze of crime-scene techs reminded Hailey of the hundreds of similar scenes she'd visited as a felony prosecutor. It all seemed so familiar . . . second nature to her.

The front door to Fallon Malone's apartment was wide open, but flanked by burly uniformed officers. Kolker didn't need to badge them by flashing his gold detective's shield; they recognized him.

"Lieutenant." One of them spoke a greeting, somber under the circumstances.

"Morning, Rourke. All the crime lab staff here?"

"Yep. Got here about twenty minutes ago. We held them off for you to take a look first. They're in there, though."

Stepping over the threshold, Kolker called over his shoulder, "She's with me, Rourke."

"Roger that, Lieutenant."

The first thing that struck Hailey was the sheer size of Fallon Malone's apartment. It looked as if two full floors had been gutted to make a spectacular front entrance, vaulted clear up to at least forty feet, painted stark white. A huge open doorway straight ahead was at least twelve feet high, easily fifteen feet wide, and opened into a den. To the right of the entrance was another open doorway leading to the dining room. Inside was an over-the-top white marble sculptured table, ten white upholstered chairs situated around it, and a fantastic abstract art sculpture, pure white, as its centerpiece. Hailey couldn't make out a specific form, but it looked expensive.

Up the entrance hall's winding spiral staircase, the harsh white walls bore only one embellishment, a canvas bearing the likeness of Fallon Malone, but painted in bright neon colors. Looked like a Steve Penley. Must have cost thousands to have that commissioned.

The Penley was the only injection of color in the entire apartment, so far as Hailey could see from the entrance. Like the walls, the floors were matching white marble. A faux (Hailey hoped) white bearskin rug covered the living-room floor and was topped by a clear glass table sitting on thick gold legs. A black-and-white book of art deco photographs was the only thing on it, aside from a white ceramic ashtray.

Taking it one room at a time, they made their way through the living room, then to an adjoining room where a group of uniformed and plainclothes officers were waiting. A tech handed both Hailey and Kolker scrub gowns and footies to put over their shoes before they went in.

"She was always claiming she had stalkers, but no one took it seriously. There was never a note, a threat, anything. I think she just wanted to look as if her fans were mad about her, and when she heard other stars had stalkers, she just had to have one of her very own. Like a pet." The tech kept talking.

Hailey stopped in her tracks. "Fallon Malone had a stalker?"

"Probably not. But I read about it a few months ago in *Snoop*."

"Good to know." Kolker scribbled a note in his notebook and reached for the footies. "Where's the coroner's people?"

"On their way. Don't want us to touch anything."

"Good."

Both Hailey and Kolker put on the blue paper gowns and footwear over their street clothes and carefully entered. Also painted stark white; the den, however, featured a deep red sofa with a matching furry red rug and red accent pieces.

The walls were covered in framed magazine covers from all over the world. Fallon graced each one. On one she was in full riding gear, standing beside a chestnut-brown stallion; another showed her lounging on a beige satin sofa, and many of the others were head-and-shoulder shots. There were dozens of them, the shots taken over the years. And she was absolutely gorgeous and provocatively posed in all of them.

Hailey suddenly noticed that all the conversation among the cops who had gathered at the entryway to her gym just beyond the den had ceased. No one said a word. It was the same atmosphere as at a funeral home viewing, hushed silence. When Hailey entered the exercise room, she understood why.

The gym was state-of-the-art, featuring an advanced set of cardio machines you'd only see at the country's best spas and exercise clubs. Custom-built cabinets, all white of course, housed a series of weights and barbells, exercise balls, and yoga equipment. The walls, like those in the den, were covered with framed magazine covers, each one with Malone on the front, but in this room, all the covers were from women's health and fitness magazines.

The room also featured two large flat-screen plasma TVs. Both were still on. One had a Lifetime movie playing, and the other was running QVC home shopping. Lifetime was on mute. The QVC model was showing her hands, one of which bore a sparkling fake diamond cluster and matching bracelet.

There was an exercise bike, a treadmill, and in the center of the row, a behemoth of an elliptical. And there was the cause of the hushed silence, even among hardened veteran cops and detectives.

There she was. In stark contrast to the stunning photos of her lining the walls, so beautiful, so perfect looking, was Fallon Malone, lying skewed across the machine, clearly in the middle of a workout at the time of her murder. She was wearing metallic-silver lycra tights with a T-shirt covered by a baggy navy sweatshirt. She wore white socks and seemingly brand-new white Nike Airs.

Her body was prone, but twisted across the machine. Her feet were still in the vicinity of the machine's foot pedals, but her body had fallen over, apparently slamming into the machine's front piece before falling to the right side. She actually appeared to be staring with the one eye still left intact, unblinking, up toward the QVC hand model.

Her mouth was completely gone, now only a gaping hole. Hailey could see her entire mouth cavity, all the way back to her wisdom teeth. A blood-spatter pattern began there on the elliptical, spraying across the machine's front digital display of time, speed, and heart rate, and further. Hailey walked toward the wall bearing the TV screens.

"Kolker, here's some pinpoint spatter." She pointed to it with her right hand, fingers spread out like a fan.

Kolker walked over to see. Hailey continued, "You'll get the angle and trajectory from this, given her height when on top of the elliptical, and the machine's distance from the wall. Better bring in the blood expert, too, in addition to CSI. So he or she won't be testifying only from pictures at trial. They'll have actually been here. The defense won't be able to say that."

"Good idea. I'd have just used CSI."

"They know their stuff, but just to impress the jury. The spatter expert needs to string it. You know, secure a string wherever we believe the shot was fired and pull it taut along the trajectory path, ending where the bullet would have landed." Kolker made notes.

Kolker turned back toward Fallon. It was a gruesome sight. Hailey went with him and came to his side just in time to see his jaw clench. For a moment, she thought he might tear up. The room went quiet.

"Let's keep the techs out." Hailey said it quietly, breaking the silence in the room. "And look around on the floor before anybody else steps in here."

"Okay. Guys, hold up just a moment. We'll check the floor first."

The CSI crew hung back in the den. Hailey and Kolker got down on their hands and knees, each at an opposite corner, and started examining the floor. The room was silent once again, except for the soothing tones of the QVC anchors interacting with callers and each other. A good fifteen minutes passed as Hailey, touching nothing, searched around and under the gym equipment as best she could.

"Tooth." She called it out, squatted in front of the elliptical, only a foot or so away from where Fallon lay.

"By the way, you're an official police consultant now," Kolker said as he continued to inch across the floor. "Okay? Otherwise, I couldn't have a civilian here on the scene."

Hailey was busy scouring the floor.

Kolker was on his knees, making notes about the tooth Hailey spotted. Photos would be taken of the entire room in the state in which it was found, and then photos made with numbered markers beside each and every piece of evidence they uncovered. He then came over to where Hailey was now on the floor, flat on her stomach again, still looking under the elliptical.

She looked up from the floor to see Kolker staring at the QVC screen.

"What? You're going to buy CZ diamonds off QVC?"

"No. We got our bullet."

Taking both her hands, Kolker pulled Hailey up to a standing position.

"Wow. Clean," Hailey remarked.

The bullet had torn a small, neat hole just below the equipment bolting the plasma TV screen to the wall, where it could easily have been missed. They both stood for a moment, looking back and forth from the elliptical to the bullet lodged in the wall.

"Trajectory path right from the door, directly behind the victim, through her head and into the wall."

"Yep, she probably never even saw him."

"I just wonder who the hell could make it through the lobby and up here into Fallon Malone's apartment."

"Somebody who knew what they were doing. Nobody saw a thing, not the doormen, building maintenance crew . . . nobody. No sign of forced entry; it had to be somebody who knew how to get in unnoticed," Kolker responded.

"Or somebody she knew. Somehow. I'm not saying they were bosom buddies, but it was somebody that knew her, all right."

"Agreed."

"Plus, the mode of death. There's no sign of robbery or argument. She's fully dressed, so probably no sex assault. That leaves some pretty defined motives . . . anger, jealousy, revenge, hate . . . or, of course, murder for hire. But that's a long shot. Usually just happens in the movies. And . . . from the looks of it, the killer's a do-it-yourselfer . . . no accomplice, just one shooter. Only one person entered here, I'd put money on it . . ."

"I didn't know you were a gambler, but I agree with you." Kolker was still examining the floor for evidence.

"I was about to say I'd put money on it *if I were a gambler.* Which I'm not. I don't even play the lottery. I don't trust politicians to run anything."

"I figured." They both broke into laughter.

"You know, we shouldn't be laughing over Fallon Malone's body. Doesn't she have a family? They're going to be devastated."

"I know, Hailey. But I see so much evil in the world, it feels good to laugh at something."

"I know, sometimes we'd end up laughing at anything while we were waiting on a verdict. You know, the courtroom staff, the court reporter, the sheriffs, the cops who work the case hanging around for the verdict. I guess that's what they mean by gallows humor. You can get so overwhelmed with it all, sometimes you just laugh at anything."

The two got quiet again, looking down at the body. Fallon Malone's beautiful face was nearly gone, blasted out of her head with a single bullet from behind.

Even if she could talk, she likely couldn't name her killer.

She never saw it coming. He shot from behind.

"Hailey, you said you don't trust politicians. I have a question for you. Could you ever trust anybody? Anybody at all?"

Hailey looked up at Kolker, taken aback. It was an intensely personal question. Since Will's murder, it wasn't so much she didn't trust anyone . . . She just couldn't risk getting close again. To anyone. Losing love again, be it friend or lover, was just too much for her to even consider.

Instead of lashing out at him with a biting or sarcastic comeback, like she normally did whenever someone brought up anything that touched on her and Will, she actually smiled. "That's a good question, Kolker. Tell you the truth, I haven't even considered trusting anybody for so long, I'll have to think on it and let you know."

The room got quiet again.

"So guys, ready for CSI techs? Plus, the morgue guy is here. They brought the whiz kid with them." A uniformed cop broke the silence from the doorway.

"Who's that?" Hailey asked. Who else would want to come see a dead body?

"He's the rising star over at the Medical Examiner's Office. Did the initial autopsy on Prentiss Love and then did a second autopsy on Leather Stockton for Suffolk PD. He's the one who managed to find just enough of a bullet sliver in Prentiss's brain cavity to get a bullet match, God bless him." Kolker had heard a lot about this guy. All good.

"That's odd. The actual MEs hardly ever come out of the office." Hailey thought it out loud.

"Wish more of them would. It couldn't hurt. We just called him over because he did the report on Prentiss Love and a second autopsy on Leather Stockton. I'm beginning to think he's starstruck, a little over-enthusiastic. But he's certainly making a name for himself," Kolker responded. As a second thought, he threw back over his shoulder, "Send him in now! But make sure he's got on booties, gown, and gloves."

"Don't worry, Lieutenant, I think the kid actually brought his own!"

"I'M SO EXCITED. DON'T YOU WANT TO KNOW WHY?"

"Why?" Hailey asked into the phone, knowing full well Tony Russo would tell her whether she wanted to know or not.

"We just got exclusive video. A two-year-old smoking pot! Can you believe it? *A two-year-old smoking pot!* I died and went to heaven! TV heaven!"

"TV heaven?"

"Yes! Don't you get it by now? It's guaranteed ratings!!! The viewers won't be able to take their eyes off it! I can't stop watching it! I'm playing it again right now on my monitor! You should see it! But that's another conversation. That can wait. Right now, we *have* to have you on the Fallon Malone show."

Hailey said nothing and continued reading the *Post*.

"You have to do it! Please? It'll be flat without you. Nobody on the show will have the guts to challenge Harry or that obnoxious defense attorney, Derek Jacobs. He's so sleazy."

"If he's so sleazy, then why do you have him on the show?"

"Sookie makes me. Plus, he just called his own press conference to announce that he's representing all three victims' families."

"Representing them for what?"

"He didn't say. But knowing Derek Jacobs, he'll find somebody to sue."

"I didn't know the women had children." Hailey couldn't believe she'd missed that fact.

"Oh, none of them do. Jacobs will sue on behalf of parents, aunts and uncles, cousins, grandparents. You know, loss of a family member. Wrongful death. Maybe the yoga studio or the apartment building or the Hamptons mansion should have had better security. I don't know how he'll sue . . . but he'll find a way . . . Trust me!"

"That is so wrong. It gives lawyers such a bad name."

"So, come on, *please*? You'll like it because we have video of Fallon's apartment from Harry's last interview with her."

"Please what? What did you say about an interview?" Hailey was no longer paying attention. She was reading an article about a mugger stalking little old ladies all over the East Side.

"Please do the show! The interview . . . Harry did it about six months ago. Hailey, *listen!* I don't think you're paying attention to me!"

"Okay, I'm listening." Hailey kept reading the article about the mugger. The mugger's MO was to loiter around apartment building elevators, waiting until a little old lady with her arms full of groceries stepped on, then smash up her face and take her pocketbook.

"So, Hailey . . . you have to do it! I've already got this great banner for the lower third of screen! It'll be right under your face! It reads *Inside Fallon Malone Murder Apartment!*

"Then we run video of Harry's tour of Fallon's Manhattan apartment when she did the interview! I was there with Sookie. The apartment was *fabulous.* We got raw footage of every square inch of the place, although we didn't use it all originally . . . We will today! It'll be perfect!"

"But it wasn't a 'murder apartment' then. When you did the interview and the tour of her place." Hailey hated to rain on his parade, but she felt compelled to point out the obvious.

"*It is now.*" He said it as if it made perfect sense.

Hailey was taking a long, hard look at the composite sketch of the East Side mugger. He sure looked familiar.

"Come on, Hailey . . . do the show this afternoon. We need the numbers. Our numbers nearly double every time you're on the show and we talk about the serial killer. Plus, you won't even have to be on the set with Harry or that sleaze-bucket Derek Jacobs."

"Hmm. Not remotely tempted yet."

Russo acted like he didn't hear her. "It'll be fantastic. Fallon had Harry over for a one-on-one about her movie career."

Even over the phone Hailey could picture Tony, sitting at his desk, pumping out sincerity. All the while he'd be typing furiously into his desktop computer and sending messages over his Black-Berry.

Hailey was still processing everything she'd observed at Fallon Malone's apartment. She'd stayed for a couple of hours, going over evidence with Kolker at some diner where they all seemed to know him pretty well, brought them both lemon meringue pie, and then refused to let him pay.

It had been a long time since Hailey had had lemon meringue pie. She ate the whole piece. It reminded her of home, in Georgia. It tasted just like her grandmother Lucy's.

Prying her mind away from her grandmother, home, and lemon pie, Hailey said, "Listen, I'd love to do the show. I would, I really would. But I have to see two patients, starting in about ten minutes."

"Hailey, give me a break. Did I tell you I had to go set up a live shot in Boston last night and the hotel put me in a room next to a dog? A dog, Hailey . . . a dog."

"So? What's wrong with a dog?"

"Well, first of all, I could smell it."

"You could smell a dog through the walls?"

"Yes. I could. I could definitely smell something shaggy. But even after I asked for a quiet room, they put me next to a dog. I called the front desk at 2 a.m. and held the phone to the wall so they could hear the yapping. Of course, I had them move me to the Presidential Suite. So, is it true you were at the Malone crime scene today?" he asked suddenly, tossing a little bomb into the conversation.

"How did you know *that*?" Hailey finally looked up from the *Post*, stunned.

"I have my sources."

Tony Russo being coy didn't fit at all. He had a habit of blurting out everything that crossed his mind. Tony's thoughts were like gum in a gumball machine. They automatically went from his brain down to his mouth, then were spit straight out. No filter whatsoever.

"No BS. How'd you know?"

"If I tell you, will you come on to the show? You can move a patient . . . or we can delay taping an hour or so. The crew is there all day anyway."

Tony should've been a lawyer. Always an angle. But Hailey really wanted to know if one of the cops or techs at the scene was a leak to the press . . . most likely paid for information. This was a serial murder case and any leak or impropriety could end up affecting a jury verdict down the line. Even the tiniest of improprieties, much less the big ones, could come back to haunt a case.

"You're quiet . . . does that mean you'll do it? I'll tell you who told me you were there!"

"Okay. I'll do it. Now who told you?"

"It was just Matt and Clark, two of our producers. I sent them out for Starbucks and they saw a lot of cop cars at one of the high-rises. They walked over and saw you coming out with a cop and getting into a car. They asked around and the doorman told them about Fallon. Which is why we need you!"

"I'm not saying a word about what I saw."

"We just want you to talk about murder cases and the string of D-Listers that bit the bullet lately."

"That's not funny."

"What's not funny?"

"Your pun. 'Bit the bullet.' They were all shot in the head."

"Fallon was shot in the head too? Man! I didn't know that!"

Hailey wanted to kick herself. She'd unwittingly let a fact slip out. She'd have to be more careful on the show.

"I really don't know that, I was at a distance, I couldn't really tell." Hailey tried to cover.

"Whatever. Head, chest, back . . . I don't care. Fallon Malone was murdered and so were Prentiss Love and Leather Stockton. Think the same person killed them all?"

"Come on. How would I know?"

"Now that you're doing the show, I feel so much better. I had Italian last night, and there was some dried red sauce on my fork. Before I started eating. They gave me a fork with somebody else's food on it. I almost had somebody else's food on my lip. I swear I've felt like vomiting ever since."

Hailey decided to ignore another of Russo's stories about his nausea. "Please, don't drag out that horrible gold lamé blouse again. I'm not wearing it, plus it smells."

"How about red velvet? I have that, too. It's got a sequined lapel. You'll love it. It'll look great on air."

"Okay, I said I'd do the taping, but you have to stop with the red velvet and sequins."

"Promise. No red velvet."

"Or sequins." She had to be specific with Tony Russo.

"Or sequins." He tried to sound glum. "You're too prim . . . Will you at least unbutton the top button of your shirt?"

"Bye, Tony." She clicked off and went to change clothes. Hailey was smiling on the way to her bedroom closet. Tony was growing on her. Maybe she even liked him.

Staring at the rack of clothes hanging there neatly, she wondered briefly why she bothered to look. Of course, she'd wear solid black, like she always did. Anything else would be inappropriate, given the topic.

There was no way it wasn't the same killer. That much she knew.

But who could possibly hate all three women enough to tear their brains out of their faces with a single shot?

I N LESS THAN TWO HOURS, HAILEY WAS BACK IN A DARKENED STUDIO, clutching a stack of research on serial murders and news accounts of the three murders she'd read and printed off her home computer. She sat completely still, staring into a blank camera. Suddenly, she heard a male voice in her ear.

"Hailey, can you hear me all right? Got everything you need?"

It was Tony Russo in her ear from the control room. "I'm fine, but I could use a cup of hot tea, skim."

"On the way! And remember, Harry just *loves* it when you fight with him! It's great TV! The numbers will shoot through the roof!"

Hailey knew for a fact that Tony was outright lying and trying to "produce" her again. It was very clear Harry Todd hated it when she corrected him or argued with him. He always looked just like a deer caught in headlights, and until somebody coached him in his ear, he couldn't think of a thing to say back to defend himself.

The show's theme music started playing in her ear and the screen before her lit up with "program," what the viewer would see. Various video clips of Harry Todd flashed across the screen . . . Todd interviewing a former president, Todd cooking with a tall, brunette domestic guru, both wearing matching aprons and laughing . . . Harry Todd walking along the streets of New York City being mobbed by adoring fans who just wanted to touch him.

If they only knew . . . Hailey thought it but would never say it out loud. She waited for the intros and for Harry Todd to begrudgingly throw her a question when it came her turn to take the side of the police. She knew he'd make it as much of a hardball as he could muster.

She wasn't worried. After practicing law for years and handling more homicide cases than she could remember, she'd basically prepared for this her entire life. Harry Todd, on the other hand, was just reading cue cards.

After tossing an opening question to a tall, blonde female reporter dressed in a gorgeous red cashmere coat and matching scarf, standing on the street outside Fallon's apartment, Todd, of course, went to the defense attorney to the stars, Derek Jacobs. Jacobs was seated in the studio a few inches from Todd himself. The two looked extremely casual and friendly, like they'd just had a long meal and now were kicking back for drinks and cigars.

Fallon Malone's death was simply sport to them. Something to talk about. The fact that she'd been brutally murdered, just like the others, meant nothing to these two.

Hailey grimaced. At that precise moment, the camera showed her face, as if the control room had been waiting for a twitch or a sneeze. She quickly erased her expression. She took a look at the panel . . . the beautiful blonde reporter; the left-wing nut, Yale Professor Robert Seefeld; a crime-scene-specialist-turned-TV-talking-head; slimy looking Derek Jacobs; and the ringmaster, Harry Todd. They all smiled widely, displaying shockingly white smiles. They had to be caps or veneers. No teeth were naturally that white.

Hailey just couldn't bring herself to turn on the big smile she knew was expected of her. What was there to smile about? The awful fact of the murders, grim news that should depress anyone, was just another hot topic for Todd and his crony, Jacobs. The panel moved on swiftly to Fallon Malone's failing movie career, inanely discussing her last movie and her "sex goddess" image. Hailey remained silent, but knowing Todd's show as she now did, Hailey deduced this was just a ploy by which they could justify showing a clip of Fallon washing the Vette.

It was *no* way to treat a murder victim. No matter how the public viewed Fallon Malone, she'd been viciously gunned down through no fault of her own.

Hailey broke in, speaking for the first time. She'd been warned Todd hated to be interrupted. It broke his train of thought, such as it was, and it was hard for him to counter original thoughts not written on his yellow cue cards and printed questions.

"You are all making a mockery of Fallon Malone's murder, and it's wrong. She is a crime victim. Would you want people to laugh in the same breath they talk about your murder? I wouldn't."

Her spontaneous tirade stopped Todd cold. He looked around to see if one of his pals was going to defend him. They didn't.

Todd turned his attention to Hailey. "With us is Hailey Dean, former prosecutor, who has been at the Malone crime scene. Is it true she was shot in the head?"

"I will not comment on anything I observed at the scene." Hailey was stone-faced. "But I will confirm your reporter's story that Malone was murdered in her apartment."

"Assuming they catch the guy, I guess you're ready to string him up as usual, right, Ms. Dean?" His tone was sarcastic, as if there were something wrong with jury trials followed by sentencing for cold-blooded murders.

"I'd have to hear the facts at trial, Harry. But if your reporter is accurate that Ms. Malone was unarmed and shot from behind with no chance to defend herself, and if there is no affirmative defense such as self-defense, accident, or insanity, I think a jury's consideration of the death penalty would be appropriate. Of course, any lawyer worth his salt would already know that the state of New York outlawed the death penalty."

Todd's response was fast. "How does it make you feel, Ms. Dean, to send someone to Death Row? Have any of your targets actually been put to death?"

If he was trying to make her feel bad, it didn't work.

"That would have been a decision made by a jury after hearing facts and evidence on some of the most heinous, most brutal murders ever seen in the halls of a courthouse. It was my job to offer that alternative to jurors, an alternative they had the right to accept or reject."

Hailey heard Jacobs try to interrupt. She didn't stop. "And just for your information, Harry, so you don't continue to mislead your viewers, regardless of what Mr. Jacobs and the professor on the panel today have to say on the subject, most of America believes that certain murders, depending on the atrocity of the crime, do warrant the death penalty."

Todd's face was beet red and Hailey spotted perspiration on Jacobs's upper lip. It beaded through the thick makeup they'd caked onto him.

"And as you may or may not know, death row appeals take up to twenty, twenty-five years to complete. So the answer is no, as of today, none of the convicted murderers I put on jury trial have sat in Old Sparky *or* gotten the needle . . . *yet.*"

She knew instinctively that her references to "the needle," or death by lethal injection, as well as her use of the term "Old Sparky," as if the Georgia electric chair was somehow an old friend of hers, would irk Todd and gang.

Someone in Todd's control room mistakenly pressed the wrong key and Hailey could hear the directions being thrown at Harry Todd over and over. "Get out! Get out! Go to break! She's doing it again!"

On camera, Todd looked confused, and the other two men on set, Derek Jacobs and Robert Seefeld, looked like they'd bitten lemons.

"Just read the prompter, Harry. *Read the prompter.*" Hailey overheard the voice as it continued in Harry Todd's ear.

"When we come back, exclusive! *A look inside Fallon Malone's murder apartment!*" Against all bets being waged in the control room, Todd did manage to read the words right in front of him.

The show's music suddenly geared up and played over the famous clips of Fallon Malone washing the Vette. Then there was a dissolve to police cars swarming outside her penthouse apartment just as a van drove onto the scene. NEW YORK MEDICAL EXAMINER'S MOBILE UNIT was emblazoned across its side underneath a depiction of a large, gold police shield.

Hailey looked down at the bottom of the camera's monitor where the precise time down to the second was displayed in dimly lit red digital numbers. Only twenty minutes had passed.

It was going to be another long hour.

 **31**

"**M**R. ANDERSON?"
"Yes . . ."

"Lieutenant Ethan Kolker, NYPD. Do you have a moment to speak to us?"

The next morning, when Scott Anderson answered his front doorbell, he certainly didn't expect to find Lieutenant Kolker flanked by two huge NYPD uniformed officers on either side of him. The three of them at the edge of his front door practically blocked the morning sun behind them. It was only 7:30 a.m. and Anderson was still in the sweat pants and T-shirt he'd slept in the night before. His dark hair, usually perfectly coiffed, was still tousled from sleeping.

Kolker flashed his badge, the gold shield reflecting a seventies-style light fixture hanging from the ceiling behind Scott Anderson there in the foyer of his suburban home. It looked like an agglomeration of clear, crystal icicles hanging in a mass, lit from inside its center. His ex bought it years ago. After nine years together, she left with half of everything he'd made off the PGA tour, the house in Boca, the two dogs, and the Porsche.

He got the house note and the crystal light fixture. All because of a fling. It had been nothing to Scott. It was just a girl who sold sandwiches at the Masters down in Augusta. An Augusta local, for Pete's sake. It wasn't like he would ever leave Rachel for her. He could barely even remember her name. Or any of the others, for that matter.

His ex found out about the sandwich girl. One night when he was a little late coming home, she hacked into his cell phone and heard messages from the girl. Scott's contention was that his wife had no right to listen to his private voice mails . . . that she'd violated his Fourth Amendment right to privacy.

Note to self: *Never use your birthday as the numeric code to your voice mails.*

"Hello, gentlemen. What's up? Somebody get their car egged again? I swear, I didn't do it! I don't even like eggs!" Scott Anderson flashed his best smile, which even this early in the morning was dazzling white, thanks to several sessions too many at a teeth-bleaching franchise.

"Got a minute?" the tall one with the tan, standing in the middle, answered. He didn't smile back.

"Sure. Come on in."

At first thought, Anderson assumed he'd keep them on the front porch just outside his front door. He was afraid they were like vampires; you had to invite them in and once they're in, you're a goner. But neighbors would be slowly driving by, starting their commutes to work and pre-schools at any minute.

No need for them to see the three men, two in uniform, on his front porch. A quick glance at the street in front of his yard confirmed the three had arrived in an unmarked car, thank God. He ushered them in and with one more sharp glance toward the street, Anderson closed the front door behind them.

He stepped ahead of them and took them through his empty living room. The hardwood floors were bare, no rugs and no furniture. Just one lamp sitting on the floor in the corner. It had once sat on a beautiful end table, whose top was decorated with several tones of inlaid wood, just at the arm of a deep navy brocade sofa.

All the living room furniture was gone the afternoon he came home to discover Rachel gone with most of the household goods. He'd dashed to the phone and dialed the 800 number to his checking account.

Empty as of twelve noon that day. Not even one penny left in it to keep the account open. The only thing of any value she'd left in the house was his beloved water bed in the master bedroom. He'd had it since his bachelor days.

She'd left it all right. But only after she stabbed it repeatedly with a kitchen knife. The carpet beneath the bed was soaked and, after a day or two, had the foulest smell to ever hit his nostrils.

And all the crotches had been cut out of every single designer suit he had. They were worth thousands. His tailor managed to save a few of them. You could only spot the mending if you stared really intently at his crotch.

The cops . . . after leading them through the empty living room, Anderson ushered them into the only room he'd furnished since the divorce, the den. Should he offer them coffee? He only had instant. He better not, it would only encourage them to stay longer.

"So. What's this all about? The eggs? I didn't see a thing and, luckily, my SUV hasn't been a target . . . probably some kids."

"Mr. Anderson, it's not about eggs." The tall one in the sports jacket was doing all the talking. He'd taken out a little spiral notebook from somewhere and held a pen in his right hand, poised over the paper. The tan guy, Kolker, looked straight at him. He never seemed to blink. That was disconcerting. Especially this early in the morning.

Damn. He was like a lizard. The guy never blinked. Scott Anderson waited for the other shoe to drop. He didn't have to wait very long.

"When did you start your affair with Fallon Malone, and when was the last time you saw her?" Kolker changed neither voice inflection nor facial expression. And he still didn't blink.

What the hell? How did they know about Fallon?

Scott knew the shock registered on his face. Kolker continued.

"We know you two got together sometime last week, but we're trying to pinpoint just how many hours after you saw her she was murdered."

Anderson stood up. "Murdered? Fallon murdered? What are you talking about? She's fine . . . I'm supposed to see her . . ."

"Sit down, Mr. Anderson," Kolker interrupted. "If you could just focus on the last time you were with her. You seem to be the last one to see her alive."

Anderson sank down into the leather center of his pit group. He stared blankly at the morning edition of ESPN.

"I can't believe she's dead. What happened?"

"You don't watch TV?" All three cops looked pointedly at the jumbo-tron just feet away, already up and running at 7:30 a.m.

Anderson leaned forward to pick up the remote control sitting on the thick, glass-top coffee table. He clicked the TV off.

"I do. But only ESPN. And nobody's said a thing about Fallon. Did you say murdered?" He'd never had a girlfriend murdered. Not that he knew of, anyway. This was a first. Scott Anderson took a deep breath and tried his best to look broken up.

"She was shot execution-style. Single bullet to the back of the head. And according to video surveillance in the hall of her apartment, you were there in the twelve hours before the ME set time of death. We're waiting on lab results right now. If the coroner finds sperm . . ."

"*Sperm?*" The thoughts in Anderson's head were all crashing together like a pile-up on the interstate, one plowing into the other and into the other without ending, each one as violent a crash as the one just before it.

"Then it's only a matter of time before we get a DNA match."

Anderson showed absolutely no expression whatsoever. He'd seen just enough true crime on TV to know that any expression was likely to be construed as guilt.

"I don't know anything about DNA." He looked up to meet Kolker's gaze. "I was there just to return her sunglasses. I gave her a few golf lessons out at the club, and the last time she was there, she left her glasses. I was heading into the city anyway, so I dropped them by. As a courtesy."

"You weren't having an affair? That's not what her driver tells us."

That S.O.B. Scott had instinctively disliked Fallon's driver. Sitting there flanked by cops, he tried hard to remember just what had gone on in front of the driver . . . not that much, as he could recall.

"And, while we're here, Mr. Anderson, were you acquainted with Leather Stockton?"

Scott answered quickly, "The actress? The blonde? The Leather Stockton that was on the TV show? The cop show?"

"Yes . . . That would be the one."

Anderson didn't hesitate. "Absolutely not. Never met the lady."

The three cops exchanged looks across the coffee table. They were surreptitious about it, but Anderson caught them. He acted like he didn't.

"Well, think back. We were just flipping through a few videos of Miss Stockton and happened to spot you out at the Pebble Beach Open last year. Oh, let's see, how long ago was it?" Kolker looked at the short, stocky one. And actually, Hailey had been the one to spot it. She'd volunteered to go through reams of videos while the cops worked the streets.

"Lemme think, Lieutenant." The cop acted as if he actually had to think . . . as if they hadn't talked about it the whole drive out to Scarborough. "Pebble Beach . . . Pebble Beach . . . That woulda been a few months ago. Yeah . . . I'm pretty sure."

"You were on camera with her at the ninth hole. She was interviewed about the charity throwing an event. You even put your arm around her. I believe you said a few words into the camera yourself. Any of this ringing a bell, Mr. Anderson?"

Kolker locked onto him with those eyes. They were just barely blue. The irises were actually more white than blue, like a husky dog. Creepy.

"Well, as a golf pro I do travel around the country for different golfing events . . . Let me think . . . Now that you mention it, I do believe I recall Ms. Stockton was there."

"She was there all right. And you had your arm around her."

"Did you happen to know Prentiss Love, too?"

Anderson knew when it was time to clam up. This had gone too far. He should never have let them in the door. He didn't have to. He knew that much from before. Back before he was married, one of the women he was dating had charged him with battery. She had always been a pain in the backside anyway, always complaining. He didn't know why he dated her in the first place. It was nothing, and in the end, she dropped the whole thing. It never even went to court.

It had taken quite a bit of "convincing" her on his part, though.

After that, Scott Anderson knew all about the cops. They were all asses and they were stupid to boot. He, Scott Anderson, didn't have to say a word.

"Hmm. Prentiss Love . . . Prentiss Love . . . that name rings a bell. A singer, right? Or was she on one of those soap operas? I don't know who she is . . . You know, gentlemen, I'd be happy to talk to you some more, but I have to get to work."

"It's our understanding you don't have a lesson scheduled until around noon today."

Damn! Had they called the club? Just what he needed . . . to have his bosses in on this whole thing.

"Oh yes, that's right. But paperwork. You know how it is, officers, the damn paperwork . . ." His voice trailed off and his face remained completely unconcerned.

He was pulling it off.

"What paperwork?"

Damn! What the hell?

"Oh, the usual," Anderson answered without a pause. "Time sheets, PR work, the usual."

"So, you did or you didn't know Miss Love?"

"No, I never met the lady." Oh crap . . . he'd said it again. That was the same thing he'd said about Leather. He quickly added on, "If I'm even thinking about *the right lady . . .*"

The cops sat silent for a moment as if they were giving him a chance to reconsider his answer. He didn't.

"Mr. Anderson, do you own a gun?"

"Well, I do, but it's been so long since I've held it in my hands, I can't even tell you the caliber."

"Think back." They weren't letting go.

Scott Anderson pinched his lips together and looked down at the floor as if he was deep in thought.

"If you've got it handy, we can just take a look at it."

"Actually, it's at the club."

"Okay, we can ride along with you and take a look there."

"Now that I think about it, I believe my ex-wife, Rachel, took it with her. That's right . . . she's got it. She pretty much cleaned me out of house and home when we split."

None of the three said anything, so he kept talking.

"You know . . . *women.*"

"Right. We have her address on East 65th Street in Manhattan. Is that right?"

Damn. They'd already checked her out.

"I believe that's it. We're not really in touch right now."

The room went quiet. He got the sense they were waiting on him to keep talking.

Anderson was the first to stand up. Then the three stood up, too. Anderson turned his back and walked toward the front door. He hoped like hell they were following him.

As he opened the door, he turned and to his great relief, they were there with him in the entrance hall. They were leaving. Thank God.

"Thank you, Mr. Anderson. We'll be in touch."

His body was flushed with relief; his knees actually felt weak. He gripped the handle of the front door for strength.

"Oh, yes. Anything I can do. And I'm so sorry to hear about Ms. Malone."

"We knew you would be."

The three turned and headed down the front porch steps.

"He's sorry, all right. Sorry she had a camera outside her front door," the uniformed sergeant muttered to Kolker, who was walking along to his right.

"Yep. You pegged it. He's lying through his teeth. We need that time of death and the DNA match. We might have our man."

"So, warrant on his house and the wife's apartment?"

Kolker responded, "Doubt we'll need one for her. She'll be only too happy to help us pin this on her ex, from what I read in the divorce papers."

"Okay. But I'll get the paperwork ready."

"Good idea." Kolker kept walking along with the other two down the front walk to the unmarked squad car.

He went on, "And get one for the country club where he works. Pretty swanky place. We'll need a warrant, but once we show it, they'll be nothing but smiles. Don't get me wrong. It won't be because they like us. They'll just want us in and out as fast as possible. Don't worry, we won't get a tour of the place or an invite to lunch on the terrace."

Just as they were approaching the car, Kolker asked without turning his head either way, "Is he looking?"

Paddy looked back over his shoulder up at Anderson's house. He immediately spotted a tiny, slight movement in the heavy curtains covering the living room window that looked out onto the front yard.

"Oh, yeah. He's looking."

"Straight on? Or is he hiding behind the curtains?" Kolker opened the car's driver side front door, not looking back at the house himself.

"Behind the curtains, for sure."

"And I noticed he didn't follow us down to get the morning paper. It's been sitting at the edge of his front porch steps since we got there. He didn't want to be questioned for the time it would take to lean over and get the paper. And now he's hiding behind the curtains? Yep. We just may have our man."

Kolker took the wheel, one cop in back, one riding shotgun. He cranked up and eased away from the front of Anderson's house. When interviewing a potential murder suspect, better to work in teams. Anything could turn on a dime and go sideways.

"He still looking?"

"He's still looking, boss."

"Good."

Kolker eased into surprisingly heavy traffic for a cul-de-sac in a suburban neighborhood.

Lots of station wagons, big heavy sedans, and mom-type SUVs. Everybody was heading to preschool.

Anderson didn't fit here. Something was wrong.

Kolker looked back at the house, back at the curtains in the front window.

Something didn't fit. He knew it in his gut.

Scott Anderson . . . golf pro. Something was wrong.

IIIIIIIIIIIIIIIIIIIIIIIIIIIIIIIIIIIIIIIIIIIIIIIIIIIII **32** IIIIIIIIIIIIIIIIIIIIIIIIII

H AILEY LOOKED THROUGH THE TINTED WINDOW FROM THE BACK of the black limo GNE sent to pick her up after her last patient of the day. It was Mazz again. As with her other clients, they'd continued regular phone sessions and Skype while she had been in Atlanta.

Mazz was a high-priced CPA-turned-financial-guru with a stable of wealthy clients. Hailey had long suspected him of criminal activity. Today, Mazz was kicked back in an Armani suit that had to have set him back at least three thousand dollars. Hailey saw the tag on the inside of the jacket when he took it off and hung it on the coat rack standing just inside the door to her office suite.

She'd prepared his coffee just as she heard the buzzer alerting her he was downstairs waiting to be let up. She'd learned Mazz liked his coffee piping hot, loaded with heavy cream and four packets of sugar. Even with all that cream and sugar, he stayed rail thin. Must be the stress of criminal enterprise.

"You look tired, Mazz. Bad night?"

"Oh, Hailey. If you only knew. It was the monkey again."

"Oh, no! The monkey . . . What happened this time?"

As if she didn't know. An evil carnival monkey, actually an IRS agent in disguise, had plagued Mazz for over two years now. Typically in the dreams, two chunky IRS agents chased Mazz through variations of an intricate maze. Sometimes he was lost between high hedges, sometimes he'd be caught in a stone labyrinth, sometimes wandering through a dense forest, and sometimes going through a series of rooms connected by elaborate hallways and secret trap doors.

Whenever Mazz thought he'd eluded the gang of IRS agents, all dressed in dark blue polyester suits with rayon-mix ties, the monkey would literally jump out of nowhere onto his back, screeching loudly.

"It was the house again."

"Oh, no." Hailey kept her face completely expressionless, as usual when reliving Mazz's monkey dreams.

"Were you a fly this time?"

"No. I was a bird."

"Well, that's good. At least they weren't picking off your wings again."

"That's true, Hailey. They couldn't tear my wings off. But Hailey," Mazz began twisting the Hermès bandana he always pulled, neatly folded into a square, from his back pants pocket. "I tried earlier to fly away out one of the windows . . . but it was locked.

But I didn't feel like a fly . . . I was more of a . . . a . . . falcon. Some sort of bird of prey. I was definitely not a fly this time. But I crashed into the window and then I had human legs again. I looked down and saw them running. I turned around, and it was the big guy chasing me, the one with the incredibly plain navy suit."

Mazz always described what other dream characters were wearing in great detail.

"Poly-rayon tie again?"

"Oh, yeah."

"Hmm," she said, nodding, "no natural fibers . . . again." Hailey made a note.

"So I got to my hiding place, you know, behind the metal file cabinets down in the furnace room at the bottom of my office building." She nodded. Same place he always ended up.

"Hailey, they didn't find me. They disappeared. I could hear their feet, running away down the halls till it just went silent. And then I woke up." Mazz was soaked with sweat. He looked across the three or so feet that separated them, she in a wingback chair facing the window, Mazz on a buttery-colored sofa beside her. His expression was one of amazement . . . disbelief. How could he be so confounded by the same dream he'd been having for over a year?

"I think the fact that you were not a fly, didn't have your wings torn off, and actually had human feet and legs is a huge step forward."

"Totally agree, Hailey."

"But what do you think, in your real life, triggers the dream? The IRS agents, the running, the monkey?"

Mazz suddenly looked extremely uncomfortable and pulled at the neck of his shirt.

"Hailey, that's a tough one. I forgot to tell you, I gotta go early today." He had practically leaped off the sofa and headed to the door.

The limo lurched over a pothole. Hailey looked up at the canopy of trees overhead as the car slowed down after following a long, winding driveway that went straight through a swath of apple orchard. After over an hour on the expressway, she was here, at the mansion of Sookie Downs.

It was a monster, set far off the main highway, down a winding one-car driveway in the center of a huge apple orchard. Parked in a circular drive at the front exterior, the thing loomed over them.

"I think you're supposed to wait." Hailey leaned toward the front seat and spoke through a plastic partition between herself and the driver.

"I'll be right here." He said it reassuringly from his spot in the front seat behind the wheel. She had no idea why she'd been summoned, but her curiosity caused her to agree to come.

"Thanks." Hailey slid across the long, leather backseat, pushed open the heavy car door, and stood beside the limo, looking all the way up to the top of the home. It was more like a castle than a home, complete with turrets on the left and right front sides.

Turrets? In East Hampton? Who knew.

There was a tall and impressive set of steps leading to the front door and Hailey climbed them to ring the bell. She could hear it plainly, echoing a series of chimes.

No answer.

She waited a few moments, then pressed the bell again. After a few more moments of waiting, Hailey could hear movement and then the front door swung open. Just over the threshold stood a short, dark-haired woman dressed in formal maid's attire.

Hailey was taken aback. She'd never actually known anyone who had servants in their home . . . servants who dressed in uniforms as if they were working at a luxury hotel. The woman smiled through the open door at Hailey. She wore a long-sleeved, light blue dress, covered by a crisp white apron with black, rubber-looking shoes so as not to make a sound as she made her way around Sookie's mansion. The uniform was topped off with a little white kerchief-looking headpiece, almost like a mini-mantilla.

"Good afternoon. Are you Ms. Dean? I'm Consuela and Ms. Downs is expecting you. Please, come in."

The woman was pleasant. Hailey stepped in to follow behind after she gently shut the front door and motioned to Hailey to come along.

The entrance hall was cavernous with a hardwood parquet floor. The ceiling was vaulted, and a huge crystal chandelier hung down from its joist in a thick, wooden beam that went from one end of the hall's overhead surface to the next. Hailey's footsteps sounded out loudly as they crossed the entrance hall into a formal living room. The carpet was baby blue and the furniture looked antique and uncomfortable. Across the distance of the room, Hailey looked ahead into a den.

Although it was just as large as the living room, it was only a little less formal, with a brownish sofa and chairs whose centerpiece was a large stone fireplace. It fleetingly brought to mind the Manhattan penthouse apartment of Fallon Malone, not in the schematic or color scheme, but because every wall was covered with shots of its owner.

Framed photos of Sookie Downs with every sitting president dating back to the fifties, when she was a little girl, were prominently displayed. As a child, she appeared in the photos along with her father, who was pictured in full military regalia.

Consuela stood silently behind Hailey, also gazing at the wall of photos. She must have seen them a million times. "Please, have a seat, Ms. Hailey. Can I bring you anything? Would you like a glass of wine? Ms. Downs is very proud of her collection."

"Her collection? Of what?"

"Fine wines." Consuela looked as if she were confused Hailey did not know she was referring to wine. "Ms. Downs collects wines from all around the world. She even has a climate-controlled wine cellar . . . I'm sure she will show it to you. She can control its temperature by remote!"

"Oh, my, remote-controlled temperature in her wine cellar. Now that is really *something*. But, no. Thank you." It was way too early to be hitting the wine. The woman looked disappointed, as if she'd specifically been instructed to make guests happy.

Hailey quickly added, "Maybe later?"

Since Consuela still looked worried, Hailey decided to ask for something. "Let me see then . . . may I please have a cup of hot tea? With milk? Skim if you have it . . ."

The woman smiled broadly, as if getting a cup of tea for Hailey would absolutely make her day. "Oh, yes, Ms. Hailey. I'd be happy to get that for you. What type of tea would you like?"

"Irish Breakfast . . . I don't guess you have that on hand. It's so much harder to find than English Breakfast or chamomile."

"We do have it, as a matter of fact. Mr. Russo called to tell us it's one of your favorites, and Ms. Downs insisted we have it for you today. I will be right back. Here, Ms. Hailey, sit here. It's the most comfortable chair in the house and Ms. Downs wants you to be comfortable. She is on a call and will be right along."

The comfy chair was located directly in front of the wall of fame, and whoever sat there looked directly into dozens of Sookie Downs' posed "candid" shots. In just moments, Consuela was back with a full tea service on a silver tray. She handed a cup of piping hot Irish Breakfast to Hailey and left the room again.

Hailey was left alone to examine all the presidential photos on the wall. Hailey looked back to the first one to the left again. It must have been one of the earliest. Out on a landing strip of some sort stood a tall, lean man who was dressed in military garb and obviously Sookie's father.

Looking carefully, Hailey recognized immediately the significance of the embroidery on his shoulders. There were four stars on either side. He was a four-star army general. Extremely rare.

In his arms, he held what was clearly, from the photos, his only child. Beside them stood President Dwight D. Eisenhower. Hmm.

Hailey quickly calculated that, based on the picture, Sookie must be at least in her fifties.

Wow. The miracle of modern science. Hailey would have guessed Sookie to be in her forties instead of mid-to-late fifties.

Hailey could see the resemblance of Sookie, the child, to Sookie Downs, the woman full grown. But over the years, that similarity had become much more vague. Mousey brown hair as a child turned red somewhere in her twenties and instead of dulling over time with age, it became more and more vibrantly red. It was plain to see, when photographs taken over the years were displayed side by side, that extensive work had been done on Sookie's eyes, nose, chin, neck, and cheeks.

She looked altogether different than she had early in life, but still, the same gray eyes stared out from every photo. Overall, the effect was pleasing. Sookie was an extremely attractive woman, tall and thin with shoulder-length red hair and a physique toned by years on the tennis courts, and then later, whatever the scalpel could offer.

Next in the row were more shots of Sookie and her dad, but with JFK, LBJ, Nixon, and Carter. Then, the photos' backgrounds changed, from out in the field with her dad to shots with the *Harry Todd* background behind her. There were Reagan, Bush Sr., Clinton, and George W. Bush, each standing with Sookie. Then there was an Obama event with Sookie in a formal gown along with the President and Harry Todd in tuxedoes at some sort of gala.

The rest of the wall was literally covered with photos of Sookie, with all sorts of celebrities, stars, and dignitaries, ranging from rock bands to ambassadors to screen legends and politicians.

Impressive.

Having given Hailey enough time to soak in all the photos and framed news and magazine articles about Sookie and *The Harry Todd Show*, the woman herself breezed into the room as if the timing wasn't intentional. Hailey briefly wondered if she pulled the same effect on every guest before making her entrance.

"*Hello*, Hailey!"

Hailey turned. Sookie was perfectly made up and her gleaming auburn hair had obviously just been blown out. She was tricked out like a twenty-year-old in $800 Christian Louboutin spike-heeled shoes with red soles. Hailey recognized the label on her "distressed" jeans and remembered seeing them priced at over $500 a pair. The ensemble was topped with a bright pink cashmere sweater that came just above her belly button. Even her nails were perfect, each one gently rounded on the tip and lacquered to match the pink cashmere.

Hailey stood up and extended her hand. Sookie held it lightly and briefly, her palm and fingers cool and dry to the touch.

"So! I finally get to meet the woman the *camera just loves*! You're absolutely wonderful! Harry *loves* you! Thank you for coming all the way out here . . . I hope the drive wasn't *too horrible* . . ."

"Oh, no. It wasn't bad at all. And I got lots of work done on the way."

"You worked in the car?"

"Oh, yes . . . I dictate patients' notes right into a little hand-held recorder. I take the information from entries I make during sessions, then send it to a transcription service. It comes back to me within a day or two, all neatly typed and ready for the patient's file."

"Oh, my. You're so . . ." Sookie paused, searching for the right word . . . "*industrious!*" She kept on a light smile and sat down gracefully on the deep sofa parallel to Hailey's seat. As Sookie sank into the sofa, Hailey took the cue and sat again in the chair facing both Sookie and the wall of Sookie photos. Suddenly it struck her that there wasn't a single picture of the woman's children on display. Somehow, Hailey couldn't imagine Sookie Downs ever being pregnant, but apparently she was, twice.

"How are your children?"

"Oh, they're wonderful! Just wonderful! They attend St. Pius private school. It's really the best out here, but I just hope they don't fill them up with all that *religion*! I don't want them to be freaks!"

Hailey was silent. Some of her happiest memories were those involving her little Methodist church back home. She'd practically grown up there, running up and down the halls, exploring the quiet sanctuary while her mom practiced away on the organ. Oblivious to Hailey's silence, Sookie went on. "You know, I just love your hair. Who does it? It looks so natural! I have mine touched up in the city . . . costs me a fortune."

Hailey opened her mouth to speak, but Sookie kept talking.

"Consuela . . . please bring out more hot water for Hailey." She directed her voice toward what Hailey presumed to be the kitchen area.

"You have a beautiful home, Sookie." While neither the interior nor the exterior was anything Hailey would have wanted for herself, it was . . . *big*. Big and formal.

"Oh . . . thank you, dear. *Architectural Digest* has featured it more than once. We just *love* it. Would you like a tour?"

"That would be great." Hailey followed along behind her hostess and headed toward the large staircase in the foyer. Climbing the stairs, Sookie went on.

"So you must be wondering why I brought you out to the house. We've really enjoyed having you on the show with Harry. You have such a . . ." Sookie searched for the right word . . . "*spark*! Such zest, let me say. And of course, the camera *loves* you, but that goes without saying. In fact, you look better on camera than you do in person."

Hailey paused. That sounded a lot like an insult.

"Oh, please take it the right way. In this business, it's a *huge compliment*."

But by the tone in Sookie's voice, Hailey still wasn't so sure.

"This is the children's quarters." Hailey had never actually known anyone who had "quarters."

Sookie walked rapidly down a hallway at the top of the stairs. Hailey heard her own cowboy boots clunking along in stark contrast to the staccato of Sookie's stiletto Louboutins against the gleaming wood floors. Her hostess then waved her right arm upward in a *Wheel of Fortune* gesture. Hailey looked in the general direction in which Sookie was pointing and saw a huge light-blue bedroom full of every conceivable toy known to man. There had to be forty stuffed animals sitting on a pale green sofa facing the foot of a painted blue double bed.

Standing at the door to the room, Hailey did a double-take. At the far edge of the sofa sat a little boy. Just as Hailey noticed him, he looked up, and they met gazes. For a moment, Hailey had mistaken his small form for one of the oversized stuffed toys.

"Hi. I'm Hailey."

The little boy just stared back through a pair of thick glasses, regarding Hailey with a steady gaze.

Sookie spoke over her shoulder as she continued down the hall, never slowing down. "Oh, that's Kyle. He always has his nose in a book. I keep telling him he needs some fresh air. I wish he was interested in sports. Here's Emily's bedroom. The decorator was fabulous! Even if I have to say it myself!"

Hailey still stood at the boy's door. He looked so lonely, sitting there clutching his book. He kept looking at Hailey, as if he wanted her to come in and play. Actually, she would much rather do that than continue the tour she was being given.

"Want to come with us, Kyle?" She gave him her gentlest smile.

The boy shook his head "no" and looked back down at his book. She paused another moment, but he never looked back up at her. Hailey trailed along behind Sookie again. Between the two bedrooms was another giant room, this one a bright-yellow playroom. Murals of various nursery rhymes were hand-painted on the walls. Each child's bedroom had a door opening into their mutual playroom.

Next was Emily's room. It was predictably pale-pink and done—or overdone would be the better word—in a princess motif. The girl's bed had a royal theme and a glittery, golden crown painted on the wall over its headboard, a large, capital "E" for Emily in the center of the child's fantasy coat-of-arms.

"She charged me thousands for the headboard, but there's nothing else like it out there. It's an original."

Anything Hailey could have said at that point would have either been an outright lie or a likely insult to Sookie's taste, so Hailey followed her own rule ... *when in doubt, say little and do less!*

Down a long hall and across a semi-formal reading area as large as Hailey's New York apartment, came yet another long hall. All the floors were covered in thick Oriental rugs. Even an amateur like Hailey could tell these were the real thing. Given their size, number, and quality, the rugs alone had to cost over a hundred grand.

They turned left toward the front of the mansion's façade and into a foyer that opened into Sookie's sleeping quarters.

There at the doorway, Hailey stopped in her tracks.

Sookie's bedroom was straight out of a 1940s Hollywood movie. A huge California king-size bed was the centerpiece of the room, adorned with a gorgeous custom-made pure, thick, beige, raw-silk duvet with lavish brocade trim around the bottom. It matched perfectly a brocade bed skirt peeking out from underneath the silk cover, so as not to offend anyone with a possible glance at the hardwood floor underneath the bed.

The pillow-show was in full swing in Sookie's bedroom. Her bed alone had to have twenty pillows of different sizes and shapes artfully arranged against the massive mahogany headboard. Above the bed was a floor-to-ceiling sheath of the same beige raw silk, twisted into a triangle, its point at the top. The upper tip of the silk triangle was secured to the wall by a large, rounded, mirrored medallion. Its facets caught the light in the room, casting tiny bright bits of light across the smooth floors and thick rugs in front of the bed.

There was a fireplace directly in front of the bed, about thirty feet away from its matching mahogany footboard. About twenty feet to the right of the bed was a sitting area with two love seats and a big cushioned chair, huddled around another fireplace. A highly embellished Louis XIV writing desk sat in a corner, as if Sookie were just about to put quill to paper. Photos in what looked to be sterling silver frames were carefully positioned on the writing desk.

"My. I've never seen a bedroom quite like it." At least Hailey was honest.

"Really? I just love it! It's so . . . romantic!"

Sookie led her across the bedroom to a closet that was at least the size of Hailey's family's living room back home in Georgia. For a closet, it was massive. What first struck Hailey was that it looked like an ad for California Closets. The closet was designed to look exactly like a high-end dressing room with a cushioned seating area and several full-view multi-paneled mirrors.

"Oh . . ." Sookie laughed girlishly ". . . my private dressing room for my clothes and shoe collection! It's designed exactly like a Gucci changing room I once visited in Paris! Isn't it *fabulous*? Julian just *hated* it!"

Was Hailey supposed to know who Julian was?

Hailey stopped briefly to examine Sookie's shoe collection. Once again, she'd never seen anything like it. There had to be hundreds of pairs of shoes, all stacked in lines. There were shoes in every color of the rainbow, and then some. They were perfectly preserved, each with a shoe tree inserted and a pink sachet cushion wedged down onto every sole. There were evening slippers, boots, stilettos . . . even some lined in mink from what Hailey could surmise. Hailey recognized some of the labels from fashion magazines. A single pair, Hailey knew, could cost over a thousand dollars, and there had to be two to three hundred of them.

"Julian . . . He's in yachts. That's my ex . . . but that's another story." Sookie now responded to Hailey's unspoken question. But Hailey wasn't about to touch that one with a ten-foot pole, though she had a feeling Sookie was going to tell her anyway.

She was right.

"He ruined my life and the lives of our children over some tramp from Barbados. She's in college, for Pete's sake . . . *college!* She's a *co-ed!*"

"Oh, dear . . ." It was all Hailey could get out before Sookie began a tirade about Julian, walking out of the room and assuming Hailey would trail along behind her.

And of course she did. What else could she do? Had she really traveled all the way out here to look at a ridiculous shoe collection?

Along the hallway were framed articles and news stories. Even if Sookie's name was only mentioned once in the entire article, her name was highlighted with yellow marker, and the article was set in an ornate frame. Many of the articles were in fact about Harry Todd and only mentioned Sookie as being his executive producer, yet they were all mounted and framed as if each and every article was about Sookie herself. Lighting inlaid flush with the ceiling shone down on the articles and photos.

Sookie turned left and started down a grand, curving set of stairs, covered in yet another thick runner. The hand railings, like the staircase Hailey had climbed up, were of rounded mahogany, shined to a dull sheen. They went back through the main foyer and down yet another staircase headed toward, as Sookie described it, her *absolutely fabulous wine cellar.*

By now, Hailey was pretty sure this was not the first time Sookie had given a tour of her home. Opening a tall door with a key hanging obviously around the doorknob, Sookie led Hailey down another wide set of stairs with the same mahogany rails on either side. The steps were steep and on the walls on both sides was an expansive display of more photos of Sookie's dad. Also hanging on the walls were various mementoes he'd brought back, obviously from time spent overseas in the military.

There were multiple shots of him in Burma, placing him in the Burma Campaign during World War Two.

Along the stairwell walls were animal horns of some sort, multiple black-and-white photos of Burma itself, postcards in frames, even a saber and its leather sheath encased in glass. One of the few color shots showed him posed, standing behind the wheel of a jeep wearing no shirt, deeply tanned, with a red-handled pistol stuck down the waist of his military fatigues. He must have been some dad. Whatever his fathering skills, his military prowess had helped catapult his daughter into the upper echelon of society and politics. Hence, her job at GNE.

What followed was nearly a full hour, an excruciating fifty minutes of Sookie waxing on about wine. As they trudged back up the stairs, Sookie finally came to the point.

"So, I was thinking . . . you must get terribly bored in your little psych practice down in the Village. All those patients, all their miserable problems, it must be awful! We'd love to have you join our show as a regular contributor . . . taking the police or prosecution side of course."

Hailey was stunned at her rudeness. But Sookie was apparently so extremely self-absorbed, she clearly didn't realize how insulting she truly was.

What a boor . . . was Hailey's first thought.

"Actually, they're neither miserable nor boring. They are all fairly wonderful people. I've grown very attached to them and it would be extremely difficult for me to leave them or even cut back on their sessions."

The guided tour of her mansion was clearly over. Apparently, it was time to get down to business. Sookie turned, quite clearly stunned someone wouldn't jump at the chance to appear regularly on *The Harry Todd Show.*

"But, darling, *you'd get paid.* Certainly another paycheck wouldn't hurt anything . . ."

Hailey looked around the monstrosity of a home Sookie held out on display. "I don't need the money that bad. And if you're suggesting that I get paid to take a certain position, even if it is the side of the state, my opinion is not for sale. But thank you so much for your kind offer. I'm extremely flattered, Sookie."

"But we could make you a *star. Don't you understand?* I could make you a TV star, Hailey." Sookie's gray eyes were widened and fixed on Hailey's face.

"Don't get me wrong, it's a lot of fun appearing on the show. But I don't want to peddle my opinions. I think we should just keep it as it is. When you need me, call me and I will do my very best to make it happen."

They were now standing exactly before the front door. Out of nowhere, Consuela appeared with Hailey's coat.

"Well, you certainly have your principles! But I'm not giving up so easily." Sookie's smile was fixed.

"Thank you for the tea and the lovely tour of your home. It's unique!" Hailey continued to try not to lie.

Sookie awkwardly leaned forward and gave a sort of air-kiss to the side of Hailey's head. An air-kiss was something Hailey would absolutely not do under any circumstances, so she just smiled again as best she could. Consuela ushered Hailey out. But, just before she made it down the front steps to the driveway, Hailey heard a loud crash on the other side of the front door, inside the foyer. It sounded like glass smashing.

"Little bitch! I can't believe she turned me down!" She heard Sookie yell it out, apparently to no one in particular. There were a few seconds of silence, followed by a door slamming somewhere in the bowels of the house.

Hailey looked up and saw Conseula at the corner of one of the front windows. She smiled apologetically at Hailey.

Hailey turned and made her way toward the limo, waiting there in Sookie's circular front driveway.

"Poor kids . . ." It was all Hailey could think. *"They don't have a chance . . ."*

IIIIIIIIIIIIIIIIIIIIIIIIIIIIIIIIIIIIIIIIIIIIIIIIIII **33** IIIIIIIIIIIIIIIIIIIIIIIII

MIKE WALKER OF *SNOOP* KICKED BACK IN HIS BRAND-NEW Longhorn. It was a Barcalounger power recliner with generous proportions and soft, rounded arms. They were the "motion furniture" specialists and every single one of their products either reclined, swiveled, rocked, glided, or had some special combo of moving features. Walker's Longhorn was spectacularly comfy and fully automated. After the fat paycheck from the Leather Stockton murder photos, he couldn't help but splurge.

He loved his Barcalounger. He rubbed the soft curved arm with his fingertips. He'd always wanted one but could never really afford it. Now he had one, and she was a beauty!

His wife, Marjorie, had objected at first, based purely on aesthetics. But this baby was so swank, you'd never even know it was a recliner! He even chose the nailhead-trimmed, large-scale Vintage option with a deep-tufted back and turned legs with a stained cherry finish. Fashionable and functional!

What's not to love?

The Longhorn purred into three different positions with absolutely no effort at all by using a control panel tucked between the arm and the seat cushion. After discussing it in-depth with the Barcalounger sales rep, he even went all the way and went for the optional leather-seat cushion upgrade. And it was all top-grain leather . . . He could tell.

The Leather Stockton murder photos had been viewed all around the world and *Snoop* was having a field day, going after any and all outlets that used any of the pictures without their consent. That meant even more money for *Snoop*.

Walker told his bosses he'd used old info from a longtime source, a doorman at the L' Hermitage Park Towers, where Fallon Malone lived, to get inside her apartment and get even more murder photos. Years ago, the same doorman had spilled to Walker about the servants' entrance to Malone's place. The maid's door wasn't caught on the hall's surveillance camera because it used a kitchen entrance that opened up into the high-rise's common stairwell.

Walker had used the info to catch a big-time movie director, who happened to be "happily married" at the time, sneaking in and out of Malone's apartment. That was back when Walker was a young hotshot who'd do anything for a story. Now that he was older, a few gray hairs had popped up, but he cured that with his Just for Men hair color. "Darkest Brown" was his shade . . . Even his wife didn't know about it.

Now all these years later, Walker knew exactly how to get photos from inside Malone's apartment without his minion turning up on grainy surveillance video. And nothing had changed. Malone still left her spare key under a ficus in the hallway like she used to. Hadden was in and out in less than fifteen minutes. Piece of cake.

Hadden's shots netted Walker another fifty grand from *Snoop*. They were stunned Walker got the first photos of Stockton still dead on the murder scene, plus the gurney shots were primo. As to the shots of Prentiss Love dead in her SUV, he told his bosses he was tailing Love 24/7 in order to catch her boozing, hopefully at a public bar. He'd said he had to have a private eye stay on her day and night due to her unusual drinking habits. That's how Walker explained the fresh shots of Love behind the yoga studio. He even got them before the *Post*.

The bigs at *Snoop* never bothered to ask too many questions. They obviously understood he had a true journalist's integrity.

Naturally, he had to pay Hadden out of his own paycheck, but other than that, the three murders had pulled him out of the red and put him not just in the black, but in the pink. The good thing about Hadden was he always showed up pretty quickly no matter how late he had been out snookered the night before, and importantly, he never asked questions. Walker liked that in a photog. Just snap the shot and keep your yap shut.

And now, there were even rumors that if Walker came through with another big story get, he could be in the running to topple the mag's executive editor, who'd been in place nearly fifteen years. That was a record at *Snoop*.

The TV was on low, one of the morning shows droning on in the background. Same old, same old. Weather, Washington, women's health, and a stupid cooking segment.

Walker pressed the hidden automated control panel stuffed conveniently between the chair's rounded arm and the seat cushion. The Longhorn made a gentle humming sound as it reclined him nearly prone. He *loved* this thing.

Where would the story go next? Walker was about to doze off there in the Longhorn with the TV on low. He could see *Snoop's* headline now . . . *"Madman Serial Killer Stalks Silver Screen Beauties."* Wait . . . no . . . the headline should be *"Who Dies Next?"*

Brilliant!

Snoop hadn't had a good Death Watch in over two years. They could use the Death Watch headline and place red-hot actresses underneath, suggesting they, too, had been labeled for murder! It would be in all caps across the top of the mag. He'd have the sole byline.

The news. Man, what a business.

||||||||||||||||||||||||||||||||||||||||||||||||||| **34** |||||||||||||||||||||||||

I T WAS HOT AND DARK AND THE SHEETS WERE TWISTED AROUND Hailey's waist like ropes. There at her bedroom door stood a figure, partially shrouded behind the door frame, only the left half of the body, head to toe, visible. The intruder was silent, seemingly content for the moment just to stare across the room at her as she lay sleeping.

Although the intruder made no sound or movement whatsoever, the feeling she was not alone woke Hailey with a start, and she sat straight up in the bed, instinctively reaching for the .38 she kept in the shoulder holster hanging on the bedpost beside her pillow. She tried her best to peer through the dark of the room, lit only by dim, milky moonlight filtering in from behind the bedroom window shade.

Hailey saw her standing there. Hayden Krasinski. She stood staring without blinking. Her face was pale white but blue around the mouth and her eyes bulged out of the sockets as a result of a strangling death. Her neck looked shrunken halfway between her jaw and her clavicle, the result of a powerful ligature strangulation.

On the front center of the old hooded sweatshirt she wore so often was a huge blossom of dark red blood that had seeped through her clothes, the result of a searing, double-pronged stab wound to the back. She had been left to die over a year ago, face-down in slushy ice of a Manhattan back alley, and blood from the stab wound that punctured her lungs, staining not only her T-shirt and sweatshirt but the ice lying beneath her.

And here she was at 1 a.m. in Hailey's apartment, high above the city. How did she get in? Hailey had locked up tight and set the alarm, a new feature in her apartment she'd added after Atlanta defense attorney Matt Leonard had come after her. Not to mention his client, Clint Burrell Cruise. Hailey convinced a jury to send him to death row for the murders of eleven young female prostitutes, but between a bad cop and a bad judge, the case was reversed on appeal and Cruise walked. He was last spotted in New York City.

Hayden just stared, her blue lips twisted into a curve. First smiling, she then opened her mouth to speak, but at that precise moment, a gush of blood came pouring out, a result of the piercing of the lungs, the blood involuntarily pushing upward through the throat and out the mouth. Hayden looked shocked, alarmed, afraid when the blood poured out of her mouth and downward onto her sweatshirt, leaving a wide, deep-red trail from the neck of the sweatshirt down.

She looked up from her shirt to Hailey and began to scream . . . a bloodcurdling scream. Hailey leaped out of the bed and ran toward the door, to Hayden, and just as she got there . . . Hayden dematerialized, simply vanishing, particle by particle, into the dark of the apartment.

Hailey stood rooted to the floor, not moving an inch. Her mouth seemed locked open, her heart beating wildly in her chest, sweat pouring down the front and back of her neck and into the white T-shirt she'd worn to bed that night.

It took several minutes for Hailey to understand what had happened.

It was a dream. It had to be a dream. Hayden and Melissa, both her longtime patients, both murdered in a plot to discredit and frame Hailey Dean. Matt Leonard had, in fact, murdered the eleventh hooker and let his own client, Clint Burrell Cruise, take the fall. Only Hailey had access to all the files and all the facts of the murders, and although she might have failed to put together the pieces, Leonard believed otherwise.

So he'd come after her. Her clients were the collateral damage. It was all Hailey's fault, or at least she believed it was, on nights like these. This wasn't the first time she'd had nightmares where she was visited by Hayden or Melissa, although she always prayed each visit would be the last.

There was no way she could go to sleep now, icy chill replacing the heated spikes flashing through her body just moments ago. She trudged toward the kitchen, .38 held down and close to her right side. She wanted to check the apartment . . . just to make sure.

The lights were still burning brightly all across Manhattan, and the dark sky rose above it. There were a million points of light sprinkled across the high-rises and office buildings. The Crown Building, Chrysler Building, Citigroup Center's sloping peak, and of course, the spike of the Empire State Building, were all lit up in the night for tourists and residents alike to adore. Looking down onto the city somehow gave her comfort tonight.

Hailey switched on an eye of her gas stove and put on the kettle to brew a cup of tea. Heading back to her bedroom, she picked up the notebook she was keeping on the serial killings . . . the "murdered D-Listers," as Kolker called them.

Once in her bedroom, she settled back into her bed with her hot tea, propping herself up against pillows. Opening her notebook, she clicked on her bedroom TV. A few days before, she'd spotted Malone's golf pro at a charity event Leather Stockton also attended. Not much, but it was something. Earlier that evening, she'd been reviewing clips again for Kolker. They were a mélange of various appearances the three women had made. Hailey stared at the screen, sipping her tea. Her blue pen rested in the center fold of the notebook, inviting her to start work.

She watched the first thirty minutes of one of the Prentiss Love DVDs without making a single note. There were award speeches, red carpet events, interviews about various projects, especially her gig on *Celebrity Closets.*

The next DVD was of Prentiss's funeral. It was pure Hollywood. Several blowup head shots that must have each stood eight feet tall hung by nearly invisible strands from the top of the auditorium where the public service was held. They were stunning. The place was packed with special friends and family sitting in reserved seating up front.

They'd all filed in one by one or in little knots of two or three. There was a little bit of a stir when Prentiss's yoga instructor came in with his boyfriend. Apparently, all her entourage knew she had a huge crush on him and had invested quite a bit of money in his studio as well as his plan to build a "yoga empire." No one, not even Prentiss, knew he had a boyfriend. No doubt Prentiss Love's investment decisions would have been far different if she had known that tiny detail. An argument broke out between one of Prentiss's girlfriends and the yoga instructor, and the boyfriend intervened.

It wasn't pretty.

Anyway, after that bumpy start, the service got under way. Hailey watched the whole thing intently, but found nothing of merit to report back.

She got up and headed to the kitchen to heat up more water. Brushing past her doorjamb, Hailey got a chill. In her mind's eye, Hayden had just been standing there. Hailey's eyes burned and tears welled up in them.

Had it all been her fault? Would they have been alive if it hadn't been for their connection to her, Hailey Dean?

Climbing back into bed, she clicked the remote to start the next DVD, then took a sip of tea, holding the cup with both hands. She could hear the wind blowing outside her window high up in the sky.

The old, familiar ache was spreading from her chest up to her throat, and it felt like she'd swallowed a huge lump. No matter how hard she tried to get away from the pain of Will's murder, it just kept coming back. As a psychologist, her mind told her that the new wave of grief she was feeling was simply an aftershock from the murders of Hayden and Melissa, her patients.

Her heart didn't care why, it just hurt.

Leaving Atlanta and her career as a felony prosecutor had seemed like such a great idea at the time, and for a few years here in Manhattan, it actually seemed to have worked. But now, not only was the pain over her patients' deaths dredging up the old grief from Will's death, she was alone . . . completely alone. Again.

Hailey swallowed hard to try to get rid of the lump in her throat. She wiped her eyes and face, now wet with tears, with the edge of the bed sheet, and took a sip from the cup of tea she'd been clutching.

She stood up. Walking over to her bedroom closet, she opened it with one hand, still holding the tea in the other. She carefully set it down on the closet floor. There in the corner. There it was. Hailey just looked at the white cardboard box. She didn't need to open it to see what was inside. She just wanted to look and see that the box was still there. She knew what was inside.

Her wedding dress, still beautiful and pristine, still made of silk the color of champagne. With the gown would be her veil, both gently folded away between layers of crinkly tissue paper, and placed in the white cardboard box. She'd never sealed the box, just in case she wanted to take them out and look at them just once in a while. But she never let herself do that. It would be too risky.

It always seemed to end up there in the corner of her closet, not far away at all. The white cardboard box had taken on its own identity over the years, and although she never lifted the lid, she carried it like a treasure . . . a reminder of another life and another time, a fresh-faced girl who grew old too young.

She used every ounce of self-control to step away from the closet, to shift her thoughts away from Will and Melissa and Hayden, and attempted to focus on the stack of DVDs still left to sort through. She headed back to the bed and the remote, rewinding the part that had already played while she was thinking of Will, and not Prentiss Love, Leather Stockton, or Fallon Malone.

She started with the raw footage of the *Harry Todd* shoot. Tony had gotten all of it for her, including the parts that never made air. She saw the tour of Fallon's apartment, and it was just as beautiful and jaw-dropping as the day Hailey saw it herself. Fallon spent a lot of time standing on the front staircase landing, directly in front of the towering Penley portrait of herself. It was magnificent and Fallon worked it to her best advantage.

Then there was a segment where Sookie positioned Fallon in the kitchen as if the actress were whipping up a homemade dish. Trying their best to get a flattering shot of Malone, Hailey glimpsed Tony Russo and Sookie several times in the background hovering over the shoot. But after much fidgeting with lighting and positioning and such, the segment fell flat when Fallon admitted she had no idea how to light her gas stove.

The viewers weren't stupid. Fallon Malone was not the Betty Crocker type. The minutes dragged by and Hailey learned nothing new. The wind was howling outside, screaming up and down the avenues, and gusting off the street all the way up to Hailey's apartment windows.

She pushed a different DVD into the player and tried her best to focus on Prentiss Love as she thanked a group, mostly men, at what appeared to be a memorabilia event. Love seemed entirely genuine when she spoke out to the crowd. There was no doubt in Hailey's mind that she loved her fans.

They may have been the only ones who really loved her back. Prentiss had been notoriously unlucky in love.

She was absolutely beautiful, standing there at a mike stand almost as tall as she was, dressed in a gorgeous white halter dress, her hair falling in long waves around her heart-shaped face.

Multiple posters of Prentiss hung behind her . . . shots from her latest CDs, publicity photos, you name it. In each one she was more stunning than in the last. Beside her sat a desk at which she could sit and sign photos, autograph books or ticket stubs, or basically whatever memento with which the fan approached her. The footage was date-stamped nearly two years before a single bullet seared through Prentiss Love's mouth and face.

The camera panned out at the enthusiastic crowd, most of whom looked as if they were hanging on her every word. They were mostly twenty- to thirty-something-year-old white males. They all looked, lovesick, at the object of their desire, Prentiss Love.

It was then that she saw it. The camera operator had gone out into the crowd when Prentiss stopped speaking and made herself comfortable at the desk to start the signings. One guy after the next spoke into the camera about how he'd always loved Prentiss Love and couldn't wait to get her signature. Each one, three in all, had a story about Love that was basically just a variation on the same theme . . . adoration. But it was there, in the background.

A man standing on the outskirts of the crowd, not really noticing the camera at all, staring intently up at the stage where Prentiss Love sat happily signing away, schmoozing with her fans for $25 an autograph.

Although he wasn't speaking into the camera himself, there was no mistaking him, standing there. He wasn't in the line for an autograph, just standing at a distance, never averting his gaze from Prentiss Love.

It was Scott Anderson.

RANCIS LAY BELLY-DOWN ON THE LIVING ROOM FLOOR BEHIND his mother's sofa. Right now, it was the only thing between him and the Feds at his front door.

The rug at the foot of the sofa smelled of something . . . what was it? He'd never been quite this close to the fake Oriental rug before, certainly not close enough to get a good whiff of it. *What was it?*

From his vantage point, looking through the legs of the sofa and across the floor, Francis had a perfect view of a tiny slice of light between the floor and the front door. Staring hard, he was convinced he detected movement outside on the front porch.

Then he heard it. Muffled voices. The jig was up. The Feds were on his front porch. His mother had always said this would happen. Crazy old bat.

What would he tell them? He'd used various computers all over town, actually, all over the country to stay in touch with his lady loves. And he'd used so many different names. He had multiple screen names and all of them only knew him as "Jonathon." He'd never divulged his real name. Names didn't matter to Francis . . . Only feelings mattered.

The multiple screen names should throw the Feds off to some degree . . . but Francis knew he'd left a track a mile wide. Flowers, gifts, candy, Valentine's Day cards, birthday cards, Christmas gifts, you name it . . . It could all be traced back to Francis, or at least to Jonathon, anyway. They'd nail him. He knew they would.

Cards, flowers, candy . . . What did that prove? *Nothing!*

Without the murder weapon, they had nothing! Nothing but evidence that Francis was in love . . . granted, with several different women . . . but in love all the same. What would they bring before a jury? A Valentine card?

Francis thought of his guns . . . all of them stashed away over at Crestlawn Sacred Grounds . . . just yards away from his mother's plot. They'd never find them. Without that, absent an eyewitness or a confession, what would they have?

Although the murders were nothing but a blurry vision in Francis's mind, actually more of a big, black blank, he was absolutely sure he would not have been so careless as to have eyewitnesses. And no way were the Feds getting a confession out of him.

In fact, he'd already turned down and dog-eared the number to his old public defender's office in the yellow pages. He'd even gone so far as to write the *Miranda* warnings in ink on the inside of his left arm from just beneath his wrist nearly to the inside bend of his elbow.

He'd also written the lawyer's number directly beneath *Miranda* in case the Feds used the phone book to beat him. The Feds were famous for beating people with phone books.

The voices rose on the porch.

Didn't they have to knock first?

Probably not. Francis was pretty sure that good manners were not mandated in the Constitution. They may even have gotten a "no-knock" proviso in his arrest warrant so they could beat the door down with a battering ram if they wanted to. Nothing could stop them.

Francis just had to stay strong and not confess. Stay calm. Stay cool. Keep it together.

Plus, in all reality . . . How could he give a confession? He couldn't remember anything.

It was all his damn mother's fault. If she hadn't forced, or tricked, all the mind-altering drugs into his system, he wouldn't be having blackout spells in the first place. Much less days upon days where he couldn't remember a thing.

How the hell did he put all those miles on his car? Francis had figured it out the night before. There were nearly exactly enough miles on his mom's Saturn to prove he'd driven to each one of the murder locations. And it would only take a cursory look at his Chevron gas card to prove he'd visited them all numerous times in the past.

Plus, Francis had cashed his disability checks from the government at banks all around the country. So, bottom line, he'd definitely left a paper trail connecting him to countless locations where the ladies had been for one reason or another.

Concerts, appearances, walks on the red carpet, Francis had been to all of them. Granted, he'd always stayed in the background; he wasn't there to upstage them in their moments of glory. He was just there for support.

He'd even managed to get several shots of himself with each of the ladies. True, they were usually far in the background while he held his cell phone camera out in front of him, taking the shot at arm's length, but they were in the photos together for sure. Those photos were some of Francis's most sacred treasures, next to Leather Stockton's underwear of course, and he'd be damned if he'd erase them off his cell phone memory, Feds or no Feds.

Some things a man just had to fight for.

Oh, yes. His mother was probably looking down at him right now, shaking her finger disapprovingly. She'd always told him women would get him in trouble. With him lying on the floor hiding behind the sofa so the Feds wouldn't pick up on even the slightest movement inside the house, Francis just knew that she'd be saying, *"See? I told you so!"*

Just then, the spooks on the front porch slipped something under Francis's front door.

Oh, hell! What was it? Was it some type of psychotropic drug that would make him talk and tell all about his relationships with the three dead celebrities?

Francis could definitely detect a strange odor. There was no way out now. Wasn't it illegal to use sodium pentothal to get the truth out of a suspect? Wasn't that only in injectable form? Could it be reduced to a powder? Was that what they'd slipped under his front door? If so, were they all outside on the front porch wearing gas masks so they, themselves, would not be affected by the truth-telling powder . . . just Francis alone?

It was suddenly stronger. He felt dizzy. Damn the Feds to hell and back.

Francis crawled around the edge of the sofa. From across the expanse of the living room floor to the front door, maybe twenty feet or so, he spied the packet slipped under the front door. Straining his eyes in the dim light filtering in from outside, he could barely make it out.

He inched closer. The floor was hard against his elbows as he made his way completely around the sofa.

It wasn't sodium pentothal after all. It was a thin copy of both *Awake!* and *The Watchtower* magazines, religious weeklies distributed liberally by the Jehovah's Witnesses spreading the word.

Why wouldn't they leave him alone?

Then all at once it hit him. He recognized the smell. It was emanating from the carpet at the foot of the sofa from years and years of exposure to odors wafting out of the kitchen.

It was his mother's favorite dish, veal and peppers.

Oh, how he hated her. Her *and* her damn veal and peppers.

CASSIE LAKE WAS IN TOWN. THE SINGING STAR HAD SHOT TO stardom as a young girl singing with her sisters and brother. The siblings were talented all right, but there was no doubt she was the star. With long frosty hair tumbling over her shoulders, she had a beautiful voice and a squeaky-clean reputation as a devout Catholic. She was a teetotaler who married young and had four children almost immediately, one after the next.

Then, of course, came the eventual divorce, weight gain, admissions to depression and secret drinking in the linen closet of her Miami mansion. She was now on the wagon, and an AA advocate, and about to kick off a Vegas show that would reunite her with her two sisters and brother on the stage again after nearly fifteen years.

She flew into the city solely to perform with the Rockettes in their Christmas Spectacular at Radio City Music Hall and absolutely *nothing would do* but for Tony Russo to get her booked on *The Harry Todd Show* while she was here in town. That way, they wouldn't even have to pay for a flight!

He planned to pitch it to her as a way to pump up sales for her new book on getting clean and sober. He'd also promised she could relentlessly plug her singing performance with the Rockettes and her new Vegas act set to kick off in the New Year.

The morning shows would probably get her first; they always did because of their huge numbers. But Tony could probably convince her to do *Harry*. His numbers were right up there and with *Harry*, it would be Cassie Lake for the hour! Not the three or four minutes the morning shows could offer between hair and makeup segments, and news briefs glossing over pain and suffering around the world.

But, of course, what would *really* happen once she got on the show, is that Harry would ask her all about her alcohol and drug dependency, her recent breakdown over her divorce, and the sixty pounds she managed to pack on in one year.

Tony could hardly wait.

Tony was crouched down against the cold, waiting outside Radio City Music Hall in order to catch her when she came in to practice. The grandeur of the building was totally lost on him, but every single thing about it was larger than life. It was one of the largest indoor theaters in the world, and the marquee alone covered a city block. The walls and ceiling were sweeping arches, with the Great Stage mounted on hydraulic elevators for special effects. A fourth elevator raised the orchestra, and a shimmering gold stage curtain teamed with the "Mighty Wurlitzer" organ to thrill audiences. Spiraling fountains of water, clouds, fog, even thunder, magically appeared on stage thanks to an elaborate system sourcing steam from a special Con Edison plant.

None of it meant a thing to Tony Russo. He had to take off his winter gloves and reach deep into his coat pocket every time his cell buzzed, which was constantly. Sookie was dialing his cell phone every few minutes to find out if he'd made contact with Cassie yet.

He looked across the street at a little Greek diner, where he saw people scurrying in and out with steaming cups of coffee. Usually, he'd only drink Starbucks, a grande half-caf, dry, skim cappuccino with extra foam, to be specific, but under these circumstances, he'd take anything.

If Russo had a dime for every black limo that drove past Radio City, he'd be a millionaire. Every time one of the cars barely slowed down, he jumped up out of the crouch position and lurched toward it in his attempt to get to Cassie before her driver got around the car to open her door. She'd of course be on the curb side of the car with the driver on the opposite side. So, bottom line, Tony would definitely have time on his side, *if* and only if he spotted her car in time.

After texting Sookie for the millionth time that he was in fact in position to catch Lake, the moment came. A white stretch with heavily darkened windows pulled up. As its wheels grazed the curb, his hackles raised and a tingle went down his body. He was a booker to the core . . . He knew deep in his gut. It was her.

Tony made a lunge for it and just as he hoped, the driver had unlocked the back doors from the fingertip controls on the driver's arm-side panel before he got out of the car to walk around and open the door for his passenger. In the thirty seconds it took the guy to open his door, put his feet on the pavement, close his door, and make his way around to her door, Tony had already opened the door and handed her a bouquet of two dozen yellow roses, her favorite.

He did his research.

With the other hand, and flashing his most sincere smile, Tony whipped open an umbrella to hold over her head.

"Miss Lake, Tony Russo, chief booker for *The Harry Todd Show.* I'm such a huge fan, all the way back to the old days and *The Lake Family Hour.* I just had to deliver these flowers myself. I always loved you in those bell-bottoms, and remember that furry vest you wore that time? Can I get you some Throat Coat tea? I know it's your favorite . . . I just happened to bring a box of it with me just in case this cold weather bothered your throat . . ."

How he got it all out in one gulp was a mystery. He had his GNE ID security badge hanging around his neck and on prominent display so she would see he was legit and wouldn't be scared away.

Tony held out his hand just as the driver made it around to the back edge of the stretch, clearly intent on throwing his chubby little body to the curb. He could do it, too. The driver was a hulk.

Tony concentrated on Cassie's face and forced himself to keep smiling and not turn away from her to look at the burly man to his left.

Just as the driver grabbed Tony by his upper left arm, Cassie reached up from the depths of the cushioned limo seat and took Tony's right hand.

"You, Mr. Russo, are a saint. And yes, I'd *love* some Throat Coat. I can't believe you remember that furry vest! And I adore Harry's show! I haven't seen him since his big birthday bash . . . How *is* he?"

He had her.

Taking her hand and tucking it into his left elbow, he held the umbrella over her head as they made it into Radio City. Entering through the front doors, Tony adroitly closed up the umbrella and quickly but naturally slipped his elbow back in its earlier position entwined with Cassie's elbow. Winding through the twists and turns of RCMH, they made it down a long hallway back to Cassie's dressing room. She opened the door with a key and clicked on all the lights. It was a warm and cozy room, made attractive by rose-colored walls and floor lamps on either side of a sofa pushed against the longest wall of the room.

As if he had been working out of the dressing room for months, Tony immediately made his way across the room, opened a cabinet over a tiny microwave, and pulled down two coffee mugs, which he then filled with spring water from a jug dispenser standing in the corner of the room. Dunking two tea bags of Throat Coat into the cups, he set the microwave and turned back to Cassie, who was sitting in a chair before her stage mirror, light bulbs surrounding it now turned on.

"Light cream and one sugar as I recall?" Tony Russo was pretty good at what he did. That would be sucking up, of course. He kept every known detail about anyone who had ever appeared on *The Harry Todd Show* in his desktop. He could access most of the desktop information from his BlackBerry; hence, he knew exactly how Cassie Lake took her tea the last time she did *The Harry Todd Show*, which was precisely four years and two months before. He'd checked it that morning before he set out for RCMH and then checked it again as he sat crouched, waiting in the snow under the marquee outside the building.

Stirring with a plastic spoon he found in a plastic cup beside the microwave, he brought over the tea and set it down in front of her.

"Hey! Even under these lights and no makeup, you look great!"

She smiled at him. It was genuine. Of all the celebs that had ever been on *The Harry Todd Show*, she had been one of the most real, the most sincere. All the good works, the family values, all the talk of God in Heaven and clean living, she really meant it. Falling off the wagon was a huge personal defeat for her.

Lake was for real.

Tony almost hated to set her up for the show.

"Cassie, you *have* to come on with Harry to push your book! It's *fantastic*! *I loved it!* It's going to help so many people!" His voice took on its usual whining, pleading tone. He looked straight into the mirror and into her eyes.

It was truly incredible that he could look so sincere, even knowing Harry would likely bring up all the sordid details of her divorce, her bulimia, her drinking problem, and of course, suggest she had been a hypocrite preaching family values all those years before all the time she spent alone with a bottle of Scotch in the linen closet came to light.

"Tony Russo, you know you make it really hard to say no . . . but with my schedule here . . . you know . . . the Radio City show, the book signings . . ."

"Then, don't! Don't say no! We'll tape around your schedule! Whatever you want! And Harry would *love* to bring out a baby grand and have you sing at the end of the show . . . whatever you want! The viewers will *love it* and the book will sell like hot-cakes!"

"It would mean a lot to me . . . Harry's show really sells the books . . ."

"That's exactly right! It does! Showcasing your book on Harry's show could put you back on the *New York Times* top ten list! Wouldn't that be great?"

"It really would . . ."

"Oh yes! I forgot to ask you! How are the children? They're growing so much! Any of them following in Mommy's footsteps? Anybody want to be a singer? Please tell me you have pictures with you!" Tony really was shameless.

"I do, as a matter of fact! I carry a little album in my makeup suitcase! Let's sit on the sofa and go through them. Want some more hot tea?"

"I'd love some!"

Tony Russo was in Heaven. Snuggled together on the sofa, the two drank hot Throat Coat while Tony listened to stories about each of her four children, their braces, their schools, their manners good and bad, how they'd handled the divorce . . . by the time they'd gone through the huge binder of photos . . . Cassie Lake's appearance on *The Harry Todd Show* was a lock.

It was like taking candy . . . from a baby. He couldn't wait to call Sookie.

"IT WENT GREAT!"

"How can you *say that*?" Cassie Lake was in tears as she left the studio.

Tony was right beside her, his arm again entwined in hers. Actually, it hadn't been bad at all, since Harry was, basically, in his starstruck, sucking-up mode.

But the few questions he'd read off his yellow cue cards regarding her divorce, her admitted alcoholism, and her eating disorder had really upset her. She'd addressed it all in her book, but talking about it unnerved her. It wasn't until Harry read one of the last questions about how the divorce devastated her two-year-old that she really broke down.

Tony almost felt bad.

"You *emoted*! There's nothing wrong with that! America will love you for it!"

"I thought we were just going to talk about the Radio City show and the book . . . I didn't think it would be so . . . *personal*. I mean the questions about my relationship with my ex-husband were bad enough, but the ones about the *children* . . ." Cassie couldn't finish her sentence for sobbing.

Tony offered Kleenex.

"Well, I think America is going to love you even more for this interview. And the photos you shared with us, the ones from the photo album . . . They were just *so wonderful*!"

"You know that's the first time I've ever let them all be pictured on TV . . ."

"And we are so grateful!"

Tony walked her all the way to the limo, helped her in, handed her a wad of Kleenex, and slammed the door. He waved half-heartedly at the car as it eased away from the curb and into traffic. Whew. That was done. The taping was over, and Lake was safely, albeit in tears, headed to LaGuardia for the next outbound flight to L.A., and the show was in the can. And it would be a hit . . . the numbers would be huge!

Walking back through GNE's thick glass doors, he felt a presence fall in step with him. It was Sookie. She'd actually driven to meet with Lake beforehand and watch the taping from the control room.

"Brilliant! *Brilliant!*" I can't believe you got her! And she started crying! She could hardly make it through that horrible song you got her to sing! Did you write up Harry's cue cards? I know he didn't think of those questions himself! And the photos!!! How'd you *ever* get them? She never shows her kids on air!"

"I learned it all from you, Sookie! All from you! Want to have lunch?"

He almost hated to ask. Every lunch in the city was followed by a shopping spree of some sort and Tony would end up being bullied by Sookie into buying her things again.

"No . . . I can't. I'm super-pressed for time."

"You're coming back for the Cassie Lake edits?"

"No way. You'll have to handle it. I've got an appointment I can't rearrange. It'll go into the evening and I doubt I'll be on cell. Can't you handle it on your own? Oh, and did you pick up that stuff for me from the drugstore?"

"Sure did!" Tony had worked all his life to be in the world of TV. It had been his dream since he was a little boy watching sitcoms alone on the floor of his family's den. TV was wonderful, magical . . . a whole different world from the one he lived in. Being part of it made him feel wonderful, too. And if he had to run errands and pick up laundry and get Sookie's lotions and potions at the drugstore . . . so be it. He never complained.

"I have the receipt." He knew she wouldn't expect him to expense it.

"Oh, you cover it, I don't have any cash. Anyway, Cassie Lake, *what a get!* It'll go straight on the air!"

Tony walked her all the way to the glass doors and then out onto the sidewalk. He looked around for her usual driver in a sea of black limos, but then, a candy-apple-red Porsche Boxster Spyder pulled up to the curb. At the wheel was defense attorney Derek Jacobs.

"Hi, Sookie! You look fabulous today! Nobody wears a miniskirt like Sookie Downs. I've said it a million times." Charm just oozed out of Jacobs.

"Hi, Tony." Jacobs added it as an afterthought, and the effect wasn't lost on Tony Russo.

Sookie's face visibly brightened. "Hi, Derek! What are you doing at GNE?"

"I had a meeting around the corner. Want a ride?"

"Great!"

"Hop in."

The two were off in a moment and Tony Russo watched as the Porsche's red taillights disappeared around the corner. The celebration over the Cassie Lake booking certainly was short-lived.

But, hey, what was Tony expecting? A medal? Sookie was always all about the next show. In a couple of days, she'd forget all about how he was hunched down in the snow for hours waiting for Lake to show up. She'd forget all about how he had to sweet-talk her and hold her hand and look at countless family photos of her kids crammed into a thick album . . . how he sought out, bought, and made her special Throat Coat tea. It would just be another show, another rating.

Tony's BlackBerry buzzed. It was an e-mail alert from the show's editorial producer. A guy had just thrown battery acid onto his ex inside a cell phone store in New Jersey. A show producer was on her way to the hospital.

His heart raced and he nearly clicked his heels together as he practically ran back inside and headed for the elevators.

||||||||||||||||||||||||||||||||||||||||||||||||||||||| 38 |||||||||||||||||||||||||

"SO, YOU'VE GOT A BULLET MATCH ON ALL THREE: STOCKTON, Love, and Malone? And you've got Scott Anderson connected to all three, and lying about it. Why would he lie about it if he were on the up-and-up? There's got to be *something* there . . ."

Hailey stood at the widest window of her apartment, the one facing the West Side. The sun shone down brightly on them through low-hanging clouds, making the buildings sparkle in the morning light.

"Exactly," Kolker said. "Why lie unless there's something more nefarious involved other than just a fling? From what we can tell, he's had plenty of those. Just usually not with dead girls."

"Other than knowing them, and actually having an affair with one of them, Malone, what else do we have? Let's see, he was the last person to see Malone alive, a history of alleged violence on women, a wife and a girlfriend. We have him lying about Stockton at Pebble Beach, *that we know of*; there may have been more between them . . . Then we've got him basically stalking Prentiss Love at the Memorabilia Fair at the Javits Center."

"I can't believe you found that clip, Hailey. That's incredible. You basically found all the hard evidence we've got on him."

"No way. The best thing so far is him on the Malone security cam. Thank Heaven they hadn't taped over it already."

"They would have, but they just hadn't re-set the camera yet. We lucked out. And, true, the security cam is great evidence, but I can't make a case out of a couple of house calls. I know you stayed up late sifting through it all."

Hailey thought for a split second and decided to leave out that she'd woken up with her heart pounding from another nightmare about Hayden's and Melissa's murders. "I was just lucky when I found it."

"You always say that. Look, Hailey, thanks. I really mean it."

"No problem. I kind of miss working cases. So tell me about Scott Anderson. He's good-looking, I can see that from the video. But what's he all about?"

"Lives alone . . ."

"Of course. They usually do . . ." Hailey was automatically beginning to profile him in her mind. White male, early thirties, college educated, single again after a divorce, split on bad terms, living alone, house pretty much bare, based on what Kolker had told her earlier . . .

The buzzer rang and Hailey left the window and walked over to the intercom linking her apartment to the front desk.

"What's up, Ricky?" She spoke clearly and directly into the intercom on her kitchen wall.

"Hailey, you order food?"

"Yeah. I got a hungry cop up here."

"Okay. I'll send him up."

"Thanks, Ricky. I ordered you a pastrami. Get it out."

"You're the best, Hailey. Thanks."

"And there's a cherry seltzer water in there too for you."

"Thanks, Hailey."

Hailey smiled, picturing Ricky diving into the brown paper delivery bag from the diner across the street.

She looked at Kolker. He was making a disgusted face.

"What's wrong?"

"Ugh! Cherry seltzer?" He looked like he chewed poison.

"Yes, Ricky went on a diet and exercise kick a while back. After a few weeks, he stopped the diet and exercise. The only thing that stuck was low-cal seltzer water!"

They both laughed again and Hailey answered the door, signed for the food, and brought it back to the kitchen to lay it out on the kitchen counter.

"So even if you prove he knew all three, or at least knew two and stalked one, had an affair with one of them, maybe two, what else do you have? Although I gotta tell you, that's pretty strong circumstantial evidence linking him to all three women . . ." Hailey pulled bottled waters out of the bottom of her fridge.

"That's right. I mean, come on, what's the likelihood one guy is going to be linked to all three dead women? Practically zero."

"Don't know and don't care. Statistics are not allowed in as evidence. I only care about what I can put before a jury. What about prints?"

"Nothing. Nada. Zilch. This guy knows what he's doing. I brought in the best, and nothing."

"Get the outside of the car? Up around the window? The doors at the pool house? The light switch in the pool house? The chair where Stockton was sitting?"

"And then some."

"What about the doors and light switches at Malone's place?"

"Done."

"Any glasses out in the kitchen you could check for prints or DNA?" Hailey was grasping at straws now.

"The place was clean as a whistle. Turns out the maid had just come the day before. We looked over the whole apartment, bedroom and bathrooms included, for glasses. Matches, cigarette butts, you name it."

"Bathroom door handles and light switches? Just in case he went in here? Was her bed made?"

"Checked all the bathrooms and, no, her bed was not made. But it was only unmade on one side, the side she slept on."

"How could you tell?"

"Glass of wine there from the night before on the bedside table and a stack of *Variety* magazines. Looks like Fallon Mallone was seriously looking for a comeback project."

"Hmm." Hailey's mind was racing. "How about the gun? The murder weapon?"

"Well, you'd think the killer would dispose of it somewhere close to the crime like they always do. The fact that he hasn't makes me think more murders are coming."

"Me, too. But this guy will never get rid of that gun. If he hasn't already tossed it, he'll keep using it. It's one of his signatures. He's used it in all three. The gun matters to him. Or else he'd probably ditch it." Hailey watched as Kolker dug into his turkey sandwich. She unfolded her own and began pulling out some of the lettuce that was piled on so thick she could hardly bite the thing.

She really didn't even want the sandwich. What she really wanted, she couldn't have. Right now, anyway. She wanted collard greens. The kind from home.

Hailey had been to all the great New York City restaurants and, yes, they were truly great. Italian, sushi, Chinese, seafood, American cuisine, vegetarian, raw, she'd done it all. But nowhere could she find collard greens

That very morning, she'd tried to get some in a grocery store. Of course, the produce clerk had to ask his boss what they were. When the manager showed up in the vegetable and fruit corner of

D'Agostino's grocery store, he said they rarely got them due to lack of demand.

The manager then sagely advised she try the pet shop around the corner. When Hailey threw him a puzzled look, he responded, "Don't you have a pet iguana?" Turns out, the only reason New Yorkers ever buy the stinky greens is so they can chop them up and feed them raw to the little lizards who, apparently, would kill for a plate of collards just like Hailey would.

Good to know.

Thus, the turkey sandwich. "So, bullet match, no prints. Cell phone, text, or e-mail links?"

"One link other than Scott Anderson. Some kid by the name of Jonathon Kent. He apparently wrote all three, but from what we can tell from his e-mails, he's a high school kid with major crushes on the women he sees on TV. Seems pretty harmless. But it's odd he was writing all three."

"That is strange. Almost as odd as Anderson being connected to all three. What's this kid writing about?" Hailey lived by the rule that there were no coincidences in criminal law.

"Oh, let's see." He took another bite and washed it down with water. "School, classes, movies he's seen. Asks a lot about what they're doing, where they're going, always seems to have caught their last appearance, even rents their stuff and watches it and comments. Asks all sorts of questions about movies, sets, co-stars, whether they date anyone, you know, the typical things a high school kid would ask a female TV star."

"I don't think it's 'typical' that a high school kid is in close touch with one female TV star, let alone three female TV stars. And for your information, Malone was a screen star. A has-been, true, but a screen star nonetheless."

"True." Kolker wolfed down the last bite of sandwich and kind of looked around like he was still hungry.

"I made a lemon pie last night. Want some?"

"You cook? I had no idea!"

"Yes, I do, pretty much whenever I'm hungry," she joked back.

"But New York is a take-out and delivery town!"

"I know. But sometimes I just want some home cooking. Anyway, do you want the pie?"

"I never turn down lemon meringue pie."

Hailey went to the fridge and pulled it out. She handed him a plate, a knife, and a fork. Only a tiny sliver was missing from the pie.

"You sure didn't eat much of it."

"My eyes were bigger than my stomach. It's all yours. Back to Jonathon Kent." Hailey saw Kent as much more of a possibility than Kolker did.

"Have you been able to locate this kid Jonathon through his texts? They've got to come straight from a phone. A cell phone has to be listed to *somebody*. Right?" Hailey was trying to think of everything.

Kolker nodded. "Done. He usually e-mails, but when he does text, we think it's from a disposable phone or a phone card."

"Oh, Kolker, that's going to be hard to run down. There's a million ways to beat a text ID. You can always sign in to Yahoo! or AIM with a fake name, and text whoever you want, and it's free. Or you can use a different SIM card. And the disposable cell phones are a whole other animal. You don't have to sign a contract or have a credit card, and they're next to impossible to track. Even terrorists use them to detonate bombs, much less some high school kid. Much less if he's spoofing the number. Then we're really in trouble."

Hailey thought for moment before she went on. "He's either awfully smart or he's cheap and doesn't want to pay monthly rates for a cell phone. But you've started locating where the cell phones and cards were sold, right?"

"Right. Louisiana."

"Hmm. If this 'kid' is down in Louisiana, that makes him a lot less of a suspect than Anderson, who's right here under our noses. So other than school and classes, what else does he talk about?"

"His dog, Ringo."

"Ringo?"

"Yep. It's a Maltese. And it has a heart condition."

"Okay. He talks about a Maltese dog named Ringo with a heart condition. Anything else? Like about visiting?"

"Not that we've seen. Yet, that is. These e-mails go way back. At least two years or so."

"*Two years?* Now that's a dedicated fan! Or a stalker, wouldn't you say?"

"Good point. It's just that the content of all the e-mails and texts are so benign, we don't see Jonathon Kent as much of a threat."

"Kolker, *please.* Everybody's a suspect right now."

"Okay, you're right. I'll step up the heat on Jonathon Kent. Poor kid. He's got Hailey Dean after him now."

"Thank you very much." She said it with a smile. "Tea or coffee? I'm having some."

"Sure."

"Which one? Tea or coffee?"

"Whatever you're having. Thanks, Hailey."

"Okay. So it's a no-go on the cell phone. What about e-mail? That should be easy. It's amazing to me that in this day and age, people think their true identity and location are hidden. You'd have to live under a rock not to know that the IP address of the computer used to send the e-mail can be uncovered and traced. It can lead directly to a person. Your people know about the IP addresses, right? Every computer connected to the Internet has, or shares, an IP address. You know, a series of four numbers from zero to 255, separated by dots. Every time this so-called 'kid' e-mails, his IP's included on the header."

"But you can block an IP. It's interesting you'd bring that up. He must not have a home computer. He's sent e-mails from all over. His IPs are in California, New Jersey, Louisiana, even Connecticut, and some from right here in the city. We think he is in the school band and they travel."

"*The school band? You're kidding me!* He's been right here in the city?"

"Just once or twice, and it wasn't around the time of the shootings. That we know of."

Hailey gave him a look of incredulity. Jonathon Kent was turning into a real suspect.

Kolker went on. "And we know he's using free e-mail accounts: Hotmail, Yahoo, and Hushmail, so there's no credit card linking back to an account payment, like with AOL."

"Where did he set up the account? They're usually set up at home or work. Then you'd have the IP from when the account was first set up . . . right?"

"Right. But again, I don't think this kid has a home computer. He uses several different accounts, and they've all been set up at computers in Internet cafés, libraries, you know, public . . . where hundreds of people use the same computer every day."

"Different cities?"

"Different cities."

"Hmm, that's some band he's in." She said it pointedly. Kolker started to look embarrassed. Hailey was right.

"By the way, what instrument?"

"What do you mean, what instrument?"

"What instrument does he play in the school band? French horn? Trumpet? Tuba?"

Kolker stopped short. He looked straight at her for a moment. "You know, he never said."

"He tells the dead women he travels with the school band, but he doesn't bother to tell them what instrument? There's something wrong, Kolker. Don't you see it?"

"*Hailey, he's a high school kid.* He's not the killer! Listen, come over to the station and read the e-mails. You'll see for yourself. This is not the killer."

"How do I know who he is? Until I see him with my own two eyes, I don't know who, *or what*, he is. A kid in the school band or some freak . . . *We don't know, Kolker.*"

Kolker sighed. He suddenly looked tired. "You know what? I think Anderson's our man. But just to make you happy, I'll put the heat on the guys to find Kent. Okay? Happy?"

"Happy. Look, you asked me to help, right?"

"Right. And Hailey, we need to look under every stone. I learned the hard way. The day I arrested you and you punched me, I deserved it. I was wrong. I don't want to make the same mistake again, with Anderson. Just promise me one thing."

"What?"

"No fat lip this time?"

Hailey thought for a few moments.

"I can't promise anything right now. Let's just see who Jonathon Kent turns out to be. There may be another fat lip on the way, depending on who Jonathon Kent really is."

"Okay. At least this time, I've been warned."

THE BUSBOY LOOKED TWICE. THE NIGHT AIR WAS COOL FOR NORTH Hollywood and the alley behind San Pietro's Italian restaurant was pretty dark this time of night.

There was once a streetlight illuminating the area surrounding the restaurant's back door, but it had burned out long ago and was never replaced. Didn't really need it though; the only reason he came out the restaurant's back door this late was to toss garbage into the alley for pickup the next morning. He dropped a cardboard box full of trash from the kitchen, then shoved it closer to the metal Dumpster with his foot.

Billy Ryan was addicted to cars. His bedroom at home at his mom and dad's house was cluttered with stacks and stacks of *Motor Trend, Car and Driver, Automobile,* and *Road & Track.* As long as he worked and stayed in school part-time, his mom didn't mind.

Looking out and down the alley, he spotted what he believed to be the car of his dreams, still sitting where he'd seen it earlier that evening. He glanced down at his watch. The car had been there since around 8 p.m., he was pretty sure, and now it was nearly midnight. He couldn't see the driver's side; it was next to the alley's other wall, but earlier, a guy had been sitting in the passenger seat, so Billy didn't want to get too close.

San Pietro's closed that night as usual at 11 p.m. on the dot. Why anybody would want to eat dinner that late was beyond him, but whatever. The Hollywood types ate at all hours of the day and night.

Anyway, the car.

She was a dream. It was one of the brand-new Mercedes CLS550s. It was one of the most expensive cars in the world. He'd only read about them in magazines. It was the new color too,

Alpine Rain Metallic. This baby was *tricked out* . . . somebody had taste.

But who would leave a car like this alone in an alleyway? It was just begging to be stolen! The rims alone were worth a couple of thousand. They were definitely specialty rims. He was at a distance, but if his eyes didn't fail him, he was spotting four Revolver Chrome Wheel Rims. Wait . . . were they the Hyper Silvers or the ADR Emotions? Either way, they were worth thousands.

He wanted a closer look.

He was dying to check out the car. Instinctively looking both ways first, he stepped out and walked across and down the alley. The car shone in the moonlight and Billy Ryan was thrilled. That is, until he got a little closer.

Less than a foot away from the car, Billy doubled over and began vomiting violently. When he managed to stand up straight again, it didn't last. Waves of nausea swept over him and the smell of his own puke hit his nostrils. He couldn't stop retching.

Stumbling back from the car, he wiped his hands on the sides of his pants, leaving streaks of vomit on his pants legs. Reaching into his back pocket, he pulled out his cell phone and punched in the digits.

A female voice answered on the other end.

"You gotta hurry. There's a woman, she's dead. Her face is shot off."

Billy Ryan managed to give 911 Dispatch his location just before another bout of retching began. Rescue arrived within about fifteen minutes, and LAPD was right on their heels.

The senior cops jumped from the squad car and hurried across the alleyway to the dead body, the car now opened by the rescue team. One of them went straight to Ryan, who was now sitting in the alley, his legs sprawled out in front of him, his back leaned up against the restaurant's rear brick wall beside the trash cans. He was still puking, but much less violently. The cop didn't seem to care about Billy puking.

"You the kid that found the body? What did the passenger look like?"

"I don't know ... All I seen was dark hair, maybe brown or black. I couldn't really make it out." Billy wiped vomit from his chin.

"What did the man look like? You had to see something ... white, black, tall, short, mustache, beard?"

"All I saw was he had black hair. I think he might have been white, I don't know. I saw his head from behind. I didn't want to get too close, you know how rich people are about their cars ..."

The cop looked disgusted. No help at all. He glanced down the alley at the others.

There was no use trying to resuscitate her. Half her head was gone. Blood lay in a congealed pool in the car seat and there was a spray of blood on the driver's side front window. Whoever shot her had either reached in the passenger side door or ... had been sitting in the car with her.

The rookie stayed in the squad car and ran the tag plate to the Mercedes. He should have known the dead girl was Cassie Lake. The tag was custom.

It read "I SING."

I T WAS 6:30 P.M. HAILEY WOULD SOON PACK HER THINGS, LOCK UP her little office overlooking the gingkos in the brownstone's back courtyard, and catch the Number 6 train uptown to her apartment. If she was lucky, the wind would let up in time for a jog along the East River.

There had been a nineteen-year-old with an eating disorder who binged and purged nearly every day. She obsessively took notes on each bite she put into her mouth and, late at night while her parents were sleeping, she'd gorge herself on anything she could find. Whole cakes, an entire rotisserie chicken, large meat-lover's pizzas called in to be delivered while the girl waited at the curb in front of her folks' house, dressed in nothing but her robe and pajamas.

Then came a young Wall Street executive dealing with the loss of his younger sister in a car crash. He was overcome with guilt that he had worked so many hours the last few years and never made much time for seeing his little sister other than on holidays, if then. Now he'd never have the chance.

Hailey ended the workday with a forty-year-old woman who'd just caught her live-in cheating, again. She was trying to rationalize that the entire thing was somehow her fault and find a way to stay in the four-year relationship, holding out for marriage.

"Lori, you have to confront what's happening." Hailey had tried her best to encourage her to face the fear of starting over.

"But I'm afraid I'll end up old and alone! Aren't you?"

Hailey knew better than to bring her own loneliness into the mix. She didn't want the session to degenerate into a sob-fest. Years had passed since Will's murder just before their wedding and still, Hailey had no interest in another relationship.

She'd dated plenty, but it never felt right, and she always ended up breaking it off and hurting someone's feelings. She'd concluded that maybe it was better just to be alone, and was actually pretty happy with that. She'd just let down the dentist in the office downstairs, Adam Springhurst.

They'd had nearly two dozen dates, movies, dancing, dinners, Broadway, music . . . They were all great. But for Hailey, it just wasn't going anywhere. After every date, even if it had been wonderful, she felt even lonelier for Will than she had before she went out. It just wasn't worth it, and she felt something akin to relief when she opened up a tiny bit to Adam about why she wanted to call it off. *It truly wasn't about him.*

Adam took it well and was still friendly and upbeat when they bumped into each other around the neighborhood where they shared office space in the same renovated brownstone. Thank goodness.

Lori went on. "It's been four years. I've been with Reggie *four* years."

"Lori, before you go down that road, let's re-examine. You say you've had suspicions since year two. You've busted him twice before. There's a pattern. Can't you see it's not about you? Do you really believe that somehow you can change him?"

"But, Hailey, don't you know the likelihood of a woman my age getting married this late in life? It's more likely I'll be killed by a terrorist!" Lori dissolved into another fit of sobs.

Hailey came out of her chair and handed Lori another stack of Kleenex. "Lori, I'd love to get my hands on whoever started that saying. I've heard it so much, I've actually researched it. It is absolutely not true."

Lori stopped sobbing, for a moment. Hailey seized the opportunity and kept talking in a low, calm voice. "It's been thrown around as fact for so long, people actually *believe* it now. I think it came from some idiot at *Newsweek*. Probably a twenty-three-year-old man! It all springs from the theory that the more education a woman has, the longer she waits to marry. That's it . . . the whole she-bang."

"Hailey, *I have a master's and a Ph.D.!* I'm definitely dying alone!"

Hailey wisely left out the stats that women born in the late 1950s and still single at thirty had only a 20 percent chance of marriage, and the numbers only got worse with age.

"No! Don't say that! Haven't you heard of self-fulfilling prophecy?" Even though the likelihood of terrorist murder was *much lower,* Hailey decided that any talk of death by terrorists was not a good move at that particular moment.

"No need to make a rash decision; it's just that Reggie has a pattern, which suggests it *will happen again.* Come on, men are everywhere out there, especially for someone who's smart and beautiful . . . and that would be *you.*"

Lori's self-esteem had taken another beating. But for the moment, she seemed to be calming down a tiny bit. "Come into the kitchen and let's make some coffee. You want regular or decaf?"

"Decaf. I'm too upset for caffeine."

Hailey was busy at the coffee maker and had her back to Lori. Turning around with two cups of hot coffee, she glanced up at the tiny TV sitting centered on top of the fridge. She kept it on the news networks; right now, it was on GNE, the volume on mute.

Hailey froze. A giant red banner covered nearly the entire bottom third of the screen. America's sweetheart, Cassie Lake, was found murdered in a North Hollywood alley behind an Italian restaurant. Gunshot wound to the head. Right now, the screen was showing close-up video of her rehearsing for one of her Vegas comeback concerts.

A chill went down Hailey's spine. Could it be the same killer? No . . . no way. This guy only killed in and around Manhattan. Cassie was found dead in her car in Hollywood. But the similarities were striking. Cassie was a woman, like the other shooting victims. She was also a celebrity. She was beautiful, white, female, and as of recently, single, too. She was a D-Lister like the others, trying to make a comeback.

Lori carried her cup of coffee back into the den and set it down on a mosaic coaster on the edge of an armchair table between the sofa and Hailey's worn, wing-backed chair, a floor lamp at its side. Lori reached over to gather her coat, hat, and scarf off the back of the sofa, where she'd laid them when she first came in.

Setting down her own mug, Hailey helped Lori with her coat and gave her a reassuring hug.

"You are going to know when the time is right to make a change in your life. You're already thinking it over, you'll see." After another tight hug, Hailey closed the door gently behind Lori and heard her light steps going down the stairway.

Hailey immediately reached into the pocket of the soft, amber-colored sweater she was wearing that day to pull out her Black-Berry. She would not allow herself to even glance at it when she was with a client, and was very rarely tempted to do so. She saw its red light blinking, indicating messages or calls. One quick glance said it all . . . three calls from Kolker. It could only mean one thing.

The bullet matched.

Hailey instinctively went to the window and dialed Kolker's cell, staring out at the tops of the gingko trees waving in the chilly wind there in the back courtyard.

He picked up. "Have you heard?"

"Just saw it on TV. Does the bullet match?"

"Oh, yeah. It matches. We sent shots of the markings by e-mail and they've already confirmed out in LA. It's him. He followed her all the way from New York to California just to put a bullet in her head. Why didn't he do it while she was here? Whatever, it doesn't matter. Hailey, I hardly know where to go next with this thing."

"We'll figure it out." Hailey tried to sound confident.

"I'm out of time. We've got a monster on our hands and I'm no closer to an arrest than I was last week. Can't find the ex-husband. Her kids are just finding out now. The grandparents are telling them. Man, I'd sure hate to be in that house right now. Can you imagine?"

Hailey didn't bother to point out that yes, she could imagine the grief and pain and shock of losing someone you love dearly. Kolker had to feel the same way about his sister, Susannah.

"Kolker, it's going to be awful, and it won't end today. Those children have a lifetime of having to cope with this ahead of them. I hate it too, so much."

"I feel sick in my gut. If I'd already cracked this thing, Cassie would be alive right now . . . home with her kids." Hailey heard his voice break. "But this time, Hailey, he screwed up. He got messy. He finally got spotted. The busboy says it was a man with dark hair, and by the dimensions of the car seat, about five-ten to six feet tall."

"Get the LA CSI stat. They've got to get a hair sample. It may be the only way to place the passenger, who's likely the killer. You said she was shot from the passenger's side, right? Not through the driver's-side window, like Prentiss Love?"

"Right, from the passenger's side."

"Stippling on the skin?"

"Correct. Stippling."

Upon firing the bullet, hot gases from exploding gunpowder, and microscopic metal fragments from the bullet and the gun barrel themselves propel out of the muzzle. In contact range wounds, hot gases and particulate matter blast into the skin along with the bullet, charring the skin and depositing along the wound track or on the skin itself, leaving a lacerated appearance.

"Well then, if there's stippling, it had to be somebody in the car. Gunshot residue only shows up when the shooter's less than three feet, usually, that is. And stippling says it's a contact wound, gun to skin. But anyway, we gotta get the hair. If there's a nucleus, a root, we can get full-on DNA. Even if there's just a shaft, we can go for mitochondrial DNA. They have to comb that passenger side of the car."

"I'll put in a call when we hang up."

"Oh, and have you thought about sending the ME out? That young guy with the long ponytail . . . Emory what's-his-name? Wouldn't hurt to have a little consistency on all of the post-mortems. He can just assist if the local LA coroner objects . . ."

"I thought of that. As luck would have it, he's actually already in LA, sightseeing or something. Now there's a coincidence."

"That *is* great timing on his part. You know, Kolker, the DNA off the hair, if it's there, could make the case. Although we've gotta have somebody to *match it to* . . ."

"I know, it's a great lead, but if I could have only moved a little faster . . . we could've saved Cassie Lake . . . those kids of hers . . ."

"Kolker, stop. You can't do this. A lot is riding on your shoulders right now. You're not responsible for this, the killer is. Look, come get me. I'm at the office. You can get me faster in a squad car than it would take a cab to get me uptown to you. Wait, no, I'll grab the subway. I'll meet you at Lex and Fifty-first in twenty minutes. Okay?"

"I'm on my way, Hailey."

"Wait! Don't hang up . . . Where's Anderson . . . Scott Anderson? He's definitely got dark hair."

"We can't find him." A knot formed at the pit of Hailey's stomach.

"What about his car?" Her mind was ticking through all the possibilites.

"Still looking. Tried home, work, last known girlfriend's place . . . nothing yet."

"Have you thought of LaGuardia?"

"Patrol cars on the way right now."

"JFK and Newark?"

"Done." His voice was clipped.

"What about the Westchester County Airport? He lives a lot closer to that one . . . Right?"

"You got me. I'll send somebody up there right now."

"Okay. See you in twenty. Same car?"

"Right. Unmarked."

They both clicked off without the unneeded pleasantries of formal goodbyes. Hailey felt a sense of urgency as she grabbed her coat out of the closet situated in the foyer of her little office suite. She locked the door behind her and, holding her hat and scarf in her hand, took off down the stairs, not even pausing to wrap the scarf around her neck against the wind.

"ACTUALLY, NO, YOU DON'T HAVE TO BEG." HAILEY'S CELL PHONE was perched on top of a stack of homicide investigative reports and set on speaker mode. Hailey kept reading files but talked in the cell phone's general direction.

"What? I can't hear you." Tony Russo practically yelled it into the phone. It was a good thing Hailey had her cell on speaker and, consequently, it was several inches away from her head . . . and eardrums.

"I must have the worst reception in the world. You know you'd think cell phones would give you great reception in Manhattan. I mean, it *is* the capital of the world, right? But no, instead of being the best . . . It's absolutely the worst."

Hailey didn't have the energy to commiserate on the tragedy of bad cell reception. Years of dead bodies, crime scenes, and victims' families had taught her plenty of lessons about what things were worth complaining about, and in her mind, bad cell reception wasn't one of them.

"And this is exactly why Sookie should have thrown so much money at you that you'd have no choice but to go on the show's payroll. That way, I wouldn't have to beg you every time there's a crime and justice story and we'd have you locked in. It would be your *job*, you'd *have* to come in. Then I wouldn't be on this horrible cell phone with its horrible reception."

Tony had talked himself in a circle and lost his train of thought. "What was I saying, anyway?"

"I don't know." Hailey turned a page and looked at the LA Medical examiner's detailed drawing of the Cassie Lake murder scene.

The ME investigators typically did a diagram complete with measurements down to the foot and inch . . . the length and width of the alley, how far the car was parked from the wall, how far it was from the nearest light, details that could become important at trial.

It seemed the car could have easily been parked much farther down the alleyway so as not to have been detected so soon. The body's evidence suggested Cassie had only been dead a few hours.

Had the killer wanted her body to be found when it was, at San Pietro's closing time? Eleven p.m. on the West Coast? But this time, he got sloppy; he was possibly spotted, at least from behind. The best evidence would be tracking down the passenger, believed to be a white male with dark hair, five feet ten to six feet tall, based on where his head was positioned in the passenger's seat. That was, of course, according to the busboy.

Tony piped in. "Oh, yeah. I remember. I was saying I could have sworn I heard you say I didn't have to beg you onto the show this time."

"Your phone is fine and so is the reception. You don't have to beg. I am just sick about Cassie Lake. I want to address the killer directly and Harry Todd's show, as ridiculous as I think he is, will actually give me that opportunity. I've got a very strong feeling the killer's soaking in every single detail about him that hits the airwaves."

"You're going to send a message? To the killer? On *The Harry Todd Show*?" Tony was thrilled, of course. His mind was racing . . . what was the best headline for the lower third of the screen to maximize its sensational appeal? Of course . . . *Message to Killer!* Short, sweet, and scary! He *loved* it!

"Yes. I am. That he will be caught and when he is, he will be looking at the California death penalty. He could get by with time behind bars as long as he stalks and murders defenseless women in New York, but California's a whole different story. California's not afraid to give the death penalty; it ranks right up there with Texas and Florida. So he's made a big, big mistake. When he sees the needle, maybe he'll remember the faces of the women he murdered and the children he left behind without a mother."

Tony was struck. Hailey was for real. She really meant what she said and that was rare in the TV business. Now, if he could only get her to say all that on-air.

"But Tony, it's way past time for your taping. How will you get the Lake murder on the air?"

"We're trying to track down Noel Fryer right now. We want to go live at eleven tonight. I've been trying to run him down for three hours. Anyway, I can go to his number two if I have to. Really, Sookie should be dealing with this but she pushed it off on me.

Probably better that way anyway. Look, where are you? Can you come now?"

"I'm at the Midtown North; I'll grab a cab. I want to go get some coffee first."

"Okay. See you!" They clicked off.

Hailey unfolded her coat, hat, and bag and headed toward the precinct's old elevator. Waiting for its doors to open up and take her down to ground level, Hailey looked down at the old, tile floor. It was worn and yellowed. Oh, the stories it could tell if only it could speak . . . all the killers, thugs, and thieves this hall had seen, along with crime fighters dating back decades.

Out of the elevator, across the precinct lobby, and onto the street outside, the cold, fresh air was bracing, but it felt good after poring through the Cassie Lake case file. Hailey wanted to go for a run out in the cold night air right then and there, but she'd agreed to head across town to GNE for the late-night live shoot.

Traffic was light in the city for a change, and with the cab driver darting this way and that between cars, they pulled up at GNE headquarters in minutes. She paid the cabbie and turned toward the glass front.

There in the lobby, standing in front of the long security desk, was Tony Russo, hunched over his BlackBerry. A closer look revealed he had one BlackBerry wedged between the top of his left shoulder and his ear, his neck crooked downward to keep it in place. In both hands, he was feverishly working another one, thumbing messages with all the speed the two short inner digits could muster.

Even though he'd come down to secure her onto the set ASAP, he didn't notice when Hailey walked in, and looked up only when Hailey touched him on the shoulder.

"Holding up okay?" She knew he'd been working nonstop putting together the Cassie live show that night. Due to the angle of his neck, Tony gave an abbreviated nod of "yes," but didn't stop talking into his shoulder where the BlackBerry was pinned in place. He did, however, pause to hand Hailey a two-page synopsis of the night's show he'd left sitting beside him on top of the security desk. Hailey looked down at that night's show guests.

Russo had managed to cobble together quite a cast of characters for the show: Cassie's family priest; her aunt; reporters out in LA, no doubt standing by at the alleyway where she'd been murdered; Hailey to explain the investigation and criminal law; Derek Jacobs to repeatedly admonish everyone that the killer was presumed innocent; and, believe it or not, Billy Ryan, the busboy who found Cassie's dead body.

Hailey was surprised the state's eyewitness was telling his story before the trial, but there was no legal way to stop him. His appearance on *The Harry Todd Show* would definitely be fodder for cross-examination at trial, much less if he sold his story to the tabloids. The tabs had been the ruin of many a Hollywood witness after they'd sold their stories or photos, having made money off a crime. Juries don't like someone making money off murder.

Still talking to somebody on the other end about getting a satellite truck into the alley behind San Pietro's out in LA, Tony nudged her toward the elevators and up they went. As Tony still worked the phone, trying to arrange wedging a fat satellite truck into a narrow alley behind a restaurant two thousand miles away, Hailey looked up at the two flat-screen TVs flush against the elevator's wood-paneled walls.

At that precise moment, an ad for *The Harry Todd Show* flashed across the screen. It showed Harry and Cassie sitting across from each other there at his desk in her last interview before her murder. Then it flashed to her singing at the end of the show, which then dissolved into a video of the alley with her car parked in it, surrounded by police, blue lights swirling atop squad cars, and yellow crime-scene tape across one end of the alleyway.

The elevator doors opened and the two made their way down a maze of hallways to a darkened control room that looked down on the *Harry Todd* set. The control room was in chaos, in preparation for the live show set to start in just over an hour. The show could be taped, making it an easy job to edit out all of Harry's snafus. But tonight was live; they couldn't afford any errors. A show producer was back in Harry's dressing room at that very moment trying to tutor him on the facts as best he could. If he'd just stick to his cue cards, everything would be fine.

"Hold on just a minute, Hailey, and I'll take you to your studio. I just need to check the banner."

"Okay." Hailey stood back against the wall and watched staffers rushing by, their arms full of stacks of papers, carts of video, and steaming cups of coffee. The volume in the room suddenly lowered and Hailey turned back toward one of the control room's doors just in time to see Sookie Downs enter, arms crossed over a clipboard full of show notes she held to her chest.

She looked perfect as usual. Makeup, purple stilettos to match a deep burgundy miniskirt paired with a pale lavender silk blouse . . . it was all impeccable. Her hair, usually blown out long and perfectly trimmed, was pulled back in a sleek ponytail hanging just below her shoulders.

Sookie spotted Hailey and immediately made a path to her. "Hello, dear. How *are* you? Excited about the live show tonight?" Sookie always put the emphasis on *are*, as if speaking to someone who had been extremely ill.

Hailey extended a hand and Sookie held out her own. Looking down, Hailey spotted a thin line of dirt under all ten of Sookie's nails. Sookie Downs . . . dirt? Did she garden? She loved plants? "Thank you for inviting me on. Sookie . . . What happened to your nails? They're always so perfect . . . Do you garden too?" Hailey nodded toward Sookie's nails.

Sookie looked down and smiled. "Yes, as a matter of fact I do! I was planting daisies out in back of the house. I love them. Gardening takes my mind off stories like this awful case. Poor Cassie Lake."

"I know, I feel so bad for her children." Hailey realized this was the first time the two had discovered a single thing in common. Gardening . . . plants . . . the outdoors . . . maybe Sookie wasn't the plastic Barbie Hailey had first thought, after all.

"Poor things, they must be devastated." Sookie's tone had gone flat . . . almost bored, and at the same that she spoke, she was scanning the room. "Has anyone seen Noel? Noel Fryer? I've turned the building upside down looking for him. He's always hovering when we go live, so irritating, but the one time you need him . . ."

Sookie, looking annoyed, didn't finish the sentence, letting it just hang there. A couple of the producers looked up to shake their heads "no," then promptly returned to what they were doing.

"Tony, quick, call GNE security. He called from home earlier. I'll bet you anything he's locked himself in his condo again. Let's keep police out of it. He's becoming a laughingstock. Let GNE security handle it. Tony, get Einst Schlager on the phone. Last I heard, he was in Bahrain installing a new security system in the palace. Good luck. Bye, Hailey, I'll see you on the show."

With a quick toothy smile, she turned and left through the same door she had entered. Sookie left a cloud of perfume behind her, hanging there in the control room even after the door was closed. It smelled expensive.

ALMOST IMMEDIATELY AFTER THE CONTROL ROOM DOOR SWUNG closed, Tony poked his head back through it and motioned to Hailey to follow him. Heading down to her tiny "studio," he could hardly contain himself.

"Hailey, you just don't know. Tonight is huge for us. Sookie even showed up! And she's been AWOL with her boyfriend since the taping yesterday! When she shows up to work, you know it's big! If we get the numbers I think we will, we may go from day-time talk to a live nightly broadcast! It'll be huge!"

"I thought you said you were already huge."

"And it can't go wrong. With the interview we just did with Cassie yesterday . . . I mean, the timing! . . ."

"You told me you were already huge before," Hailey repeated. "And that you loved daytime."

"Oh. We *are* huge. But we can be huge-er. Can you hold this while I unlock the door?" Tony handed her a thick stack of show prep papers arranging satellites, studio times, commercial breaks timed down to the exact second, segment topics, and guests' names and satellite locations.

He pushed the studio door open. "Here, sit there in front of the *Harry Todd* background. They'll be in in just a few minutes to tweak your lights. Remember, Harry just *loves* it when you fight with him."

"Right." Hailey knew better. It was only too clear how much Harry Todd hated being challenged on-air. The only people that loved it when she contradicted the host were Tony and Sookie. They referred to it as "fireworks."

No one ever came to adjust the lights shining up from the foot of her chair and onto her face, but Hailey heard the show's theme music start up, and they were live, lights tweaked or not. The music melted into a long video montage of Cassie singing at various locales, then dissolved into a reporter track about the murder, and video of her Mercedes parked there in the restaurant's back alleyway.

The montage ended with still shots of *Snoop*'s front-page story. It had just hit the newsstands in the last hour. How they got the shot so quickly and got it on a cover was a mystery, but it was in full color, a long lens shot from a distance showing police huddled around Cassie's Mercedes, the EMTs standing by helplessly, and Billy Ryan sitting back against the wall.

Hailey wondered briefly how the heck *Snoop* got there before the scene was even processed, but before she could finish her thought, Tony came in her ear and told her to smile.

She gave Tony a withering glare in response. There was nothing to smile about. Just at that moment, the camera flashed to her. She saw her own angry face on the camera in front of her, but before she could assume a more neutral expression, the shot of her was over. Todd threw the first question to a reporter, who gave all the details—all the details known by the public, that is.

Hailey listened carefully. She glanced down at her notes in the darkened studio. Instead of her own notes, she saw the words "Dark Chocolate" and "Intense Red Copper Shimmer." *What?*

Hailey took a second look. She still had Tony's notes on top of her stack of research. Rather than her handwritten comments on the facts of the murder, there was a Xerox copy of a drugstore receipt for pantyhose, hand lotion, and hair dye. One look and she realized she was still holding Tony's notes, now intermingled with her own.

At that precise moment, of course, Todd fired a question at Hailey. "Why pick a public alleyway for a murder, Hailey Dean?"

From her peripheral vision, Hailey could see her own face on the screen and responded without the benefit of any notes. "I find it highly unusual, Harry . . . highly unusual. Yes, it was a darkened alley; yes, apparently no one witnessed the crime so it was isolated to that extent, but the killer had to know the car . . . and the body of Cassie Lake . . . would be found in a matter of hours. It's almost as if he wanted her to be found."

So far, no one had mentioned the caliber of the bullet or the fact that the busboy told cops a dark-haired male was in the passenger seat of Cassie's Mercedes around 8 p.m. Had those facts managed to remain known to the police only?

No. Todd then bounced from the reporter's set-up to the busboy, who promptly blurted out there was a dark-haired man in Cassie's car in the hours before her murder. Harry Todd didn't dwell on the car's passenger, apparently not digesting its import, but went straight on to ask the busboy to describe, in detail, what Cassie Lake looked like with half her face blown off.

Hailey winced. She prayed none of Cassie's family was watching tonight. Billy Ryan, clearly coached by one of the show producers, gave a description of the dead body in graphic detail. Tony Russo must be dancing a jig in the control room right now.

The music geared up underneath the segment's remaining conversation, and Todd looked into the camera conspiratorially and said, "When we come back, Cassie's private, family priest is with us, a prime time exclusive!"

"Prime time exclusive? Is eleven p.m. considered prime time?" Hailey knew little about television scheduling, but was curious. It was the first question she asked into her lapel mike to Tony during the break.

"Don't be so technical. It doesn't matter and the viewers don't know. You need to smile."

"About Cassie Lake's murder? Hey, pantyhose and lotion?" Hailey held up the receipts to the camera for Tony to see in the control room.

"It's Sookie's. I told you, I graduated journalism school so I could be Sookie's errand boy. Makeup, pantyhose, aspirin, you name it . . . I'll find it!" He said it jokingly, but Hailey knew the disappointment behind the words.

The conversation ended and Hailey could hear dead air again until the show's theme music began playing about ninety seconds later.

Todd started the second segment of the hourlong show by engaging Cassie's priest in a Q and A about the star's divorce, her alcohol addiction, and her weight problems. The priest tried his best to answer diplomatically in light of the sensational nature of the questions Harry Todd was reading verbatim off his yellow cue cards. The priest wisely continued to steer the conversation back toward Cassie's unwavering faith. Through her earpiece, Hailey could hear the control-room producers urging Todd on, trying their best to goad the priest into revealing more of Cassie's troubles on national TV.

When the pastor wouldn't budge, Todd turned to Hailey and asked her to compare Cassie Lake's murder to the other murders. She gave a recitation of what had already been released to the public. She didn't leave out a single fact, but carefully avoided citing anything she'd gleaned from police files. Hailey had a firm grasp of all the similarities, and the rest of the panel remained silent as she described the crime scenes, dates, times, and locations. She ended by pointing out the glaring difference, that the killer had struck three thousand miles away when he murdered Cassie Lake.

"Now," she concluded, "the killer's next step, and there will be a next step, can no longer be predicted."

"Go to break, go to break!" She heard Tony Russo yelling it in her earpiece and the music played over more footage of Todd's last interview with Cassie.

"Man, you know how to give a sound bite! You're a star!" Tony blared it in her ear as soon as they were in commercial break.

His words struck her cold. She was hoping to reveal the horrible truth about violent crime, not let the perfumed, airbrushed edition be the facts of record. But to the others, it was all just sound bites and video. Hailey glanced at the red numbers on the camera's digital clock. There were only a few minutes left in the show, two of which were a commercial and one, Todd droning on in a monologue at the end.

In the last segment, Todd went to a phoner, a high school friend of Cassie's who hadn't seen her in twenty years. She was absolutely irrelevant, but was apparently the best "friend" the show could dig up. The woman gave a few recollections of Cassie in high school and Harry started his monologue about the life of Cassie Lake. The show producers wisely cut him short and ended the show with a video package of Cassie set to sad, emotional music in the background.

Hailey heard the countdown in her ear, "... four, three, two, one, and ... we're out! Thank you, everyone. Great show!"

||||||||||||||||||||||||||||||||||||||||||||||||||||||| 43 |||||||||||||||||||||||||

A COMMERCIAL FOR AN ALLERGY MEDICATION CAME ON IMMEDIATELY after the Cassie video. The show was over. Hailey stood to unhook her lapel mike and take out the earpiece in her ear. Before she could get herself detangled from the set, the studio door opened, streaming light in from the hall. It was Tony, of course.

Instead of being thrilled about the night's live show, he was already obsessed about what ratings number it would likely bring in.

"The problem is that we're in the middle of NFL Playoffs." He looked peeved.

"Why is a football game a problem?" She'd unhooked herself, run the lapel mike down her blouse, and left it there on the table. The two headed down the wide hall toward the cluster of offices and cubicles that comprised the staff digs for *The Harry Todd Show*.

Tony looked at her as if she'd sprouted horns and a tail. "It's not just a football game. It's the NFL Playoffs, and it's going against us head-to-head tonight."

"People are still playing football this late at night?"

"Yes. And more important, people are still up *watching* football this late at night!" They rounded a bend in the hall and arrived at Tony's windowed office. Hailey noticed the view outside was even bleaker at night but didn't comment on it, remembering how thrilled and not just a little self-satisfied he was at graduating from a cubicle.

"Sookie's late . . . as usual. She's supposed to meet us right here after the show. Want to go with us out for drinks?" Standing behind his desk, Tony checked his BlackBerry and cell phones for word from his boss and then logged onto his computer, not taking the time to sit down in his chair.

"Drinks? You're kidding. At this hour? What are you people . . . vampires?"

"We are not vampires. We're just thirsty."

"No, thanks. I have to go to work in the morning! You TV people have it made. What are you looking up online?"

"I'm not really online, I'm looking for Sookie."

"How can you do that? What . . . Did she have a GPS chip installed in her tooth?" Hailey sank down into one of the two chairs across from the office's desk.

"Ha. No. But I wish she did, good idea. We can never round her up when there's work to do. Fashion Week was the worst. She was AWOL for twenty-one consecutive days."

"So how do you find her online?"

"I told you, I'm not exactly online. Sookie's taught me a lot, like how to locate people within the building. You have to know their security card swipe number. Then you can find the last place they swiped in. Let's see, this places her, last swipe anyway, at Noel Fryer's office. So he finally showed up. She's probably down there sucking up."

"What else did she teach you?" Hailey hadn't moved an inch. It had been a long, long day and she wasn't looking forward to the ride home in the cold. She wanted to fall asleep right then and there.

"Oh, like I said . . . a lot. She also showed me how to hack into the overhead paging system. She does it from her place out in the Hamptons all the time. She can do it from her place, the hair salon, Bergdorf's, you name it. Makes it look like she's here all the time. You know . . . 'Tony Russo, please come to Sookie Downs's office . . . please come to my office . . .' You know . . . that kind of thing. She's always faking that she's here at work. But they're on to her. They know all her tricks."

"Who's they?"

"The executives. The suits."

"If they know she doesn't work on the show and she's never around, why do they keep her?"

"The show's number one in the daytime slot. That's a huge, big deal. I guess they figure, whatever she's doing, or not doing, it works."

"They've got a point! She must be doing something right!" The two of them laughed. Russo's phone rang and he picked it up. Listening briefly, he put the caller on hold and whispered to Hailey, "This will be ten minutes, it's press about tonight's show. I have to take it. Will you please do me a favor?"

"What?" She looked at him suspiciously, joking.

"Can you round up Sookie? Noel's office is on thirty-one. His door's probably open. Just keep turning left every chance you get when you get off the elevator. Here, take my swipe card. You'll need it to get up to thirty-one and then through those big glass doors. You'll see."

"Sure. But only because I feel sorry for you having to have drinks with her this late at night. I don't think she likes me after our 'visit' out at her place. That house is a monster!" Hailey reached across Tony's desk and took the card.

Tony nodded, sat down, and took the call off mute. Hailey waved goodbye and headed down the hall to the elevators.

An open elevator was waiting and she stepped on in search of Sookie Downs. The elevator shot up the center of the building as its flat-screens played images of Cassie Lake and sound bites from *The Harry Todd Show.*

Just before the doors swooshed open . . . it hit.

Like a brick.

Intense Red Copper Shimmer . . . Dark Chocolate. Dark Chocolate . . . daisies . . . Sookie hovering in Fallon Malone's kitchen beside the service door entrance . . .

"*All I saw was he had black hair. I think he was white . . .*" You don't plant daisies in the winter. They'll die. Dark hair dye . . . hair in a ponytail instead of perfectly blown out . . . AWOL after the taping . . . dark lines under her nails. At first Hailey had thought it was dirt.

Sookie must have thrown away the box on the plane and, accidentally with it, the plastic gloves to avoid the dark hair dye seeping into her skin and nails.

Hailey stepped out into the plushest offices she'd ever seen. They looked like a Hollywood movie. Thick carpet, groupings of gorgeous furniture, with artwork and mirrors on every wall, created a lavish atmosphere that reflected the network was winning the ratings war.

Without processing what she knew, Hailey started to sprint down the halls. The next left came when Hailey dead-ended into a long, shiny teak receptionist's station sitting out in the middle of a wide expanse of thick carpet. There were no walls around the desk, its "space" only delineated by a thick Oriental rug beneath it that had to be the size of Hailey's kitchen.

That turn sent Hailey down a wide, darkened corridor. The walls were covered with gorgeous oil paintings. She slowed slightly to veer away from one in particular. It was specially lit and was positioned in an alcove of sorts apparently built especially for it. It was pop art à la Warhol and apparently an original. And expensive.

This place was over the top. Hailey instinctively darted, afraid she'd likely set off some sort of alarm. The hall ended with yet another piece of art, this time an abstract clay sculpture that stood about five feet tall. Another inlaid spotlight shined down on it and helped light the hall as she again turned left. It was all lost on Hailey, her heart now pounding in her throat.

Looking ahead of her down the dark hallway, Hailey knew she'd found Fryer's office. There were no other doors anywhere on the hall. His office must be massive, and if it was anything like the rest of the thirty-first floor, it would be entirely overdone . . . too much art mixed in theme and period, carpet too plush, heavy furniture, and an overall message of ornate opulence. Now stepping lightly, Hailey crept as quickly and quietly as she could, steadily down the hall toward the light seeping out from under Noel Fryer's office door.

Just as she raised her hand to knock, Hailey heard a groan and then a loud thud. It sounded like a piece of furniture had toppled over inside. Listening at the door, she could hear a woman's voice, strident, yet the words were muffled. Then another thud followed by a groan that sounded painful.

Hailey put her right ear close to the door and listened. Nothing. And then, a sort of groan. She tried the doorknob; it was locked.

Without a sound, Hailey turned and hurriedly retraced her steps down the hall's thick carpet. Rounding the two corners back to the receptionist's desk, she slid open the middle drawer and looked for anything that would help. Pencils, stapler, gem clips . . . no good.

Hailey felt it before she saw it . . . a grooved metal nail file. As a second thought, she lifted the receptionist's phone, dialed 9, then Kolker's cell. It went straight to voice mail.

"Kolker, it's Hailey. Hurry, GNE, thirty-first floor. Repeat . . . Hurry."

HAILEY TOOK THE NAIL FILE FROM THE DRAWER AND DARTED back down the hall. The light still poured out onto the carpet from under Noel Fryer's office door. Hailey, summoning up everything she'd ever learned from both cops and burglars, slipped the nail file between the door's knob and frame and jiggered.

Pushing the file to the right and then back to the left, she could feel the lock's workings against the metal. There was movement, but not enough to open the door.

A sound like drawers being opened filtered through the door, and a woman's voice rose again. Hailey couldn't make out the words. Then again silence.

Hailey jiggered the lock as quickly and quietly as she could, and feeling the metal grind against the lock, finally got enough traction with the file to move the catch enough to the right to gently push the door open. The office was dark except for a single reading lamp in the far corner. The room was huge and ornate, as Hailey expected it to be, the carpeted floor covered with thick rugs from all over the world, the walls boasting artwork and the shelves covered in memorabilia and framed photos of Noel Fryer with Hollywood and sports stars, politicos, and celebrities of every ilk. Hailey took it all in in an instant.

She immediately spotted the drawers of Noel's mahogany desk gaping open. A long, matching conference table against the far window was covered in notebooks and papers in disarray, and not only were the cabinet doors to a matching credenza underneath the same window hanging wide open and askew, but the cabinets had obviously been ransacked.

On the carpet in front of Noel Fryer's desk sat a pair of purple stilettos with distinctive scarlet red soles. Hailey would have recognized them a mile away. They belonged to Sookie Downs.

Instinctively, Hailey backed against a darkened wall and eyed the only other door in the room. It was across the length of the office, obviously leading to Noel's adjoining personal quarters, where he could shower, rest, even stay overnight if he wanted. Judging by the lack of doors or windows in the hallway outside his office, Fryer's personal quarters were expansive and took up the entire length of the long hall.

"You piece of shit. You tell me where the log is right now or I'll blow your greasy head off."

The woman's voice was low, almost like a hiss.

"Thank God I can finally tell you how much I loathe you, how much I've hated you all these years. You make me sick. You and your pathetic scooter and your sports cars and your women . . . your women . . . every single woman you've used in this network hates you. You're disgusting. I don't know what I ever saw in you. But I was young then . . . and stupid. But I'm not stupid anymore. Even after we were through, you paraded all your 'girlfriends' in front of me on purpose. *I hate you, Noel . . . I hate you!* Now for the last time . . . Where's the damn log?"

There was another dull thud. But this time, there was no response, no groan, just silence.

Hailey gently turned the knob to the heavy door and eased it forward just a fraction of an inch. She couldn't see much, so she pushed a tiny bit more.

There, across the room, her back to Hailey, stood Sookie Downs, still wearing the purple mini and lavender silk blouse, but now barefoot. Her hair was tumbling down her back and she was holding something in her hands, but Hailey could see nothing but her back, heaving as she breathed.

In front of her, in a deep and wide closet, sat Noel Fryer, strapped to a straight chair at both ankles and wrists, his biceps and chest also secured. The same thick, silver duct tape was wound across his mouth and all the way around the back of his head. Blood streamed down his face and his right eye was swollen, black and bleeding. Blood pooled like a lobster bib on the front of his shirt, staining nearly his whole chest a deep, dark red. His head was hanging down toward his right shoulder, and even though Hailey was now clearly in his eyesight, he didn't look up. Hailey couldn't tell whether he was unconscious.

"Are you ready to tell me, you piece of shit?" Sookie pulled back with her right arm and swung it hard straight at Noel's face. It was then that Hailey saw what Sookie was holding in front of her.

It was a gun. The handle was painted red. Hailey recognized it immediately . . . it was the one that was pictured stuffed in the pants of Sookie Downs's father in Burma. It all clicked in Hailey's head. The maroon particles were red . . . maroon-red paint particles off the gun's hand-painted butt.

Sookie held it by the barrel, pulled back like she was taking a swing at a baseball. It hit, hard at the side of Noel's temple. Downs didn't let up, relentlessly pistol-whipping Fryer back and forth across his face again and again, this time the barrel slashing across his nose with a sickening crunch. Blood squirted from the center of his face, gushing, unstopped, down to his waist. It didn't have far to go. Fryer was bent nearly in half.

"I want the log and I want it now. You're the only one with access to the company jet log and I know it. So help me God . . . I'll kill you right here, Noel. I will throw you out that window down to the sidewalk. They'll never be able to figure out what happened. Your body will be a mush. I'm giving you one last chance, you disgusting freak." Sookie's voice was pitching higher and higher, out of control.

Hailey shrank back into an alcove meant to show off a bronze sculpture perched on a rectangular block of wood. She wanted to kick herself; she'd left her cell phone on Tony Russo's desk. She'd have to cross the length of the room to get to the only phone she could spot, near what appeared to be a Murphy bed hidden within a deep wall unit covering the room's far wall.

Sookie reached forward and ripped the tape off Noel's mouth. He groaned again, obviously semi-conscious. He'd taken a horrible beating about the face and head with the butt of Sookie's gun, clearly while restrained.

"Tell me, you slimy shit. For the last time, where's the jet log?"

Noel raised his eyes to Sookie, as if he didn't have the strength to pull his whole head up off his chest.

"Sookie, don't do this. I swear, if you let me go, I won't tell a soul. We go back, Sookie, way back. Killing me will only make it worse . . ."

"Shut up, damn it! Shut up! I asked you one thing . . . where's the jet log?"

Sookie was clearly beyond reason.

"Nobody will ever put it together, Sookie. Nobody . . ."

"Nobody but you, Noel . . . nobody but you. You're the only one that knows I flew to LA and back the same day Cassie Lake was murdered. You're the only one that can piece it together. It's all your fault, don't you see that? If you hadn't threatened to cancel us, this would have never happened. You turned me into an animal that only cares about one thing . . . survival. This isn't me, Noel. You know this isn't me . . . It's something *you created.*"

"I know, Sookie. Please forgive me . . . I was wrong. Just untie me and we'll sort the whole thing out, I swear to God . . ."

"Shut up! I've listened to your BS for fifteen years. I don't believe a single word you say . . . all you know how to do is lie. I swear to God, I'm going to blow your ugly face off and nobody will hear a thing. See this thing?"

Sookie held the gun up in front of her and for the first time, Hailey realized Sookie had a black silencer attached to the muzzle.

"Nobody will hear a damn thing . . . nothing. Nobody's coming to save you, Noel. They all just think you're out nailing another intern, another celebrity, another who-knows-what . . . nobody thinks you're tied up in your office bedroom with a gun barrel in your face, you stupid schmuck . . ."

Noel opened his mouth to speak. Sookie was wild; she didn't even seem to hear anymore.

"It was for the ratings. I had to do it. You didn't give me any other choice . . ."

Sookie stepped closer to Noel, only three or four feet from his body, slumped in the chair. He was too out of it even to look up, to understand he was about to die.

Sookie held the gun up, gripping it with both hands, now aiming directly at Noel's head.

At that precise moment, Will's face flashed in Hailey's mind, his blue eyes smiling at her . . . alive, vibrant, happy . . . just before he was gunned down, shot to death. She wasn't there to save Will, he died alone. *"God help me,"* she whispered out loud, and without thinking another second, she ran for all she was worth, taking a leaping dive, her arms outstretched to tackle Sookie from behind. Hailey had to take her down before she pulled the trigger.

Hailey hit hard, and the impact of slamming into Sookie's body and then hitting the floor hard nearly knocked the air out of Hailey's lungs. Her shoulders banged into Sookie just above the back of her knees and the two careened forward. Immediately, Sookie started flailing at Hailey.

The two rolled over on the floor and somehow the gun fired into the dark. Hailey didn't have time to figure out what or where the bullet hit, but she heard thick glass shatter and as she rolled, saw the bank of windows crashing down on them.

Sookie landed on top and straddled Hailey, who now had her back to the floor.

"You! Hailey Dean! You stupid bitch! Noel thought *you* were the star. Shows how much he knows . . . *the murders were the stars,* not you! Then, you saw the hair dye under my nails . . . and you just had to say something . . . you just had to notice, *didn't you!*" Sookie screamed it out. Looking up from the floor at Sookie's face as she sat on Hailey, trying to hold her down, the woman looked possessed.

She was shrieking now; saliva flecked on her lips and spewed when she spoke. Hailey knew Sookie must have gone mad. "I thought I could let you live, that you wouldn't put it together, but now you've got to go, right along with *him* . . ."

Sookie still had the gun and, holding it with both hands, hopped off Hailey. Sookie quickly stood, backing up a step to take aim at Hailey and fire.

But Hailey was too quick, rolling over on the floor, springing up, and instinctively jumping forward, tackling Sookie again. It was kill or be killed. This time, Hailey slammed into Downs just above knee level, taking her down. Sookie hit the floor hard, the gun fell to the side of them both, and this time, it was Hailey on top. Sookie had about seven inches and about twenty pounds on Hailey, and she was fighting for all she was worth.

In the split second that Hailey had the advantage with Sookie on the floor, she used it, pulling her right fist back and landing a crunch to Sookie's left face. The blow sliced Sookie's eye and landed onto her perfectly sculpted nose. Immediately upon impact, blood spurted from Sookie's nose up onto Hailey's chest.

Sookie's head lurched toward the right along with the blow and while she was down, Hailey landed another, then another punch to Sookie's flawless, porcelain face.

In that moment, the only moment she had, Hailey rolled off Sookie, diving across the floor to grab the gun with both hands. Sookie was on her feet and rose up, springing for the gun. But now, the tables turned. Now, it was Hailey who held the gun aimed at Sookie's head.

"You won't do it. Little Miss Law and Order, you'd never pull the trigger. Listen to me, you stupid girl, I can make you a star . . . *a star, Hailey.* Look what I did for that idiot Harry Todd. Just forget what you saw tonight. Believe me, Noel Fryer deserves this and more. If you only knew what he's put me through over the last fifteen years . . . he's the devil . . . *Noel Fryer is the devil. He has to die, Hailey. Listen to me . . ."*

Hailey stood, her legs rooted firmly to the floor, pointing the gun straight ahead at eye level, just a few feet from Sookie Downs's face. She sounded like a maniac, but looking into Sookie's pale eyes, Hailey knew she wasn't crazy at all.

Sookie Downs was a cold-blooded killer.

Hailey's pause only served to egg Sookie on, emboldening her to stupidly taunt Hailey Dean.

"You know you won't do it, Hailey; go ahead, give it back to me, I know what to do with a gun, Hailey. You don't have the guts for it. After your little fiancé was shot, you can't even stand the feel of the gun . . . You don't even know what to do . . . do you?"

With that, Hailey smoothly and calculatedly, almost mechanically, lowered the gun down . . . down from Sookie's face, then further down to her knees. Without wasting another moment, Hailey Dean took aim directly at Sookie's long legs. Her beautiful long legs, legs like a foal's, legs showcased a million times in a million places, legs that seemed to bloom down out of thousand-dollar designer minis, legs she showed to her advantage whenever possible. Specifically, Hailey took aim at the right kneecap.

Staring Downs straight in the eyes, Hailey squeezed the trigger. The blast was muffled by the silencer and Sookie screamed in agony, falling to the floor. Hailey stepped back just a few steps, gun still aimed straight at Sookie Downs, now crawling across the carpeted floor toward the door.

The room was lit only by the light in the closet where Fryer sat bleeding and unconscious. Hailey raced to the phone in the far corner of the room and, barely able to make out the digits, punched the numbers 911. A woman's voice answered.

"911 Dispatch. What's your emergency?"

Before she could answer, Hailey realized the worst. Sookie wasn't heading for the door; she'd crawled across the carpeted expanse to her handbag, sitting in a chair a few feet from Noel Fryer. Before Hailey could utter another word, Sookie lurched her body forward, reached one hand into the bag, and pulled out a second gun. In a sitting position, Sookie held the gun up, aimed directly toward Hailey, and pulled the trigger.

In the back of Hailey's mind, she heard the blast and dived hard to her right underneath a long dinner table set up in Fryer's office apartment. A burning pain tore through Hailey's left side, but even then, mid-dive, Hailey took aim at Sookie yet again, squeezing off a second, and last, round.

A searing pain took over Hailey's body. The last thing Hailey Dean saw was the bottom of Noel Fryer's heavy, ornate dinner table.

WILL WAS THERE. SHE COULD SEE HIM. HAILEY REACHED OUT both her arms for him to come closer, but he wouldn't. Will smiled at her, then evaporated. There were voices . . . a low buzzing that seemed far away. She tried to open her eyes, but her eyelids wouldn't work. The voices grew louder, no longer just a buzz.

When Hailey finally opened her eyes, Will was definitely gone, leaving an empty feeling in her chest. But there were cops, uniformed and plainclothes, everywhere, swarming all over the room. Hailey could see them beyond the door in the office of the GNE CEO suite. She looked down to see she was now lying stretched out on a long, deep-blue velvety sofa off in one corner.

Glancing around the room, now brightly lit with overhead fluorescent lights as well as every floor and table lamp, Hailey immediately spotted Kolker, his back to her. He was huddled over Tony Russo, who was lying in a heap at the door of Noel's office. Noel himself was sitting up, awake and alert, the blood wiped from his face and a bandage over his eye. He was talking into a microphone held by a young, thin man who squatted on the floor while balancing a camera on his right shoulder.

Two cops were trying to attach a huge piece of cardboard to the window gaping open and framed by splinters of clear glass, what little was left after the shooting, in order to curb the blasts of winter wind gusting in. The thick carpet on the floor was covered in broken glass, shards of every shape and size.

Sookie Downs was strapped on a gurney. Her hair stuck to her head and the sides of her face in dark red tendrils. Tears were running down her cheeks and she was staring venomously straight at Hailey Dean. "Kolker, is Sookie Downs cuffed?" Hailey sat up straight and called it out loud and low across the room . . . just in case they hadn't all figured out exactly who had been shooting at whom.

Kolker stood up and turned around. He was smiling.

"Yeah, Hailey. She's cuffed." He stepped over to Sookie's gurney and pulled the thin blanket up off her body, revealing that she was cuffed to the metal side rails, hands and ankles. A thick white gauze bandage was over her right kneecap, blood flowering out through the thick cotton. She had a similar patch across her left shoulder, the sleeve of her lavender silk blouse now cut off and lying on the floor next to the gurney.

"Nice shooting, Ms. Dean. I can only assume this was your handiwork. I can't wait to hear about it." He gave Hailey a thumbs-up, as he replaced the blanket.

"What happened to Tony? Is he okay?" Hailey felt sick to her stomach looking at Tony, pale and crumpled.

"We're not totally sure yet, but we think he came looking for you, saw blood, and passed out. He's okay, just a little case of shock."

Hailey tried to stand, but settled for sitting when the dizziness hit. "Quick, Kolker. Call the corporate jet company. You gotta get the bathroom drain out of the plane Sookie took out to LA."

"What plane? And why do we need a bathroom drain?"

Hailey realized they didn't get it yet. She tried to capsulize as best she could. "Sookie took the GNE corporate jet to LA, cooked up a dinner meeting with Cassie Lake, shot her, and flew back. She colored her hair on the way. It was Sookie Downs in the passenger seat of Cassie's car. She's the dark-haired man . . . she's tall enough, right?"

"She's the man? She dyed her hair?" Kolker looked over at Sookie, who looked as if she wanted nothing more than to get her hands around Hailey's neck.

"Yes. She's the killer. She didn't want to arouse suspicion, sending Tony out for a brunette wig, so she sent him to the drugstore for hair dye instead, thinking he'd never notice the shade was brunette, not bright red. Tonight, she came here to get rid of the evidence . . . the corporate jet log naming her as the only passenger, Teterboro to LAX, the same day, right after the *Harry Todd* taping. Cassie Lake gets home around 4 p.m. California time. Sookie beats her out there by taking the GNE private jet, meets her; they head to the Italian restaurant in Cassie's car. By flying charter, she can smuggle on a gun, no metal detectors, and has the plane's bathroom all to herself for four hours to dye her hair. They probably didn't even check her driver's license, much less do a firearms check."

Kolker looked at Sookie Downs as if a light had just turned on over his head. "And speaking of the gun, it's her father's, from the Second World War. When you call LA, get them to process Cassie's car seats for red particles. They're paint . . . They're off the gun handle. Look at it, Kolker. He must have painted it with the old lead paint while he was in Burma. I saw a picture of it in Sookie's wine cellar . . . on the steps."

Kolker turned and spoke quickly over his shoulder. "O'Brien, quick. Get a warrant and get out to Downs's mansion in the Hamptons. Call Suffolk P.D. to assist. We have to get that photo before she has somebody destroy it. And seize all the computers, hard drives, search the desk, the bedroom . . . anything connected to the victims or the murders."

"Right. I'm on it." Paddy turned on his heel and left the room, already talking into his police radio.

Hailey went on. "And now that I think about it, have CSI go back over the floor at the rear of Fallon's elliptical and the rear of the machine itself. There may be more red particles there, since hers wasn't a contact wound. And, Kolker, Sookie was there in Fallon Malone's kitchen before. I saw it in the footage Tony gave me to review for you."

Sookie gave Tony Russo an evil-looking stare and all but hissed.

"I didn't know!" Tony responded to Sookie's look.

"It wasn't that long ago . . . she'd have remembered. She was there in the kitchen. She was right in front of the service entrance. She knew how to beat surveillance, probably even where Malone kept the maid's key."

Kolker injected, "But, Hailey, working on the timeline, every time I spoke to Russo about his and Sookie's whereabouts at the times of the murders, he covered for her . . ." Kolker looked confusedly over at Tony.

"It wasn't my fault!" Tony piped in, his eyes now wide open. "I covered for her all right, but it was because she was having an affair with Derek Jacobs. I thought they were over at the Mandarin Hotel in the GNE guest suite . . . it was lie or lose my job . . . and I always pick up Sookie's hair dye at the drugstore . . . in case she can't get to the salon and has a root emergency . . . I don't know anything about any *murders*!"

"I thought this was all about Noel Fryer. You mean she killed them all? Leather Stockton, Prentiss Love, Fallon Malone, Cassie Lake . . . Sookie Downs killed them all? *Why?*" Kolker was having a hard time taking it in.

"To stay on top. It's a long story, Kolker. Just trust me, get the drain out of that plane before it's too late. I guarantee you, there *will be* brunette hair dye in it. And it'll match any hair you manage to pull out of Cassie Lake's car."

Kolker turned away and began barking orders into his police-band radio.

"And find the pilot. For all we know, he's dead, too. She sure knows how to cover her tracks."

The paramedics were wheeling the gurney from the room. "Bitch! *I hate you!*" Sookie Downs called it out over her shoulder. "It'll never hold up in court . . . I'm calling my lawyers! Watch my knee, you stupid girl!" She bit the words out at the female paramedic helping to minister to her.

Just then the gurney "slipped" from the EMT paramedic's hands and banged onto the floor.

"Oops." The EMT said it calmly as Sookie screamed out in pain.

Once they got her down the hall and into the elevator, the room was calm. Noel Fryer continued detailing his ordeal into the camera. Hailey looked over in the corner and spotted Tony sitting up whispering furiously into his cell phone, shielding his words by holding his left hand over his lips and the phone. Even as he spoke, the pictures changed on the bank of flat-screens mounted on Noel's wall.

Instantly, the images switched from another political talk show with shots of the president walking across the lawn of the White House to a waiting helicopter. They suddenly cut from the White House lawn to shots of Cassie Lake singing and playing the piano on *The Harry Todd Show*, then to her murder scene, cordoned off with yellow crime scene tape, suspended in the air and dancing up and down in the night breeze.

The lower third of the screen was now covered with a huge red banner that screamed, *Breaking News! Suspect, Hamptons Socialite, in Custody for Cassie Lake Murder! Implicated as D-List Serial Killer!*

Hailey immediately jerked her head away from the screen to glare over accusingly at Tony Russo. At least he had the decency to look embarrassed.

THERE IT WAS. HE HEARD IT AGAIN. IT WAS DEFINITELY A THUMP. Downstairs.

Before Scott Anderson could roll over and turn on his bedside light, he felt hands jerk him out of his bed and throw him face-down on the bedroom carpet.

The carpet's blue fibers burned his face as he was dragged a few feet away from his bed. He felt cold steel of handcuffs snap into place around his wrists, now forced behind his back.

"I don't have anything! Take my wallet, it's on the dresser by the bed. I've got two flat-screens, they're all yours. The keys to the BMW are in the kitchen, take it . . . I won't tell a soul, just don't hurt me!" Anderson screamed it down into the carpet crushing into his mouth.

He felt a swift kick to his right leg.

"Moron. We're not a robbing crew. We don't want your car or your wallet. We wanna know why you murdered Fallon Malone and Prentiss Love. Why'd you put a bullet in their heads? Why'd you kill Leather Stockton? *She played a cop. Did you know that? Leather Stockton played a cop! And you killed her!*"

He got another kick to the shin. "And why'd you have to kill Cassie Lake? She's a mom, for Pete's sake . . . a mom!" Another kick landed on his hip and Scott Anderson grunted out loud.

Suddenly, he was grabbed by the shoulders, lifted up off the ground, and thrown back down on the bedroom floor, this time face-up. The bedroom lights were all on now and instead of looking up at home invaders wearing ski masks, he saw a gang of uniformed cops towering over him, all talking loudly at once. One was standing over near the door, reading a *Miranda* card out loud.

"You have the right to remain silent. Anything you say can and will be used against you in a court of law. You have the right to an attorney. If you cannot afford an attorney, one will be appointed to you. Do you understand these rights as they have been read to you?"

The cop kept reading out loud although no one, including Scott Anderson, could really hear him over the other cops yelling down toward the floor at him. Suddenly, one of the cops with hands the size of Virginia hams yanked Anderson up off the floor as if he was as light as a pillow. Dragging him by the arms into the den, the cop then tossed him into a sitting position onto his pit group.

Anderson was so scared, a wet spot spread across the front of his boxers. The cops looked disgusted as the urine soaked Anderson's shorts.

"Okay, you little freak . . . Why'd you do it?"

"Do what?" Anderson couldn't comprehend what they wanted him to say. "All I did was sleep with Fallon Malone . . . that's it . . . I swear to God!"

The big cop bitch-slapped him right across the face with the back of his hand.

"Don't you even say her name, you rich-boy perv! Now tell us . . . Why'd you do it? And why'd you follow Prentiss Love to the Javits Center; we saw you in the TV footage, you little freak, staring at her, practically drooling. It's all on video."

"I wasn't at the Javits Center . . ."

"Yes, you were! Don't lie! It was two years ago in the summer. We *saw* you, Anderson. Stop lying. You were there, stalking Prentiss Love!"

"Okay! I was there! I was there! But it was to see Phil Niekro! Not Prentiss Love! I got a signed baseball! It's in my sock drawer! I swear to God! Go look!"

"BS! You don't deserve to even say Niekro's name! Give me one stat on Niekro and I won't shove your mouth down your throat, just one!"

Scott Anderson's heart was racing and his face was dripping in sweat. "Knuckleball! Knuckleball!" His voice came out high-pitched like a woman's.

"That doesn't count! Any idiot could say that!" The cop drew back the big ham at the end of his arm but this time it was balled into a fist. Just before he rammed it into Anderson's nose, a cop in the corner with his radio to one ear yelled out, "Stop! Wait a minute! It's not him! He didn't do it!"

The big cop hulking over Anderson looked disappointed, but still holding his fist wound back, mid-air, he yielded and didn't land the punch still aimed at Anderson's face.

"They got the killer downtown. It's a woman, believe it or not. Some nutso TV producer. Whatever . . . It's not him."

The big cop still held Anderson pinned with his fist pulled back. "I don't believe it. This creep did something . . . I feel it."

"Oh yeah, he's a perv, all right. You ought to see the porn collection he's got hidden in his closet. But he did get the baseball." One of the rookies stepped into the doorway to the den. He held up a baseball. Niekro's signature was scrawled across it in blue ink.

"Damn." The big cop, obviously disappointed, let go of Anderson, who fell back down into the deep brown cushions of his beloved pit group. Another cop rolled Anderson over and uncuffed him.

"I would say we're sorry, Anderson, but to tell you the truth, you got off easy. We know about that restraining order that girl had against you. And we know all about your wife calling the cops when you smacked her and threatened her. Her face was a mess. And it wasn't the first time, either . . . you piece of crap."

They all stood looking at him and for the first time, Scott Anderson realized somebody saw through him . . . saw through the manners, the good looks, the bleached teeth, the scratch golf game. He said nothing back.

The cops filed out of his den, through the arched door to the living room, and out the front door, shutting it behind them when they left.

Anderson looked around. Everything was the same, nothing was out of place. How they'd gotten in was a mystery, and if he didn't have a carpet burn on his right cheek and a bruise growing on his shin, he'd never have believed what just happened.

He looked at the digital clock glowing green on top of his cable box. It was 1 a.m. Scott Anderson pulled himself out of the deep cushions of his leather pit group, stood up, and headed back to his bedroom to change his underwear.

|||||||||||||||||||||||||||||||||||||||||||||||||||||||||||| **47** ||||||||||||||||||||||||||||

I T WAS THE THIRD CIGARETTE BUTT JULES MOREAU HAD CRAMMED down the back of the pew in Aunt Matilde's crypt. "There's just no way Matilde would want to be forever six feet under with the worms and the Devil. She loved the fresh air."

Jules was dead-set on Aunt Matilde being laid to rest in the sunshine visible from the tiny slits of windows in the elaborate crypt they'd erected here at Crestlawn. Standing there, Jules took a look around the stone crypt and wondered how much the sculpture of the Holy Mother Mary had cost him, even though technically, the cost of the crypt had come straight out of Matilde's own savings account she'd earmarked for this very purpose, her eternal resting place *aboveground.*

"Jules, you're being impractical. You've always been impractical. Ever since you were a little boy, you've been impractical. Remember when you wanted to jump off the roof with nothing but umbrellas to hold us up? We both got broken arms . . . *broken arms, Jules* . . . *broken arms.* I could'a played college football if it wasn't for a bum arm. Then there was the time you thought we should be street vendors down at the Quarter. *That* was a fiasco . . ."

"I thought the tourists would *like* alligator on a stick . . ."

"I told you nobody flies in from Boca Raton or Indianapolis and wants alligator on a stick. I told you."

"Would you for one minute forget the alligator on a stick? I don't see what's impractical about Aunt Matilde being put to rest right here." Jules lit up another Winston.

"Upkeep, *ma sha* . . . . upkeep." Sensing he was making headway, he used the Creole slang for "my dear" on his cousin. "The price of keeping her here is double what the price will be if we leave her where she is . . . ad infinitum . . . Every month we'll be paying upkeep on dear *dead* Aunt Matilde's mausoleum."

The two had lived off Aunt Matilde their whole lives and now, so did their wives and eight children. She had left each beloved niece and nephew a million dollars apiece at the time of her death. Now, out of earshot of family, friends, neighbors, and priests, Jules Moreau and his cousin, Andre Regard, both dropped the guise that they cared about Aunt Matilde's wishes.

"Andre Regard, if you weren't my first cousin and we didn't share our first Communion, I would think you are lying to me. We save over a hundred grand in just ten years alone if we leave Matilde in the dirt."

"Hmm. A hundred grand is a nice little piece of change . . ." He also crushed his cigarette down behind the stone pew.

Just as the two shook hands over the agreement to leave Auntie Matilde where she was, six feet under, the Devil himself interceded, or so the rest of the Moreaus and Regards would tell it in the years to come.

When the last burning butt was crushed down into the crack behind the milky-white stone pew, the whole place blew. The sky above Crestlawn Sacred Grounds lit up like the Fourth of July and the Super Bowl half-time show combined.

Between Francis's ammo, his stash of Homemade Chemical Bombs, and the twenty or so burning cigarette butts the two Cajuns between them had crushed down on top of the homemade arsenal, the blast had to have been three hundred feet straight up in the air.

Even though the families had to bear the cost of rebuilding the mausoleum, no one complained. The Devil had risen up and roared at the world. Auntie Matilde was clearly too good, too saintly, too holy to remain in the Lower Kingdom. Her divine presence irritated Satan and agitated all his evil minions. And thus, it was decided. Matilde would have her wish and her eternal soul would no longer have to be concerned with washing away in the next flood.

Francis was sitting in his mother's favorite wingback chair, minus the doilies, his eyes fixed on the living room's TV set. He couldn't believe his eyes. He'd been up all night watching the coverage of the "D-List Killer," obsessively switching channels during every commercial break so as not to miss a moment. Rooted to the seat of the chair, around midnight, he saw two bloody people, a man and a woman, being wheeled on gurneys out of GNE world headquarters in New York City. The woman had unnaturally bright red hair and was handcuffed to the gurney and surrounded by uniformed NYPD. The man had a bandage over his eye, but was smiling broadly into the camera.

Then he saw the new blonde TV legal analyst come out walking, a little unsteady on her feet, but walking. Her arm was in a sling and she had a bandage on her shoulder. She was being helped by a plain-clothes cop holding her tightly by the elbow, his other arm around her shoulder. Images of Prentiss Love, Fallon Malone, Leather Stockton, and Cassie Lake were turning on a revolving cube on the lower right of the screen.

The killer was some TV producer madwoman . . . a tall redhead who worked at GNE. Apparently she nutted up and committed the string of murders because her show was on the verge of getting axed. Shortly after snagging an interview with one of the stars, she'd offed them in order to have the last interview of record. With exclusives like that, the ratings skyrocketed. She and that freak, Harry Todd, were getting all sorts of offers, big-money ones from other networks.

Not anymore. She was headed to Bedford or Sing Sing or wherever it is they babysit killers in New York. All the TV people should go there, Francis decided.

It had been hard enough to grapple with the pain of losing his girlfriends in such a brutal manner, all the while feeling convinced that the Feds had somehow engineered the whole thing to frame him so he would no longer be a threat to their regime. But now, he was consumed with hate. He hated Sookie Downs with all his heart and soul.

Again, Francis looked down at his hands. So they weren't the hands of a killer after all? The dreams about strangling Prentiss and Leather and Fallon . . . they'd seemed so real. He prayed to God the police had the right perp and it didn't turn out to be him after all. *Would he ever know the truth?*

Even though the sun was now up and shining brightly outside, the interior of the house was dark with the windows covered in newspaper. Francis sat with his head buried in his hands, elbows balanced on his knees in despair.

What he wanted was vengeance, and in that very moment there in his mother's wingback, he vowed revenge on Sookie Downs for killing the women he loved. Somebody had to do the right thing and kill Sookie Downs. Of course, Francis couldn't trust the criminal justice system to prevail. What a joke.

Sookie Downs must die.

He looked out from over his fingers back at the screen. Abruptly, the images switched. A live shot of a police press conference going on on the front steps of GNE in New York City was interrupted by an emergency local cable cut-in. The news alert showed a towering fire and dark plumes of smoke billowing up over a cemetery. Something about the background looked vaguely familiar to Francis. The hand-held camera shook as another explosion rocked the cemetery . . . the banner read in all caps CRESTLAWN SACRED GROUNDS CEMETERY THE TARGET OF TERRORIST ATTACK.

Francis jumped to his feet. A third blast ripped out of Aunt Matilde's mausoleum, which he knew so well, while flames roared into the sky.

Francis instantly decided this would be a great time to get out of town. Prepared to live out of his car for a while again, he hastily threw clothes into his old duffel bag, along with several cans of Vienna sausage, and, of course, the new .38 he just bought at the bi-annual gun and ammo show. He gathered up his mother's gas card and Leather Stockton's red thong, still in its plastic baggie. Gently placing them both in his coat pocket, he turned off the lights in the living room and locked the front door.

Hey . . . why not kill two birds with one stone? He could easily track down Sookie Downs once she made bond. A thought hit him . . . *Would Sookie Downs make bond?* It would be a lot harder to kill her if she didn't bond out of jail after initial murder charges.

Wait a minute . . . What was he thinking? Of course she'd make bond. It was New York City . . . even terrorists make bond in the Big Apple.

New York wouldn't be such a bad place to go for a while, anyway. Francis had a new girlfriend there who'd been coming on to him for months on the airwaves. He didn't know that much about her, but he planned to get to know her very well. She was beautiful and quite the spitfire. Francis loved that in a woman. And obviously, his new love needed him now more than ever.

Her name was Hailey Dean.

|||||||||||||||||||||||||||||||||||||||||||| **ACKNOWLEDGMENTS** ||||||||||||

First, my deepest thanks to my editor, Gretchen Young, who maintained great faith in me and conspired with me to create *Death on the D-List*. You are not just editor, but friend tried and true. (Plus your daughter will grow up to be a New York City cabbie and will be of great use to us both.) Thank you.

To Jim Walton and Ken Jautz, who are NOT the inspirations for this book, thank you for the support, the opportunities, and the friendship.

To our wonderful staff on *Nancy Grace*. To Dee Emmerson, bless you!

Dean Sicoli, my Executive Producer, "Bestie," without you there would be no HLN *Nancy Grace* and I'd probably be prosecuting shoplifting cases in night court right now. Friend, forever.

And last and dearest, thank you, David. Finally I got it . . . true love. You and the twins are the joys of my life.

And my deepest thanks to my Father God and Christ, nothing can separate us from Your Love.

ALSO BY
NANCY GRACE

NANCY GRACE GIVES THE CLOSING ARGUMENT IN *OBJECTION!*

WHERE THE HAILEY DEAN MYSTERY SERIES BEGAN...

AFTER HAVING been a victim of violent crime, Nancy Grace became a respected prosecutor for a decade in inner-city Atlanta. There, she compiled a perfect record of nearly 100 felony prosecutions and no losses at trial. Grace then joined Court TV, and for the next ten years covered major trials after co-hosting *Cochran & Grace* with defense attorney Johnnie Cochran. One of television's most respected legal analysts, Grace now hosts the top-rated HLN show, *Nancy Grace*, and is a legal contributor to ABC's *Good Morning America*. Grace lives in both New York City and Atlanta with her husband and twins, a boy and girl.

A portion of the author's proceeds from *Death on the D-List* will go to the Wesley Glen Ministries in Macon, Georgia, a non-profit ministry of the United Methodist Church that provides loving homes for the disabled. www.wesleyglenministries.org

VISIT NANCY AT: WWW.NANCYGRACE.COM